D0150218

Ace Books by Joel Rosenberg

D'SHAI
HOUR OF THE OCTOPUS

HOUR OF THE OCTOPUS

JOEL ROSENBERG

ACE BOOKS, NEW YORK

This book is an Ace original edition,
and has never been previously published.

HOUR OF THE OCTOPUS

An Ace Book / published by arrangement with
the author

PRINTING HISTORY
Ace edition / March 1994

ISBN: 0-441-16975-9

ACE®
Ace Books are published by The Berkley Publishing Group,
200 Madison Avenue, New York, NY 10016.
ACE and the "A" design
are trademarks belonging to Charter Communications, Inc.

PRINTED IN THE UNITED STATES OF AMERICA

10 9 8 7 6 5 4 3 2 1

this one is for

Susan Allison

Acknowledgments

I'm grateful for the help I've gotten with this one from Bruce Bethke, Peg Kerr Ihinger, and Pat Wrede; from Harry F. Leonard and Victor Raymond; from Beth Friedman, proofreadre, and Carol Kennedy, copy editor.

I'd *like* to thank Ray Feist for the metal puzzle Kami takes apart, but I spent far too many work hours working it out, so I won't.

As always, special thanks to my agent, Eleanor "Darth" Wood, and to Felicia and Judy.

Part One
DEN OROSHTAI

PROLOGUE

The Hour of the Hare

"YOU MAY THINK of yourself as a master chef, in Bergeenen you may have actually been a master chef, but this, my dear young cook, is Den Oroshtai, and this is your first morning in my kitchen, and as it is my kitchen, you will learn; I trust you will find the experience pleasurable as we prepare breakfast for our genial Lord Arefai and our somewhat more strict Lord Toshtai, a simple breakfast and a complex one.

"Don't think of time as a process. Think of it as a spice. You can no more measure it out as drops of water from an hourglass than you would measure spoons of pepper for a sauce; you must add just a little, tasting where possible, considering where not, until you have added just the right amount, no more, for you can no more remove excess time from a dish than you can unsalt it.

"Ah: observe: the surface of the water gently roils; it is now ready. Cradle the egg in your palm, and consider its temperature. Heat is just another manifestation of time—how long has the egg sat in the bowl of cold well-water, and then, how long has it waited on the counter? Consider it all.

"Lower the egg gently into the water, and regard it. The objective is to coddle the egg, to indulge it, to tease it at the simmer until the yolk has become thick without becoming hard, where it is still golden and languidly liquid rather than insipid yellow and tough, the white gaining form and structure without becoming rubbery and chewy.

"Good. Oh? You wish to sit and stare at the boiling water until the egg is done. How very nice—and who will prepare the rest of the simple breakfast?

"Oh. I talk too much, do I? I distract you from the brilliance of your endeavors, is that so? Very well, then; I will let you do it in your own fashion. What next? The apple, you say? Oh, good. Very good. Yes, you slice the apple gently, delicately. Very nice. I very much like the rhythm of your knife against the cutting board, and the slices are just of the right thinness to the taste of many, like that of a thin cracker.

"Your arrangement? Myself, I've always liked to snick out the pieces of core, reassemble the apple, then set it upon a bed of mint leaves, a twist of caramelized sugar to replace the stem, but I am sure that you have a better idea. Ah. Very pretty. Certainly: you've not done wrong to spread it out along the rim of the plate, like a stack of fallen tiles. Very pleasing to the eye. Ah, and you brush the apple lightly with the juice of a lemon. Very good; it will not turn brown in the air.

"And next, the oysters and sausage. A strange but interesting combination, I've always thought, wonderful if handled properly, but ever-so-dependent on preparation, and—oh, I am sorry. I do talk too much. Prepare it as you wish. Hmm . . . slicing off the top of a puff pastry, eh? Not my choice of a presentation, mind, but an interesting one.

"Yes, I do always heat the pan before adding the dab of butter, a shaking of two peppers in the pan, the barest scraping of horseradish. And then the oysters. They are fresh; this very hour, a runner arrived with them from Bergeenen, carefully packed in ice. The oysters, oh wise one, not the runner.

"Hmm . . . I would probably have opened the shells with a different knife, but each to his own; the blood will wash off, and you should be healed within the month.

4

"They do plump up prettily, don't they? And they are tasty as they sit on top of the sausage.

"Pour the tea into the mug, and the tray is ready, you think. I can but bow and nod. Very well; you may bring it in. Me? Don't be silly. When it is asked who is the fool boiled the egg to indigestibility, who is the dolt who served the apple sliced far too thinly to be properly crunched between his teeth, who is the blockhead who served the cooked oysters and undercooked sausage thick with congealed fat in a stale puffery, the answer will not be that I did it, I can assure you of that.

"You had better run, now. It is already the hour of the hare, and Lord Toshtai will be expecting his simple breakfast of egg, apple, and oysters with sausage right now. Oh, yes, the simple breakfast is for Lord Toshtai; the more complex one is for Lord Arefai, who hunts this morning. Had I not mentioned that? Oh.

"Timing is, after all, everything."

1

Morning, Breakfast, an Invitation, and Other Petty Indignities

TIMING IS, AS my father used to say, everything.

No, I'm getting it wrong, as usual. I mean, he probably still does say it—I have no reason to think Gray Khuzud dead, and less to think he's changed his mind—but I haven't seen him for some time now.

He is right, of course; my father has always had that annoying tendency. It doesn't apply just to juggling, although that's one of the places.

Consider, if you will, the knife-and-apple act. After the drunk act, I'd say it was Gray Khuzud's best. But if you put it at the head of the show, as an opener, not only will it not get the applause it should, but it will rob the rest of the show of some of its own virtue.

Not good.

Which isn't to say that there is a right time for everything. For some things there is no correct time. We all can agree that there's no good time for one's piles to act up; similarly—and contrary to what our beloved ruling class believes—there is no such thing as a right time to be woken to go hunting.

He came for me in the hour of the dragon.

I was in the middle of a dream, although even sleeping

I had been vaguely aware of somebody sliding open the panel between my bedroom and the outer room of my suite.

"Kami Khuzud—I mean, Kami Dan'Shir, wake up." Something large and stupid hit me between the shoulder blades.

Even through the shattered remains of half-forgotten dreams of soaring silverhorns and fast-picked zivvers, I could tell that the rasp was the voice of Bek De Bran, a dull and blocky soldier who had recently been reassigned to protecting Arefai, whatever that portended.

It meant something; everything always means something. The only problems are *what* and *how important is it*? When you're mingling with members of our beloved ruling class, it's sometimes every bit as hard to discover the import of supposedly minor events as it is important to know the significance of major ones.

"Lord Arefai bids you join him at breakfast."

Arguably, for Lord Arefai to have sent a member of his personal guard to wake even a lesser noble, much less a newly made bourgeois, was a signal honor. Unarguably, an invitation to join Arefai at breakfast was a great favor, no matter what it felt like, and to have the favor delivered so gently . . .

The standard way to wake a member of a lower class would be to send a servitor to kick me awake, or a soldier to poke a spear at my rumpled blankets. Sending Bek De Bran to shake me awake was a decided favor, given my status.

I tried to voice my gratitude.

"Mrph," I said.

I was rewarded by a kick.

A kazuh Warrior would have come awake at the first touch, his sword in his hand, ready to block, parry, or attack. A kazuh Acrobat like my father would have already rolled to his feet or tumbled to a one-armed handstand.

I held up a hand. "Please be easy, Lord Bek De Bran," I said. "I wake."

I sat up on my sleeping pallet, rubbing at my eyes, then

tossed the blankets aside and went to the wardrobe for some clothes. My head and eyes were so filled with sleep and muzziness that I didn't stop to marvel at it. It's hard for me to marvel at much in the hour of the dragon, the hour before dawn.

I didn't take the kick as a personal affront, although the thought of juggling his internal organs had appeal. A bourgeois can afford to be thin of skin only around middle class and peasants; cultivating a leathery exterior is a necessity if you're going to spend your time around nobility, and as a former peasant, I'd long since taken up the habit.

Not that there was anything particularly noble about the hulking creature looming above me in the gray murk that was broken only by the flickering light of the lantern he had hung on the wall in my workshop.

Bek De Bran was arrayed in full warrior's garb, from the twin peaks of the lacquered steel helmet that topped his head, to the reticulated bone armor that covered his shoulders and chest, down to the skirt of leather straps that hung about his thick waist, partly covering the kneezers and greaves, and the brass-pointed boots on his feet. His armor's finger joints clicked like dice to keep time against the shaft of his spear as he hummed a simple soldier's jig.

It seemed to me to that he wore a lot more gear than a warrior should need to go wake up a dan'shir, but I didn't mention that. For one thing, most of them seem to like dressing up in their outfits almost as much as they like singing, or beating members of the lower classes. But mainly, it's that most of them seem to like beating members of the lower classes.

I stepped into my trousers—both feet at once, the way an acrobat dresses—then pulled a nappy cotton tunic over my head. I belted it tightly across my waist with a broad black sash.

He shifted his right hand to his spear, and idly poked at me with its rounded butt end.

"Be quicker, whether it pleases you or not. The hunt awaits Lord Arefai, and Lord Arefai awaits you." Typical

9

of a member of our beloved ruling class to be impatient to start a morning of killing things.

"Shoes," I said. "I need shoes."

"Just be quick about it."

The donjon was quiet in the predawn light as we padded (well, *I* padded; Bek De Bran clomped and clicked and clacked) down the corridor, past a hallstand where a Klen vase sat, filled with an arrangement of wildflowers, a classic concentric arrangement of thorny, blood-red bantam roses surrounding an explosion of yellow daisies. As we passed, when my body blocked his view, I snatched one of the roses and tucked it into my belt, pricking my thumb on one of its sharp thorns.

As usual, my timing was faulty. Just at that moment, Lord Crosta Natthan rounded a corner.

Despite the obscenely early hour, the donjon's chief servitor was completely ready for the day, the creases in his gray silk tunic and the pleats in the matching pantaloons fully pressed, the twin points of his goatee combed and oiled, and the rest of his lined face freshly shaved, his hair pulled back and bound with a bone clip. Despite his age, his step was brisk, and his glare was sharp and alert.

Despite it all, I enjoyed the moment. I've always liked matching wits with Crosta Natthan, no matter what the risk.

"Good morning, Lord Crosta Natthan," I said, coming to an abrupt halt.

Bek De Bran probably would have chivied me along if I'd stopped for my own reasons, but not when I was having words with the chief servitor.

"And a good morning to you, too, Kami Dan'Shir," he said, with equal lack of sincerity. "I trust you didn't prick yourself too badly?"

"No, although I thank you for the concern," I said, taking the rose from my belt and tucking it through a button loop on my tunic.

When in doubt, brazen it out.

He thought about it for a moment. There is only one

punishment for theft in D'Shai; we may be hypocritical folks, but we are simple and direct in some things. The only question in his mind was whether or not my taking the rose constituted theft, in which case it was his duty to report it to Lord Toshtai. On the other hand, if I had a right to take the rose, then his reporting the matter would simply serve to annoy the lord of Den Oroshtai, and he wouldn't want to do that. Annoying Lord Toshtai was neither part of his job nor likely to lengthen his life.

I bent my head to sniff at the rose. "Part of the Way of the Dan'Shir," I said. "We appreciate beauty." Well, the use of the plural was my right; as the only known Dan'Shir it was proper for me to speak for all of us, er, for all of me.

His sniff had nothing to do with smelling a rose. "I wonder how far you will get with this Way of the Dan'Shir," he said, as he turned to rearrange the flowers, hiding the absence of the rose.

So do I, old man, I didn't say.

He had a point, of course. I didn't know how far I should—or could—push things. There are fifty-three known kazuhin, including that of the Dan'Shir. The origins of many of them—Warrior, Peasant, Deilist, others— vanish off into prehistory, when the Powers walked openly across the face of D'Shai. Quite possibly, some of the ancient kazuhin were originated by the Powers, although who can say?

But each of the historical professions traces its origin to a historical master, a historical originator, from the kazuh of the Ruler, created by the ancient Scion of the Sky Himself, to that of the Cook.

If you accept that the Way of the Dan'Shir, the Way of the Discoverer-of-Truths, is truly a Way, truly a kazuh, then that makes me the historical master of the Way, with all rights and privileges of a historical master.

Which, as we'll all recall, included the right or privilege of Veren Del Gergen, the first Painter, to lose his head from a single sword stroke when ancient Lord Egware was offended by the classic if not entirely complimentary study

11

"Kindly Lord Egware at His Leisure." Which only goes to show, I guess, that being a historical master doesn't necessarily give someone sense enough to stay away from members of our beloved ruling class.

I nodded as I walked on. "And a good day to you, Lord Crosta Natthan."

His breakfast had barely arrived, but Arefai hadn't waited for me before beginning. It wasn't that he was being impolite, but it wouldn't have occurred to him to wait, any more than he would have offered me a taste from his plate.

The breakfast cook had prepared for him a classic arrangement of the seven flavors. To the right of Arefai's plate, a steaming ceramic mug of elderbark tea provided both the hot and the bitter, while a flask of crushed fundleberries in its bowl of shaved ice to the left of the plate stood in cold, sweet contrast. An arc of melon slices had been artfully spread across the top rim of the plate, each slice separated from the next in salty opposition by a paper-thin medallion of highly spiced Patricien ham.

An even dozen oysters on sausage circled the plate, interspersed with crispy morsels of bacon-wrapped quail, rice cups brimming with salted pout roe, and some oily white fish wrapped in chumpa leaves and sprinkled with roasted sesame seeds.

The center of the plate was occupied by four ramekins, which looked to be the locally traditional four sauces: a peppery cheese sauce, so overripe I could smell the ammonia; a pale mayonnaise with dill and lemon; a thick compote of peppers, onions, and tomatoes, heavily sprinkled with basil; and a grainy brown mustard.

Delicately, Arefai extended an eating prong and speared a chumpa-leaf packet, elegantly tipping one end into the compote and another end into the dill sauce before bringing it up to his lips. He managed to take a bite out of each end without dripping sauce on his short-cropped beard or on his doeskin hunting tunic.

He finally noticed that I was just standing there, and waved me to a seat.

"Good morning to you, Kami Dan'Shir," he said. "A fine morning for hunting, is it not?"

I looked up at the sky, which was busy deciding what light shade of gray to menace me with, and out at the horizon, where dark clouds loomed threateningly—something dark clouds always do—and then decided that theatrical gestures were neither called for nor entirely safe. An occasional, very carefully chosen bit of presumption tended to charm the likes of Lord Arefai; but it was best not to make a habit of it.

"I would presume so, Lord Arefai," I said. "Certainly I wouldn't argue with your assertion."

After all, you overdressed if generally kindly idiot, I've always thought that my head is much prettier as an adornment to my shoulders than it would be rolling around on the ground and getting all dirty.

He smiled and took a bite of quail; the bird was juicy enough that he had to dab at the corner of his lips. The smell made my mouth water.

A white-clad servitor, her face holding that expression just between disdain and indifference that makes service folk think they're invisible, brought out a tray with my breakfast on it. The cook had perhaps spent less time with my breakfast than he had with Arefai's.

The tray held an apple—uncut, unpeeled, although apparently washed—accompanied by a large chunk of dark brown bread, supporting a dubious hill of butter. An unadorned chunk of pink ham lay on the plate next to the bread.

Arefai looked at it with distaste, then put an expression of polite concern on his face.

"Please," he said, "Kami Dan'Shir. You have been invited to break your fast with me; you need not await my specific invitation to begin your meal."

The way I normally began the day with breakfast was by skipping it. Later on in the morning, partway into the hour of the hare, Madame Lastret's Two Dog Inn would open on Ankersa Way, just at the edge of the Bankstreets in the town of Den Oroshtai, and I tended to take my first

13

meal there, or at Madame Rupon's. While the pay of Lord Toshtai's dan'shir was moderately generous, hour-by-hour duties had not been assigned; as long as a runner or Runner from the castle could reach me, I was unlikely to be in trouble.

I guess I should have worked out an arrangement with whoever in the kitchen cooked breakfast, instead of with Madame Lastret and Madame Rupon.

What I wished for was the old company, the juggling and foolery that always went along with meals in the Troupe of Gray Khuzud. What I wanted was my little sister, Enki Duzun, showering five eggs and an apple, while Fhilt took two spoons and kept three dollops of jam in the air until one of the Eresthais would snatch the dollops away, one by one, with slices of bread.

Well, at least this was more than peasant food. Bread and onion would have been the local peasant breakfast in Den Oroshtai, and if I'd still been a peasant, that would have been all I would have been offered by the castle servitors, most likely; certainly nothing more than dirt-food. Had I been only middle class, that might have been supplemented by a tree-fruit, an apple or a pear. As a true hereditary bourgeois—albeit, granted, the first of my line—I'd been honored with not only butter but meat. No tea, of course, nor sauce, nor game. But I wasn't a member of our beloved ruling class, after all.

Me, I prefer rooming houses, where what one eats depends more on what one can pay than upon the status of the buttocks against which one's mother once drummed her heels.

The ham was edible, although it could have stood a proper soaking; then again, perhaps salted ham with salt is a taste I've simply not acquired. I left it on my plate. The apple wasn't bad, just a bit mealy around the edges. But the bread was good and solid and still warm, and the butter was cold and smooth and rich and creamy, and that would do—for the time being. Wheedling a snack out of a cook is a skill that I'd picked up many years before.

"You don't seem excited by the idea of hunting, Kami Dan'Shir," Arefai said. "And on such a fine day."

"Hunting is a noble pursuit, Lord," I said. *You know, like pronging away at unwilling peasant girls.* I probably felt more adventurous than I should, but perhaps I was flushed with my victory over Crosta Natthan. I went on: "Perhaps if I was raised to the nobility, Lord Arefai, I'd feel differently."

"You've been a bourgeois how long?"

"Almost a month, lord."

He chuckled. "I think perhaps you might consider waiting some years before broaching the matter to my father; he has no sense of humor." He tapped himself lightly on the chest. "I, on the other hand, do. You have dined with me; you will now hunt with me."

One of the guards started, stilled instantly by a glare from the more senior.

Arefai took a final sip of tea and tossed his eating sticks aside; with a quick, beckoning flick of his fingers, he rose, not waiting to see if I was following.

We headed out of the garden, and down the path into a fine day. Two pairs of bodyguards walked in front of us, while the trio behind us kept up a marching song, the baritone taking up the verse and melody, the tenor gracing the end of each phrase with a high harmony that soared above like a bird, while the bass sang a slow countermelody that still managed to keep perfect time.

"A perfect day for a hunt, eh, Kami Dan'Shir?" Arefai gestured with a vague but possessive wave. Nobles own the day, it seemed.

Again, I agreed with him. "Of course."

He eyed me carefully; the implied reproach in the short answer hadn't escaped him.

Smiling agreeably, I ignored his look, or at least tried to look like I was ignoring his look.

I had to be careful around Arefai; since he was in some contexts such a pleasant dolt, it was important for me to remind myself that he was a blooded warrior, and worldly in the ways of statement and understatement, the form of speech called *shtoi* in Old Shai. It's never been safe to disagree with members of our beloved ruling class, even if you're a member of our beloved ruling class, and an almost formal mode of overstatement and understatement had grown up, passed on with indirectness from parent to child, from husband to wife and wife to husband, becoming more indirect, more ambiguous, and less precise as time went on, because directness, clarity, and precision could lead to trouble.

Trouble in D'Shai is often fatal.

"You seem to lack some . . . enthusiasm, Kami Dan'Shir," he said.

I had been hoping he would let it drop. I would have been happy to.

"Not at all, Lord Arefai," I said. "I'm honored that you would give me such a—" I put in the slightest of hesitations, just a moment of robbed time "—unique opportunity."

"You've never hunted?"

I weighed the odds, and decided that Arefai was not going to take violent offense at something that had happened more than half D'Shai away, so I decided that being truthful was, at least for once, the safest thing to do, and put on my most engaging smile.

"Well, no, Lord. But accidents happen. When you're walking through the roads high in the mountains of Helgramyth, it often happens that the innocent bits of wet twine you have set out the night before—"

"Snares?"

I spread my hands. "Oh, no, Lord. Simply to dry. The weather is often damp high in the mountains of Helgramyth." Of course, the need to tie the twine into a noose was not apparent, nor the need to set up a bent sapling and a carved trigger for the noose, so I didn't mention it.

He nodded. "I see."

"Well, it sometimes happens that when you're drying your twine, as the saying goes, a rabbit will on occasion tangle itself in your twine and be dead by morning. Now, even a peasant is allowed to eat dead animals he finds; that's hardly hunting."

I didn't go into how the rabbits are quickly skinned and roasted, the skin, bones, and offal buried before you swing out on the day's march, lest anybody walking along the path misunderstand and think that you'd been snaring rabbits.

"This happens often?"

"Rarely, Lord. And never within the domain of Lord Toshtai, of course." I tried on my most sincere voice.

His nod accepted me at my word.

Horses were saddled and hitched to the viny hitching trellis at the stables. Beyond, half a dozen or so matched brown horses pranced, their riders, the guards, already in the saddle.

Arefai's horse stood waiting for him, a coal-black mare, its hooves lacquered to a high gloss and crimson and yellow flowers woven into its long mane. A dull, almost taupe gelding stood listlessly waiting for me.

I didn't know whether to be jealous of Lord Arefai's fine animal and resentful I'd been given such a drab mount, or happy that I wasn't going to be bouncing on the back of an animal I'd be decidedly unable to control. The dull little gelding suited me, I decided as I climbed up the trellis and gingerly lowered myself into the saddle. While richer peasants have draft horses, horses as riding animals are permitted only to the bourgeois and members of our beloved ruling class—it would be a shame to have the head of a peasant sit higher than that of a lord—and both horses and saddles were a relatively new thing to my tender bottom.

This was the third—no, fourth—time that I had been on a horse—each time to accompany Arefai—and it was no better than the first. With every step, the saddle would try to jerk my hips forward; when the horse broke into a faster pace (a canter, they call it; I call it a personal assault) it would try to bounce my buttocks up around my ears.

Personally, I would rather have walked. That I can do well.

17

Thankfully, Arefai wasn't in a hurry this morning, so he kept his mare at a slow walk, the smaller gelding briskly stepping to keep up, prodded with a sheathed lance by one of the trailing bodyguards when it lagged.

Well, at least they weren't prodding *me*; I take what good fortune I can get.

2

The Joy of the Chase, the Thrill of the Hunt, and Other Blatant Falsehoods

THE HUNTING PRESERVE lay most of an hour's ride to morningwise of the keep: a fan-shaped expanse of forest, fields, and three lakes, some of it as carefully trimmed and maintained as the gardens in the inner court, other parts allowed to go wild.

We talked as we rode past square fields of wheat and rice—each one a standard one peden in area; Lord Toshtai divides land neatly—to where a forested ridge of low hill was broken only by our road.

More accurately, Arefai talked and I listened; his wedding with Lady ViKay of Glen Derenai was coming up in a few weeks, although it had yet to be formally announced, and he was having to take time from his other activities to supervise the preparation of her quarters, adjoining his.

I had spent a few moments in Arefai's rooms, once. His tastes were simple and really quite good. I understood ViKay's to be other than simple, and perhaps not entirely possible. If I understood Arefai correctly, it seemed she wanted her rooms floored with warm green marble; she needed privacy screens that wouldn't interfere with the air flow fitted tightly over the windows; she simply must have ancient Meșthai artwork newly carved for the headboard of her sleeping pallet; and she fully expected Arefai to supervise the installation of all of that.

I didn't voice my limited sympathy at how this was such a dreadful imposition on his time. It appeared he was forced to cut back to what sounded like a mere one full afternoon of massage, two evenings pronging peasant girls and no more than that with his concubines, and perhaps as few as three morning hunts. It's important that those of us of the lower classes show proper sympathy with the burdens of our beloved ruling class.

Lord Toshtai's chief huntsman, Garvi Denten, and his gamekeeper, Deroy Rawn, were waiting for us outside the hunting shelter, where open wooden cages and leather harnesses stood stacked neatly on the bare dirt.

I had seen the two of them only from a distance. Neither acrobats nor dan'shirs spend much time around huntsmen; this was my first chance to examine them closely.

Most men who spend their lives outdoors develop a tan to their skins, but Garvi Denten was red as a brick, and shaped like one, blocky and solid, from the thick, scarred neck where his studded collar hung loosely, to the splayed toes at the end of his massive feet. Dressed in a burlap overshirt and drawstring muslin pantaloons, he looked rather more like a peasant than a hereditary bourgeois, and a pretty disreputable peasant, at that.

Deroy Rawn, on the other hand, was dark and smooth where his master was red and rough. His skin was the color of urmon tea, his face freshly shaven beneath the well-oiled mustache that decorated his upper lip. The fingers of his hands, as he gestured at the darkness of the hunting lodge, were long and aristrocratic, the nails clean and unbitten.

A conclusion that I didn't have to raise kazuh for: Deroy Rawn was a pompous ass, despite the meaning of his name. Huntsmen are bourgeois; gamekeepers are only middle class. It's an anomaly, and if I were the Scion I'd reclassify gamekeeping as a bourgeois profession. After all, head gamekeeper is almost as common a route to chief huntsman as assistant huntsman is.

But Deroy Rawn was trying to make it look as though he were the bourgeois, and that spoke of a self-important view of his position and himself.

They both bowed deeply at Arefai as the lord dismounted.

Arefai dropped easily to the dirt and walked smoothly to the two men, while I climbed painfully down out of the saddle and staggered behind.

Well, the upper classes have to have tougher bottoms than the rest of us; they spend most of their time sitting down while somebody else does something for them, whether it's a cook feeding them, a troupe of acrobats and musicians entertaining them, or a horse carrying them. It's surprising that their women don't tend to grow immensely broad of beam.

I didn't like the sneer on Deroy Rawn's lip, so I made a calculated bow to the two huntsmen—not terribly deep, and a bit perfunctory: a bow of equals, or perhaps of a gracious senior.

"I am Eldest Son Discoverer-of-Truths," I said, introducing myself formally. Old Shai is formal for everything but names; we introduce ourselves in modern language on formal occasions, or when we are battering each other about with inappropriate formality.

Deroy Rawn was holding a bow and a packet of arrows for Arefai, and had to spread a cloth and set them down—carefully; he didn't want to let either touch the ground—on top of one of the cages in order to return my bow. His face was smooth and impassive, but I already had the idea we weren't going to become fast friends.

His return bow was a bit too shallow. The smart thing to do was ignore it, but Arefai had noticed me notice, and was watching to see what I would do.

So was I, actually. I went on, as though I hadn't finished introducing myself: "—kazuh Dan'Shir, and historical master of truth-discovery."

Garvi Denten muffled a smile as he bowed deeply, only

a hair less than he would have done before a noble. "I am Eats Chicken," he said, "Huntsman to the third generation."

Deroy Rawn had to bow even more deeply than his master. "I am Passes Wind," he said.

I take it you have not gotten permission to change your name, I didn't quite say. I could see how Garvi Denten might well want to put the gamekeeper in his place by addressing him formally when he got impertinent. Which probably meant that he had always served somebody who didn't care for him, or who he suspected didn't care for him.

Arefai had finished removing his sandals, and stood barefoot in his snowy hunting tunic and the silk pantaloons that were shirred tight at knee and ankles, but blousy above and below. They rippled in the wind, like the grasses at his feet.

He slapped his hands together. "The hunt, good Garvi Denten, the hunt. What are we hunting today?"

Garvi Denten bowed again. "Lord Arefai specified some light hunting, so I thought perhaps some quail, a fish or two, and then game of some sort." He eyed the spears leaning up against the wall of the shelter. "Boar might be possible, but—"

"One would hardly call boar hunting light, eh?" Arefai nodded. He accepted a short bow and a bundle of perhaps half a dozen arrows, the bundle secured with two twists of silver wire, while Garvi Denten belted a silver-trimmed quiver about his waist.

I unlaced my own sandals and tossed them aside as Deroy Rawn handed me a bow, bundle, and quiver, and awkwardly belted the quiver around me. What I was going to be able to do with all this was not exactly clear to me. I'd never so much as held a bow in my hands, and suspected that there was some serious sleight to its use.

Arefai set one end of his bow between his ankles and levered it against the inside of his knee to bend it into a curve, snapping the bowstring into place as he did.

That appeared easier to do than it was. When I tried it, the end slipped out and sent the bow tumbling to the grass.

With a superior smirk, Deroy Rawn strung the bow and handed it to me. "Good hunting, Kami Dan'Shir," he said.

Arefai was watching me impatiently; we set off.

The hunting trail, barely wide enough for the two of us to walk side by side, was a stone footpath leading off down the slope toward where the carefully manicured brush broke on freshly scythed grass. Each stone, individually shaped and polished to a gentle convexity, was smooth and damp beneath my feet, although it had not rained the night before.

I could almost see the huntsmen with their pails and brushes, cleaning it for the delectation of Arefai's feet.

The trail bent, then straightened. Above, huge elms towered, their arcing branches turning the path into a leafy tunnel of dark green. Off in the distance, a hairy owl ta*roo*ed, and something small scampered from branch to branch. I would have thought that a hunt ought to be conducted in silence—my own experience of walking the roads of D'Shai suggests that animals stay away from people making noise—but Arefai wanted to talk. It was his chance to play teacher, I suppose.

"It's a good idea to travel with an arrow nocked, but—" he stopped as he looked over at me. "No, no, not the big broadhead; use the half-moon arrow. That's the right one for quail."

He selected an arrow for me and helped me fit it to my bowstring, then took up his own bow and a similar arrow; it was tipped with a half-moon of sharpened steel, edged like the edge of a sword, but thin and light.

Ahead, the path widened as it opened on a grassy meadow that angled down to the pond. The flat stones circled the edge of the pond, vanishing again into a leafy green tunnel.

A waterwalker stood on one leg on one bank, its long, pointed bill in profile, as though it was looking over its left wing. My own suspicion, that one of its wide eyes watched us while the other looked for prey, was quickly confirmed when it blurred into motion. Its feet slapped in an impossibly rapid tattoo first against the muddy bank, and then against the surface of the water as it scurried across the pond, not pausing for a moment in its mad dash as it dipped its beak, then straightened, a wriggling fish momentarily in its grip. It tossed the fish high, and snapped it down before it reached the other side of the pond, only to stumble comically on the bank.

I'd seen it happen before and I saw it again: perhaps a dozen other waterwalkers rose from the grasses rimming the pond and dashed across, some catching fish, most not.

Then the pond lay silent, its glassy surface broken only by the last ripples of the birds' wakes.

Where the path broke on the meadow, it opened on a low green marble podium large enough for the two of us to stand comfortably, then bent to the right, cupping the edge of the pasture. The far side of the podium was occupied by a waist-high table where a dark silver pitcher sat, its bright sides beaded with dew to the halfway point. A tall stemmed glass stood next to the pitcher; Arefai set his bow down on the table and poured himself some of the golden, bubbly liquid, drinking deeply before he set the glass back on the table.

I was going to muffle a couple of comments—something about how I had no idea whether we were first going to see a quail as opposed to a deer and doubted he did, either; something about how I would be lucky to be able to shoot an arrow well enough to hit the *ground*—when a covey of quail took flight across the field from us, their wings making the muffled applause sound of feathers beating against feathers.

Arefai's string twanged. I wasn't watching closely enough to mark the arrow's flight, but I did see a bird fall from the sky, its head tumbling in a different direction than its body.

The body had barely bounced once on the ground when a huntsman leaped out from the brush, snatched it up, and disappeared back into the leafy cover.

"That was a plump one," he said. "And it will be tasty at dinner tonight."

Arefai's smile was modestly modest, but it disappeared when he looked down to see that I hadn't shot my arrow.

I shrugged, as though to point out that everything had happened so quickly that I hadn't had time to even think about shooting, but he dismissed it with a glare. If it had been anybody but Arefai, I would have wondered at what secret motivation caused him to care one way or another, but it was Arefai, after all.

"The arrow, please," he said, holding his hand out, palm up.

I handed him the half-moon arrow; he set it down on the table.

"The fishing arrow is next," he said, as we walked down the path to where it exited into darkness on the far side of the meadow. "We shall see if you can manage a trout."

The fishing arrow, I discovered, was headed by a triple prong, each prong barbed, and it was marked halfway up the shaft by a thin gold ring. A length of silken string was secured to the head of the arrow, which fit loosely over the shaft.

I was going to make some mention of that until I noticed that Arefai had removed the head of his arrow as though to check it, then slipped it back on.

The path snaked back and forth down a steep slope, each turn rimmed in gold leaf, until it dumped us out next to a bridge over a stream that was perhaps two manheights wide, no deeper than knee-high anywhere.

The sandy bank had been smoothed into shape and ripples had been combed into the sand. Despite the cool of the morning, it warmed my feet pleasantly.

A manheight oaken column stood on the bank, weathered and varnished to a rich texture and high sheen, a burnished brass ring projecting from its top. Arefai quickly bound one end of his silken line to the ring, paying out silk as he walked away.

Stepping stones crossed upstream of the bridge. Each

25

stone, about the width of a dinner plate, had nesting curves carved into its top, like the floor of the baths. Arefai leaped lightly from the bank to the nearest of the stones, then step-step-stepped out to the middle of the stream, nocking his fishing arrow as he did, careful to keep it clear of the line. He stood, immobile as a statue, waiting.

I took up a position on the next two stones. There were no fish in the stream that I could see, from where the water rippled just beneath my feet to where the stream appeared from around the bend. I opened my mouth to make some comment, but Arefai's glare kept me silent.

We hadn't been waiting long when the water rippled ahead, just at the bend.

Arefai drew his bow back to a light extension, where the bowstring touched the gold ring on the arrow. I pulled mine back all the way, to where the head of the arrow almost touched the bowstring. He was a warrior and I was just a newly made bourgeois, but I had spent most of my life as an acrobat, and there's something about tumbling, highwire, and flying that does give you a lot of physical strength, even more than that of somebody who spends his days chopping warriors and peasants into a fine puree.

But something about his stance impressed me. It took me a moment to realize that the only tension was in his arms and shoulders, that the muscles not involved in drawing the bow were loose and relaxed. I didn't have the slightest idea whether or not that helped with shooting, but I liked the look of it, of taut shoulders and forearms, right hand held in a clench like the talons of a falcon, the neck relaxed, the set of the feet easy and flat.

He released his string in a smooth loose, without any pluck. The bow made a deep *thrummm*, the bass note of a raw young zivver that hadn't been broken in properly. But a fish leaped from the stream, its body impaled on the barbs, then flopped down into the water, flibitaflibitaflibitting madly up into the shallow water of the bank.

For a moment, I thought it had dislodged the fishing arrow, but it was only the loose shaft. The fish lay on the bank, anchored by the barbs and the silken cord, its gills slowing opening and closing. There was a rustle in the bushes beyond the bridge, and a hand quickly reached out to snatch the wooden shaft as it washed by.

Arefai was waiting for me.

I had been so impressed with his performance that I had slackened the bowstring and let some fish slip past me, but I took aim along the shaft and pulled the arrow back to its full extension, trying to stand tall and easy, just like the warriors did.

I waited until the arrow was lined up with a large fish, and tried to loose the string with one easy motion—

"Oww!" The bowstring slapped me *hard* on my bare forearm, abrading flesh just this side of bloody, while my arrowhead bounced hard off a stone, sending the loose shaft tumbling through the air until it fetched up in the mud on the edge of the bank.

No fish.

Arefai glared at me. *What use are you?* he didn't say, so I didn't answer.

Not that I would have. A thick skin behooves us.

The stone path split four ways beyond the stream, each subordinate trail indicated by a small plaque set into the stone, and by carvings in the stone of the trail: a deer, a snake, a boar, and a dragon. A flufftailed deer's hoofprints led morningwise, curving back toward the town of Den Oroshtai and the meandering stream. Twisted indentations marking the surface of the path of the snake pointed a few grades to the south, toward Stony Buthen; the path of the boar, marked by deep hoofprints, led to the south and sunwise.

The path of the dragon, marked only by a cluster of curlicues representing a dragon's breath, led downslope, almost directly sunwise, disappearing in the trees. Perhaps a slight breeze blew out of the path, because I smelled something off in the distance, something cold enough to make me shiver.

I don't react to cold too well. "I take it we're not hunting dragons today," I said, trying for humor. I rubbed at the area where the bowstring had slapped me. Angrily red, it still hurt.

"That's not—" He looked at me, exasperated. "Ask Narantir sometime about the charms put on the paths. The path of the deer tends to lead to game for the pot: rabbit, deer, trelinger. The path of the snake is likely to pass by foreseeable danger—snakes, pit spider, razorfoot; the path of the boar leads to proof of bravery: boar, say—and make no mistake, Kami Dan'Shir, there *are* lions back up in the hills.

"The path of the dragon leads to that best left alone."

I could see the use of the first three. Fairly obvious: members of our beloved ruling class like to kill their food themselves, hence the path of the deer. They have to prove they're brave, and facing off against a lion or boar demonstrates something they can decide to call courage. Running into a dung spider or a razorfoot could help to sort out the careless.

But . . .

"If I may ask, why is there a path of the dragon?"

He looked at me like I had dung on my face. Sometimes I should learn to keep my mouth shut.

"Today we will take the path of the deer," he said. "I suspect we may find some game down there."

There seemed to be a fair chance of that, all things considered. After the fish and the quail coming along at precisely the right moment for a convenient shot, I didn't have to raise kazuh to figure that both had been prepared, that hidden huntsmen had released the quail into flight and freed a couple of fish from around the bend.

Odds were some deer stood bound and blindfolded somewhere near the path of the deer, ready to be freed and slapped on the rump, sent bouncing down the path toward our waiting bows. Taking it a step further, the odds were equally good that a backup deer was waiting.

He had his arrow in the hand he used to pull an arrow from my quiver. "Here. And try to shoot at the game this time." He gestured that I should precede him. "After you."

The path widened ahead, lined on both sides by a carpet of well-trimmed grasses.

It was hardly a surprise to me when a three-point buck soon bounded across. He paused for a moment, eyes wide.

I pulled back my arrow and let fly, again slapping the bowstring against my hurt forearm. Needless to say, the arrow went Powers-know-where, but a breeze brushed my cheek and an arrow *spung*ed into the deer's side.

The deer gave me a reproachful look and took a half step before his legs went all loose and disjointed, and he dropped to the ground, legs splaying this way and that.

A brace of huntsmen leaped out of the brush and were already dressing it out before it stopped twitching.

"Well shot, Kami Dan'Shir!" Arefai exclaimed. "Well shot, indeed!"

I turned to see him standing with an arrow nocked. Another arrow.

"I had no chance to shoot, but no need," he said. "A heart shot, and for your first time out, magnificent!" He clapped a hand to my shoulder. "The huntsmen will dress it out and lash it to your saddle; you will take it back to the keep. You must join me at table tonight to celebrate this meal. I'm sure Father will insist."

"Yes, I am sure your father will insist, Lord Arefai," I said. "I'm very sure of that."

Now I knew how a waterwalker felt. You run just as fast as you can over the surface, not stopping for a moment as you dip your beak here and there, because if you stop to think about how impossible your position is, you'll sink beneath the waves never to be seen again.

I should have known this hunting expedition couldn't have been as simple as it seemed. Thank the Powers I faced only another week of this; Toshtai, Arefai, and Edelfaule would be off to Glen Derenai for Arefai's wedding, probably leaving Den Oroshtai under the care of Dun Lidjun, and that would give me some time to breathe. Dun Lidjun didn't care if I plucked a flower, or produced a puzzle; all he wanted me to do was to stay out of his way.

Arefai, on the other hand, had been just a tad too clever, just a crumb too indirect. Not his way at all.

I should have spotted it earlier: a horse had been waiting for me. It had always been Arefai's intention that I go on the hunt with him, and it apparently had always been his intention that I kill some game, thereby giving him a credible excuse to invite a lowly bourgeois to dinner.

That was subtle, and indirect, and very much unArefai.

Things were starting to get complicated, and when things get complicated, it's good to talk them over with a friend. Sometimes it's necessary to talk them over with *somebody*.

The trouble, of course, was that I didn't really have any friends, not in the keep. The closest thing I had to a friend was Arefai, and he had just gone through a performance intended to bring me to the formal dinner that evening. It wasn't his idea; Arefai didn't have ideas. He wasn't built for it.

I didn't have many other choices. Crosta Natthan and I were hardly boon companions. TaNai and I had another agenda, and I wasn't going to complicate that.

Narantir would have to do.

3
Narantir and Other Friendly Acquaintances

A PROCESSION WAS arriving on the main road as the riding path dumped me out near the main entrance to the castle. I was bound for Narantir's workshop, intending a quick detour to leave the meat at the kitchens and the sad little gelding at the stable.

Ver Hortun, one of Lord Toshtai's soldiers, beckoned me to stop and dismount. I could almost see him debating with himself how to treat me. Here I was, only a bourgeois, but I was not only mounted but carrying an unstrung bow and a parcel that looked more than slightly like a deerskin filled with butchered meat strapped to the rear of my saddle. It didn't take a dan'shir to figure that out, what with the way it was leaking deer blood down the horse's flanks, attracting flies.

No three ways about it: either I was absolutely begging to be killed or this was authorized by at least concatenated authority from Lord Toshtai.

He decided to assume that I hadn't gone crazy, which was just as well for me. The Foulsmelling Ones of Bhorlan are said to treat insanity with herbs and magic, but we are a simpler folk, with simpler solutions.

"Meat for the kitchen, eh?" he asked, not quite looking at me. I was, at worst, a pushy bourgeois; but the soldiers around the approaching palanquin were fellow warriors, and watching them Ver Hortun's first responsibility.

The horse pranced and tugged at the reins. I pulled hard, only making it more nervous; Ver Hortun had to help me calm it down.

I nodded. "Lord Arefai invited me to hunt with him this morning. He wishes this delivered to the kitchens."

"Mmm." He nodded. "Venison needs curing or marinating." Wrapping his fingers tightly in the horse's mane, he eyed the crowd of soldiers at the gate. "It might be wise to wait here," he said, over the saddle. "Lord Minch arrives. One wouldn't want to get bound up in that."

"Lord Minch?" I asked. The name was familiar. "From Lair Tiree?"

He shook his head. "No. Another one. House Menfors from Merth's Bridge; fealty-bound to the Agami Lords. Famous archer and lecher," he said, then, as though realizing that he had talked too much, gave me a sideways glance.

I ignored the indiscretion. "Far from home," I ventured. I had found that if I was careful, if I didn't push too hard, I could sometimes make a member of our beloved ruling class treat me like I was a real person. Soldiers were tricky.

Ver Hortun nodded, his eyes on the arriving party. "He is that. On his way to Glen Derenai for the wedding."

Despite the wars that wash up and down our country like a wave in a bathtub, many members of our beloved ruling class seem to spend most of their time traveling back and forth across the face of D'Shai on any pretext available. In part, I suppose, it's a way of reconfiguring the constantly changing set of alliances that keep the Long War going at a quiet simmer most of the time. I suspect it's also largely a matter of he who can, does. Most D'Shaians grow old and die within less than a day's walk from the hovel where they're born. Then again, most D'Shaians are peasants.

The arrival of a distant noble is more of a dance than anything else, as stylized and formal a set piece as you'll find on a Wisterly stage—which is why I would normally have skipped it; dance bores me.

The chief of the visitor's bodyguard approaches to exchange a few respectful words with the captain of the guard, and to receive the implicit and sensible assurances that the local lord will not refuse hospitality to an important personage standing outside his gates, an assurance that will always be given. Forgetting—just for a moment, if you please!—the likely penalties resulting from attacking a guest, such could be more easily accomplished within the walls than without.

Think on the legends, and the history; even ancient Lord Creer made ancient Lord Dilpa welcome and fed him a fine meal before he hamstrung ancient Dilpa and threw him to the pigs, after all.

I couldn't see Minch; he was presumably further down the road with the rest of the party (and a large party it would be; members of our beloved ruling class do not travel with a pair of sacks on their backs), waiting out of sight for the expected—required, actually—invitation to stay.

The representatives of the two sides met barely a stone's throw from the gate, under the spreading limbs of an old jimsum tree, its boughs heavy with clumps of the thick, bitter nut.

Minch's chief bodyguard was almost a pastiche, a caricature of a warrior: he was a tall and rangy man, his broad shoulders straining against the dull green silk of his tunic underneath the reticulated bone armor, armor that had been coated and polished until it seemed to shine with an inner light. He stood with his legs planted arrogantly apart, a massive fist on his left hip, his right hand in front of his waist, just hovering near the hilt of his sword. I just *knew* that beneath his helmet his hair was properly oiled and pulled back into a warrior's queue, and while his visor shaded the upper part of his face, there would be carefully drawn dark half-moons of kohl under his eyes.

I hadn't heard about the arrival of a dignitary, but Minch must have been an important one, because old Dun Lidjun himself was acting as captain of the guard, and facing off against the visitor's chief bodyguard.

Superficially, Dun Lidjun wasn't much to look at. An older man, limp hair an infinitely dull gray, slim to the point of skinniness, his tunic and pantaloons unfashionably loose at the wrists and ankles, belted tightly across his hips. Narrow eyes and mouth; nose like a knife-blade. There was no overt menace in his manner; his hands didn't hover near the hilt of a sword that I happened to know was a fine Eisenlith blade. No braggadocio in it, either: the hilt was of plain wood, cord-wound. I wouldn't have even known that his sword was particularly fine if I hadn't once seen the naked blade, and I wouldn't have known it was an Eisenlith blade if somebody else hadn't mentioned it.

But then I noticed the small details; that is part of the Way of the Dan'Shir.

I saw how his thin bangs were trimmed so that they barely brushed his eyebrows; how the rest of his hair was bound back tightly into a warrior's queue. How his unshifting, steady eyes seemed to take in everything at once. How he never worked to keep his footing, even on the loose stones outside the guard station.

There's reason to believe that balance is the way of more than the acrobat.

Minch's bodyguard strode up to Dun Lidjun, his sandals slipping on the loose stones—that is, after all, why the road outside the entrance is gravelly—stopping insolently close to Dun Lidjun, less than a swordslength away. His dull olive green tunic held the small tight wrinkles that meant it had been recently unpacked.

He bowed properly. "I am Deren der Drumud," he said, introducing himself informally, which was proper under the circumstances. "I have long had the honor of being guard to Lord Minch."

Dun Lidjun returned the bow. "Dun Lidjun. I serve Lord Toshtai." The marshall of all of Lord Toshtai's forces was being modest.

"Lord Minch finds evening falling unexpectedly," Deren

der Drumud said, as custom demanded, "and he seeks shelter for the night."

It didn't seem to bother him that it was barely the hour of the horse, but then hypocrisy doesn't bother many in D'Shai, for the same reason, I suppose, that fish are not annoyed by water.

It would have been uncouth to point out that while night does many things—ask Edge of the Night if you ever have the misfortune to confront that Power—one thing it never, ever does is fall unexpectedly, nor does it fall in the hour of the horse, the hour that sits astride noon.

Dun Lidjun was not uncouth.

Behind Deren der Drumud, a dozen warriors in olive livery displaying a tree-symbol fanned out in feigned menace. The theory, of course, is that they were preparing to eagerly spend their lives to buy their lord a few moments to flee. A silly theory, granted; somebody willing to kick over the table by denying hospitality that blatantly would likely be perfectly willing to wait until the lord was within the walls of the keep, where he would be even more vulnerable.

Of course, there was a good reason and a sound motivation behind the exercise of the silly theory: If anybody made a miscalculation, it would give the warriors a chance to kill somebody. All warriors are, by definition, members of our beloved ruling class. Members of our beloved ruling class love to kill.

Dun Lidjun nodded, not briskly. "Quarters wait," he said, without the usual sort of mindlessly rote delivery of overflowery promises; Dun Lidjun was rarely on duty for such things, and, for a warrior, had little patience with form. "Be welcome," he said. He started to turn away.

Deren der Drumud's eyes narrowed. "Quarters?" He spat the word out like a curse. "I do not care for the implications of such informality, Brown Turtle," he said, addressing Dun Lidjun formally.

Dun Lidjun's face went studiously blank. "My apologies, Strong of Arm," he said, bowing. "I would have thought . . . but never mind; the error is mine." He

35

straightened. "A suite waits, a suite where incense burns softly quietly waits for Lord Minch and his company. Cool drinks sit in their glasses, dew a-beading their sides, gently whispering, 'Drink me.'

"Soft breezes, scented with rose and lemon, blow in through open windows, just for the delectation of Lord Minch's noble nose. In the bathhouse, water has been heated to a pleasant temperature just short of scalding; it waits to draw the ache from Lord Minch's supple but weary muscles.

"Just this morning, Lord Arefai, son to Lord Toshtai, has gone out in search of game that, properly prepared, might please Lord Minch's discerning palate; bird, fish, and meat are this moment being rushed to the cooks so that they may prepare it to Lord Minch's delicate taste." Dun Lidjun had already gone on rather longer than formality required.

He continued: "A dozen virgin maids, their pleasantly round buttocks straining against the thin fabric of their shifts, now bend over washtubs, scrubbing furiously at blankets and sheets that will be hung on savorfruit trees, to gather their gentle scent as they dry. Peasants plow their fields and plod through their paddies, hoping that their rice and wheat will be honored by being chosen to assuage Lord Minch's appetites."

The tips of Deren der Drumud's ears were red. He had expected the little man to quail before his displeasure, not confront him with overelegant embellishment.

"The sun . . ." Dun Lidjun stopped himself. "The sun gets no farther from the horizon as we stand here talking; be welcome."

Custom called upon Deren der Drumud to respond with polite thanks for the invitation, but he hadn't quite decided what to do when there was a sudden *snap*.

It was nothing, really; a squirrel, above, had finished with a jimsum nut and had dropped the shell, which had hit the gravel below.

But Deren Der Drumud panicked; he went for his sword, *fast*.

Dun Lidjun's hands were nowhere near his own sword, but that wouldn't have mattered. I had and have never seen anyone able to raise kazuh faster than Dun Lidjun could. There was no doubt in my mind that he could have his sword in hand before Deren der Drumud could strike. I fully expected him to take a step back and free his own weapon, block, and then cut Deren der Drumud's head off.

But he did nothing of the sort.

As Deren der Drumud's hand snaked for the hilt of his sword, Dun Lidjun, his kazuh flaring bright enough for a mindblind man to see, simply took a half step forward and laid his slim hand on Deren der Drumud's thick wrist.

There was no strain in Dun Lidjun's face, but Deren der Drumud grunted and creased his face as he struggled for a moment trying to draw his sword, desisting when he saw how useless it was.

"Control yourself, man," Dun Lidjun hissed, holding on just a moment longer. He took a step backward. "Be still, Strong of Arm. It was just a squirrel. Bid Lord Minch and his party welcome to Den Oroshtai, if it please you."

He turned about and walked away.

Deren der Drumud stared at his back for the longest time.

Ver Hortun raised an eyebrow. "And what do you think of that, Kami Dan'Shir?"

"I think Deren der Drumud is both nervous and a fool," I said, too frankly.

Ver Hortun beckoned me on. "I don't think one needs to be a dan'shir to discover that," he said. "The horse is patient but the cooks are not; you'd best rush the meat to the kitchens before dropping the horse off at the stables."

First the deliveries, then the wizard.

Narantir's workshop was in the musty basement of the old donjon, the older and smaller of the two residences within the keep's walls. The set of rooms had been used as a dungeon during the days of Oroshtai himself, but there's rarely a need for a dungeon, and certainly not for two, in Den Oroshtai; D'Shaian justice tends to be swift.

I hated the workshop. For one thing, it smelled bad. Given some of the things that went on down here, that wasn't surprising. Over near the outer wall, where a finger-high slit allowed a trickle of light into the room, a pile of bones stood in one corner under a workbench. It takes a long time to get the smell of rotted flesh from bones, Narantir once told me. Next to the workbench, yet another one of Narantir's skeletons was in either the early stages of assembly or the advanced stages of disassembly. At least it was an adult's this time.

An empty wineskin lay next to the bag of straw that Narantir used as a bed. The stone floor was carpeted mainly in dirt but partly in, well, everything else. Dirty robes were heaped in the far corner. The room was probably cleaned once every ten years or so, whether it needed it or not.

It needed it.

It would have taken an order from Lord Toshtai to get a servitor down here to muck out the room, and Lord Toshtai either wasn't interested enough to bother or, like most people, gave wizards as wide a berth as possible. I would have been willing to bet on the former; the lord of Den Oroshtai wasn't known for being reticent in his orders to his subjects, myself included.

Narantir had mounted a small, squarish, black iron cookstove on the nearest of roughhewn worktables; a slowly boiling pot of some vile green liquid sat on the grate, the wizard stirring it slowly with a wooden spoon. The thick fluid burbled and spat, but Narantir ignored the green speckling of his arm and hand.

He had been gaining weight again. His belly, always protruding, now strained against the circumference of his robes, and the fleshy wrinkles in his face were filling out. His black beard and hair were uncombed and greasy, and he had smeared something, probably lampblack, above his left eye.

He was not happy.

"Truth spells," he said, probably to himself. "Always it's the truth spells." He looked over at the small brown rabbit cowering in its wicker cage. He extended a finger to scratch at the top of its head, but it scurried to the other side of the cage. "Sorry I am, but foolish enough to disobey orders I am *not*."

I cleared my throat.

"Oh, it's Kami Khuzud," he said, as though he barely recognized me.

"Kami Dan'Shir," I said. "But it's still me. Truth spells?"

He frowned as he moved the pot on the iron grate, quietly cursing to himself when it didn't immediately stop bubbling. He pawed through a pile of tools on a nearby bench, eventually producing a pair of tongs that he used to lift the pot off the burner and onto the already marred surface of the table itself.

"Truth spells," he said. "There's been a defalcation in the village; Lord Edelfaule detected it, he says, and Lord Toshtai wants me to make sure which one of two is guilty before sentence is executed."

I didn't ask the nature of the sentence; we D'Shaians, including members of our beloved ruling class, are predictably simple people.

He sighed. "So here I'll be for the next day and a half, preparing to squat over a pentagram, knife and rabbit in hand." Narantir wasn't fond of necromancy, but it wasn't because of any delicacy of his digestion—he just liked to work with things that other people had killed.

"Who is the truth spell for?" A wave of guilt and fear did not wash over me; I hadn't done anything that desperately needed concealing, not for weeks.

"You know Madame Rupon?"

I nodded. "The troupe guested at her house," I said, gesturing toward the town. "And I've eaten breakfast at her table not unoften of late." An overofficious woman, certainly, an unattractive woman, clearly, but not the sort to get into trouble with our beloved ruling class.

"She and FamNa are in the dungeon," he said, pointing toward the wrong wall with his thumb. Narantir has no sense of direction.

"What did they do?" I should have made that *What are they accused of doing?* but I didn't.

He shrugged. "Made some money disappear, Edelfaule says."

"Lord Toshtai's eldest living son is of course correct," I said. "The heir to Den Oroshtai is unerring."

Narantir, not the most perceptive of mortals, still caught the undertone. He looked from me to the rabbit, to the pot. "It is a hidden truth, at that." He smiled. "Perhaps you would like to investigate it?"

It was my turn to shrug. "I don't know much about money."

Money doesn't overburden a traveling acrobatic troupe, and handling it hadn't been my responsibility. Which was perhaps just as well; my father insisted that I spend time enough to learn basic sums, which had taught me subtraction—subtraction is just an addition puzzle.

But complex arithmetic like division was far beyond me. To do multiplication, you have to break down numbers into their component parts, and then set them down in rows and columns and then add some parts of it together and subtract other parts out. I mean, I know some of the results—a dozen dozen is a gross, so a gross divided among a dozen people will give each a dozen. That's easy enough to figure out: you set out a square of, say, twelve pebbles by twelve. That's a gross. But real division is complicated, and I'd never learned it.

He shrugged. "It's fairly simple. There's a new schedule of rates and taxes for taverners and roomkeepers—Lord Toshtai has ordered some changes made. Instead of the taxman visiting every couple of months, the roomkeeper is supposed to collect it daily, and deliver it by runner every fortnight."

"And Madame Rupon kept it for herself?" That didn't make any sense.

He snorted, and explained. No, of course not. She had made it disappear. She had charged a deilist fifteen coppers, six fille, three shards for room and board for the week, as permitted under the old schedule. She would have put one copper, four fille, two shards away for the collectors, but Veldrum the tax collector had come by with the new schedule on his waxboard, which called for twelve, four, and one for room and board, and two, two, and one of that to be paid as tax.

Veldrum's records were clear, and undisputed. She had given him the two, two, and one, and given the deilist three, two, and two to square accounts with him.

"I don't see the problem."

Narantir snorted. "That's because you're an idiot. There's a missing copper and shard. After the rebatement, the deilist has paid twelve, four, and one; Lord Toshtai has received two, one, and two. Add it up: out of the deilist's original fifteen, six, and three, we've accounted for fourteen, six, and two. There's a copper shard missing, and she made it disappear." Narantir stirred the pot angrily.

He scratched it out on the dirt floor.

IIII IIII IIII III]]]]]] ///

"That's the original, eh?"

"Sure."

He scratched another number out.

IIII IIII IIII]]]] /

"That's what the deilist finally paid, after she rebated, eh?"

I thought about it for a moment, aided by fingers and toes. Fifteen minus three is twelve, six minus two is four, and three minus two is one.

"Yes."

He scratched another number.

II]] /

"And there's the taxes."

I nodded.

"So compare the two. The fille cancel out, but we're missing a shard and a copper. So where's the extra money, and what did she do with it?"

IIII IIII IIII II(I)]]]]]] // (/)

He circled the marks for the missing copper and shard, then threw up his hands in frustration. "I'd thought of trying synecdoche, but money is too frangible; there's no real whole for it to be part of. No chance to do relevance, and contagion isn't going to apply unless the deilist constantly walked around with exactly that fifteen, three, and six in his purse, which he didn't."

I furrowed my brow. It didn't make sense. Stealing from Lord Toshtai wasn't just forbidden, it was stupid, and while I knew Madame Rupon and her ugly daughters were not the brightest people in the world, surely they wouldn't be that stupid . . .

Would they?

"They're in the dungeon now?"

He nodded. "In the same cell you occupied, not too long ago."

Not a pleasant place. Too damp, too locked in, too hopeless. There had to . . .

I don't know what it is that raises my kazuh, and sometimes I'm not even aware that it's there.

It all started to clarify, but then Narantir—may Spennymore, one dark, moonless night, mistake him for a willing young woman—shattered the clarity.

"Out, out, *out*, with you," he said, muttering some spell under his breath. "I'm surely not going to have your zurir messing up the delicate balance of forces in my workshop, Kami Dan'Shir, you may rely on *that* without question or doubt."

I hadn't even asked him why Lord Toshtai would want me at dinner tonight. He hadn't given me the chance.

Well, when in doubt . . .

I headed up to my room for my juggling sack. It wasn't much to look at, not really, just a battered brown leather sack I'd made from a cured hide, its mouth held tightly shut by a drawstring, a broad leather strap sewed to its side so that it could be slung easily over a shoulder. Just a typical juggling sack.

Not much inside, either. Some juggling sticks, some juggling bags, a half dozen rings. Just the secret of life, that's all.

I went to my usual quiet corner of the courtyard under a spreading bolab tree whose thigh-thick branches seemed to be untrimmed, but which never quite reached toward the top of the wall, as though the gardener had taught them better, as well he may have, come to think of it. Gardening can be a high art, too. The tree provided green shade on a hot day, the light gentle hiss of wind through rustling leaves, and, in due season, a few of the fist-sized bitter-sweet fruit—but it wouldn't provide access for somebody trying to sneak in over the wall.

Most importantly, it provided some privacy. I needed to think things out, and when I needed to think things out, I need a private place to juggle.

I know that sounds strange, but it's like Gray Khuzud used to say. Says. "When you don't know what else to do, go back to the beginning." That's what my father always taught me, and that's what I believe.

My beginning was with juggling. I could argue—I'd thought about arguing—that as a dan'shir, no longer an acrobat, I should be giving up juggling, putting it aside in the same way that a peasant who had survived the challenge sword to become a warrior would keep out of the fields and paddies.

But: juggling was never my stinking rice field, my prison.

It had been my beginning; it was now my link to my past, my connection to my distant family. Juggling, of all of the arts of the acrobat, was the only one I was any good at, the only one I really cared about. I had lost several of my loves of late: my sister, Enki Duzun, to death; NaRee to Felkoi and the road; my father, Sala, Fhilt, and Large Egda to my new profession.

I wouldn't lose this one. Never. If anybody were to ask, I'd have to say that a dan'shir must juggle.

I hadn't kept any of my juggling equipment when the troupe left. The physical artifacts don't matter to the likes of what I had been. Stay-at-homes think of it differently, but I had been an itinerant acrobat for all of my seventeen years, and an itinerant finds memories to be sufficiently heavy cargo.

But an acrobat learns how to make and service his own equipment, and I'd not lost those skills in becoming whatever a dan'shir might be.

Still, I didn't need flaming wands or sharp knives or even rings. Simplicity has its virtues.

I pulled a half dozen juggling sticks from my sack, hand-carved from a few scraps of oak that I'd been able to trade with Denred Woodcarver in exchange for a thorough description of the Mesthai woodwork on the third floor of the new donjon. Denred had been allowed in the keep only once, when he became an adult, to swear fealty to Lord Toshtai; he had little to no chance of ever being in even the residence wing of the donjon.

I fingered their smooth sides, then set the sticks aside. Tempting, but no. Too complex; best to start with the basics.

Take some scraps of leather that the tanner didn't mind parting with, and add a few handfuls of dried barley filched from the kitchen, stir in a dozen evening hours with a needle and some sinew thread, and behold: a dozen juggling bags.

I took one in my hand. It felt good; just the right heft. Not so light that it would be distracted by a breeze, not heavy enough that the weight would ever be an issue.

I dropped three of them to the ground—another advantage of juggling bags instead of balls: bags stay where they fall—and kicked off my shoes as I put the other three into a simple shower. It's not just that I had use for my toes. Maybe it's my training, maybe it's that I'm really a peasant at heart, but it feels wrong to be shod while juggling.

Really only four moves create the simple shower: you throw a bag with your left hand and then catch a bag with your left hand; then you throw a bag with your right hand and then catch a bag with your right hand.

Never mind that there's a bag looping through the air toward one or another hand; it simply doesn't matter, it's not *there* yet, understand? Let the next day come when it will; let the next bag come when it will, and catch it when it comes, not before, yes?

Catch-left throw-left catch-right throw-right. That's all there is to it.

When you're showering three, don't let your mind worry about the other bag. You just hold a bag in your right hand while you throw and catch one with your left, then you just hold a bag in your left hand while you throw and catch one in your right.

It's that simple. The other bag, the one in the air, doesn't matter. When you're showering more than three, it's still the same—just catch-left throw-left catch-right throw-right, only quicker.

Keep up the rhythm, and as you add bags, pick up the pace.

That's all there is to the simple shower. You don't even have to put your mind on it; in fact, it's better if you don't think about the bag descending toward your—

I missed; I'd lost my timing, and had hurried to get rid of the bag in my left hand, throwing it too hard and high. It happens, particularly if you don't practice every day, or if you try and shortcut and start more than one bag.

No: begin at the beginning.

I toe-tossed one bag into the air and tried again. Catch-left throw-left, catch-right throw-right. Catch-left throw-left, catch-right throw-right. Better.

I worked a second and then third bag into the juggle, and then a fourth. Just the same thing only faster, just the same thing only faster, you don't have to keep track of the flying bags because they don't matter; you just concentrate on the numbers that do matter, because all that matters is . . .

I don't know whether it was the juggling or not, but I could feel my kazuh flare. This time it was like a stream of water, cold and clear as a mountain creek just melting in spring, powerful and robust as a full deep river.

It washed the mud from my mind, clarifying it all.

One by one, I tossed three of the juggling bags toward my sack—just because you're hurrying doesn't mean you shouldn't do it well—and then dropped the last one over my shoulder, catching it on the back of my heel, then kicking it up, looping it high over my head, giving me barely enough time to swoop up the sack and catch it.

I would have bowed to the phantom crowd, but *that* was part of the way of the Acrobat, and I wasn't an acrobat anymore.

I smiled. Time to see my employer, on a matter of what didn't matter.

And maybe—just maybe—to figure out what was going on with dinner tonight.

4
Toshtai, Edelfaule, Arithmetic, and Other Dangers

AFTER A LIFE spent on the road, sleeping under a canvas tent between towns, sharing a room with at least one member of the troupe in boarding houses in towns and villages all across True Shai, Otland, and the Ven, having my own rooms was a new experience, and one that still hadn't palled, despite the ancestry of my room.

Rooms, actually; my corner suite on the third floor of the service wing of the donjon consisted of two rooms, both of which seemed bare in comparison with most of the rooms in the donjon, and neither of which I had to share with anyone.

The windows of my larger room, easily ten paces by six, faced morningwise. The new workbench that Erol Woodman had built me stood under the window; a fresh sleeping pallet to be used for social purposes, the corner of one blanket folded back, lay on the floor against the opposite, a spray of yellow flowers at the head and foot. The floor was of simply polished planks of wood, unlacquered and smooth to the foot.

The smaller room, perhaps five paces by six, I used as a sleeping room. It was crowded with my sleeping pallet, a dressing table, washstand, and mirror, a laundry bin, plus a new addition: the huge wooden wardrobe that used to belong to the man who murdered my sister. But all I did in that room was sleep and change, and I've never needed much space for either.

I tossed my morning's clothes into the laundry bin in the corner. Not having to wash my own clothes was something it had taken me about half a heartbeat to become accustomed to.

I ran my thumb down the side of the huge wardrobe. Beautiful Agami woodwork, larken-built, like all the best of the Agami: each panel was made of thousands of pieces of wood, some as large as a thumbnail, some as small as a splinter, each one invisibly glued into place, fitted together like the pieces of a puzzle.

In a sense, it was a puzzle; the door was secured by a hidden catch.

I carefully depressed a piece of wood that the tip of my little finger could barely cover; there was a slight *click*, and the spring-loaded door swung open. I pulled out my best semiformal tunic and leggings and set them on the dressing stand, then quickly washed myself in the washbasin before changing.

I slipped into my new boots: dark brown cowhide, hand-burnished to a deep ruby luster, the toebox square and bourgeois, buckling tightly at the ankle. Bundi Cobbler had done well by me, even though he had charged me a good half of my first month's salary as a down payment, and I would be paying these off well through the rains.

Worth it, though. They felt bourgeois.

I was ready.

Gaining an audience with Lord Toshtai is something that's easy only if you're one of his two most senior and trusted retainers. In all of Den Oroshtai, only Crosta Natthan and Dun Lidjun had been given the right to walk uninvited into the presence, although both of them were far too sensible to do it often. A noble would request an appointment, either matter-of-factly, in the case of, say, Edelfaule or Lady Estrer, or with some trepidation, in the case of a junior warrior requesting a brideprice. As a rule, members of the lesser classes of the castle simply didn't ask for appointments. It might be seen as taking on airs; and, as a rule, avoiding the lord of Den Oroshtai was just plain sensible.

On the other hand, it's a matter of record that Lord Toshtai once ordered the headman of Swanse village killed for being too slow in reporting how badly the rice crop had been mauled by dusty blight. I didn't know what the punishment was for a dan'shir who delayed reporting the solution of a puzzle, even though it was an unassigned puzzle, and decided that I didn't want to find out.

For another thing, the Rupon execution might already have been scheduled; it would be best if the cancellation were to have a timely arrival.

I headed out the door.

The walls in the hall outside my room were paneled with Mesthai woodwork. Faces only, of course; the Mesthai woodcarvers are interested in no lesser subject matter.

I was in a hurry, but the woodwork held me for a few moments; it was too lovely to neglect.

Some years ago, perhaps back when Lord Toshtai was actively fathering children, my rooms had been a birthing suite, so I'd been told. (By Arefai, in fact, who found himself amused that a newly made bourgeois had been assigned the birthing suite. Arefai may have been something of a fool, but he was not a humorless one, even though his sense of humor was somewhat crude. As for me, I find the notion of a birthing suite on the third floor to be silly, not funny.)

The Mesthai artists had carved a cycle of conception and birth, from the passion of a man and woman at the moment of a mutual climax, through the fear and excitement and nausea of pregnancy, ending with the expression of mixed pain and joy and delight on the sweaty, slick-hair-plastered face of a woman who has just given birth, the broad smile on the face of the father, and the visage of a newborn baby grasping for breath in between lusty screams. While I liked the expression on the new father's face—his smile seemed to lay claim to the invention of fatherhood—I thought the new mother's face was the best; I reached out a finger to touch the sweat on her cheek, but drew my hand back.

If everyone who was affected by it touched it, within but a few decades it would be worn smooth, and that would be a shame, and a crime.

Life contains sufficient crimes.

"Kami Dan'Shir?" TaNai, the servitor on duty at the entrance to the residence wing of the donjon, looked up in surprise. I hadn't known she was on duty; we were at the isn't-it-an-amazing-coincidence-we-both-like-sitting-under-a-bolab-tree stage. I was slowly working around toward the mention of the fascinating flask of essence waiting in my outer room, enjoying the luxury of time and of privacy. When you're an itinerant acrobat, connections must be made either quickly, during a short stay, or disjointedly, often over several years.

This was new, and I was enjoying the process, so far.

Surprise looked good on her; the arch of her finely shaped eyebrows complemented her deep brown eyes. If I'd had the time, I'd likely have mentioned it. She had a lovely natural creamy complexion, whitened only slightly at the edge of the forehead and along her long, gracious nose. Her striped robes—made of finely woven cotton, not of cheap silk—were cut just loose of fashionable at the swell of her breast, but tight at the slim waist.

Best of all, lovely as she was, she looked nothing like NaRee.

Patience, Kami Khuzud, I thought. *There will be plenty of time over the weeks that our beloved lord is gone.* While Toshtai was not particularly generous, it would be beneath him to notice that his bourgeois attendants would have little to do in his absence. It would not be beneath Crosta Natthan, but the chief servitor's interest was solely in the smooth running of the castle, not in keeping busy those who ran it.

Her long fingers reached up and tugged at the bell rope once, twice, three times. "Please go right in."

"Excuse me?" If I'd suddenly been promoted to the status of the most senior and trusted of retainers, somebody surely would have mentioned it, at least in passing.

"He waits, he waits," she said, irritated. "With Lords Minch, Edelfaule, and Arefai."

I smiled an apology, which she returned.

Beyond the end of the carpet, across the tiled floor, one of the two guards at the huge double door pulled his door open and held it for me, while the other guard stepped through. I'm not generally told where in the residence Lord Toshtai is; I'm generally shown it.

They were waiting for me in what I thought of as the morning room; it was where Lord Toshtai had invariably been having his breakfast, the few times I'd been called in to see him early, although I understood him to use it for most semiformal visiting; its small size made it more intimate than the great hall.

The morningwise wall was openable, and in fact open, to a small private courtyard. A pretty place, filled with flowering plants, soft grasses, and fruit trees that were manicured during the night by lamplight by a team of silent gardeners.

The outer doors, when closed and locked, were as solid and sturdy as any wall in Den Oroshtai; the inner set, of light ursawood and appliqued paper, were so translucent that in the morning they seemed to glow, and even well through the hour of the ox they were still bright enough to fill the room with creamy light.

A throne had been brought in for Lord Minch; he sat next to Toshtai, a table at each of their elbows holding a flask and a tray of sweetmeats, a servitor behind each table waiting to refill the flask or replenish the tasties. I would have looked him over—I've always tried to size up strangers—but Toshtai always gets as much attention as he desires, and he wanted mine. It was all I could do to notice that Edelfaule and Arefai sat crosslegged on cushions be-

yond Toshtai, while Deren der Drumud, now in a soft
green tunic, sat near his own lord. Each had a scabbarded
sword across his lap, but that didn't mean anything, except
that the two lords were not such intimates as to neglect
formality in private.

Toshtai sat easily in his oversized throne, one flipperlike
hand resting on the carefully carved curves of the arm, the
other lowering a flask of essence to the warming stand on
the table at his elbow.

He was, as always, perfectly caparisoned, today in a
yellow silken tunic large enough to pitch as a tent, belted
neither loosely nor tightly with a broad crimson sash.

As the ancient Scion of the Sky decreed, a member of
our beloved ruling class is a ruler, a ruler is a warrior, and
a warrior is never without his sword. The ancient Scion
never, however, ruled as to what constituted a sword.
Toshtai's usual sword was a small dagger the size of a par-
ing knife, its scabbard stuck through his sash in front of
the massive belly that was more than simply large, but
somehow majestic. His face, broad and fleshy, was freshly
shaved and lightly powdered; his black hair, pulled back
by clever fingers into a fine-braided warrior's queue, had
been oiled to a high gloss.

Somebody had placed a strip of thick red rug at the
proper distance from the thrones; I stopped there and
dropped to my knees.

"I understand you sent for me, Lord," I said.

His deepset eyes narrowed marginally. They didn't belong in that face. They showed no hint of nobility or
fierceness, no trace of compassion or forbearance, none of
the calm and joviality I've always associated with corpu-
lence. All they held was intelligence, and that in abun-
dance.

His eyebrow lifted about the width of a fingernail: for
him, extreme skepticism. His hand flopped once on the
arm of the chair, a fish giving its last *flib*: I was to rise.

"You *understand*?" Edelfaule half-rose, then sat back.

I never much cared for Lord Toshtai's eldest son and
heir. He was too much a conscious, albeit thin, imitation of

his father, from the over-oiled hair down to the undersized sword. He looked like a deflated version of Toshtai; his nose was narrow, his cheeks flat, his mouth almost lipless, the skin tight across his sharp jaw. He had none of the genial naivete of his younger brother, none of the easy smile or quiet laugh, and his eyes seemed to shine with intelligence that held no wisdom.

Or maybe not. Maybe I just didn't like Edelfaule, and could only see in him what I wanted to.

"You doubt Ernal Kiunote's word on the matter?" Lord Minch put in. He sat back in his throne, crossing one crimson-clad leg over the other as his slim head cocked to one side. His tunic, cut tightly at the shoulders and hips, was of some gray textured fabric that seemed to writhe in the sunlight. A sword in a remarkably plain scabbard rested on a swordstand next to his throne; his fingers idly stroked at its hilt, as though caressing it.

Lord Toshtai's livery lips twitched.

"Not for a moment, Lord," I said, rising. "But I haven't seen Lord Ernal Kiunote today; I was on my way to the residence to ask for an appointment when the servitor at the entry told me that Lord Toshtai had already sent for me." I bowed my head, once. "I am at your service, Lord."

Edelfaule was preparing himself to take umbrage at the implicit suggestion that somebody might *not* be at the service of any member of our beloved ruling class, but Lord Toshtai nodded somberly.

"Yes, Kami Dan'Shir. I've told Lord Minch about your skill with puzzles and puzzlements, and I thought you might care to demonstrate them for him." There was a wooden box on the table next to him.

"I'm sure that would be a good choice, Lord," I said, hoping the barely implied impertinence would amuse him and not anger him. It was a good bet.

Which I won. His thick lips went up a fraction at the edges; a broad smile. "It is not the only choice, eh? You think you have a puzzle more interesting than this? Is that why you wanted an audience?"

"Partly, Lord. I also wanted to thank you for the gift of the wardrobe; it's lovely."

He didn't answer for a moment, perhaps reflecting on the meaning of me, brother to Enki Duzun, now owning a prized possession of Refle, the man who had murdered her by stealth and sabotage.

I would have preferred to have had juggling bags made from his skin, but it was too late for that. After his murderer had finished chopping Refle up, there hadn't been enough left for any such thing, and I had been in no position to be asking such boons, what with being endungeoned for the murder.

"But I do have a puzzle. Well, a puzzle's solution, Lord." I spread my hands. "I've just been talking to Narantir. He tells me that he's busy preparing a truth spell to find if Madame Rupon and her daughter stole money from Lord Toshtai and a deilist traveling through Den Oroshtai. An unnecessary truth spell, as it turns out."

Again, Minch cocked his head to one side. "May one ask what this is all about?" he asked, one finger toying with his split beard. His face was all bone, flesh stretched over it like a thin pastry wrapping a skull. A long white scar snaked around his ear and into his beard, but the rest of his skin was smooth and seemingly poreless.

Toshtai lifted his index finger slightly off the horizontal. "Permit me. I have issued a new schedule of rates and taxes for taverners and the like, and in the wake of the change, it appears some money has been peculated. Using the old schedule, the widow Rupon charged a deilist fifteen coppers, three fille, six shards for room and board for the week, putting one, two, and four away for her taxes, so she said.

"At this juncture, the tax collector arrived with the new schedule: twelve, one, and four for room and board, and two, two, and one of that to be paid as tax.

"She paid him the two, two, and one, and repaid the deilist three, two, and two."

Edelfaule leaned forward. "Which means that there's some money missing, as I discovered when I happened to investigate it. The deilist has paid twelve, four, and one; the Purse has received two, two, and one. We combine those numbers to find that of the deilist's original fifteen, six, and three, we've accounted for only fourteen, six, and two." He spread his hands. "Where are the vanished copper and shard?"

Toshtai sat silent for a moment. "Which would," he said, "seem to indicate that there is some strange magic afoot," he finished. "Where did the extra copper and shard go? Kami Dan'Shir seems to be of the opinion that he knows where it is."

Edelfaule snorted. "I am sure he does. All bourgeois know about money; they can smell it out. Tell me, little Kami Dan'Shir, as you stand there reeking of trade, tell me where your nose finds this missing money."

I don't generally like members of our beloved ruling class, and I'd taken a special disliking to Edelfaule. Not that I was going to be able to do anything about it.

So I smiled genially as I held out my empty palm. "It's right here, Lord," I said, "as much as anywhere. It doesn't exist. It never existed." I turned to Lord Toshtai. "If it please you, would you have a servant bring fifteen coppers, six fille, and three shards?"

It took longer than I would have thought, but, then again, money wasn't much used within the donjon itself, although—despite the constant comments about how the lower classes stink of commerce—our beloved ruling class has always managed to tax the lower classes heavily enough to provide for their own needs. And wants. And whims. And whimsies.

In a few minutes, a white-clad serving girl appeared, the silver salver balanced properly on her palm holding three stacks: one of fifteen oblong copper coins, another of six fille pastille, and three iron shards. Toshtai sent her to me with a finger gesture; I lowered the tray to the floor and arranged the coins carefully on the stone.

I rolled my sleeves back. I had my own pouch at my waist, and it was too late to get rid of it. I didn't want Edelfaule accusing me of having sleighted a copper up a sleeve. I could prove him wrong easily, mind, but I didn't want to prove him wrong.

"Fifteen coppers, six fille, and three shards," I said. "The amount that the deilist originally paid to Madame Rupon, I believe." I slid all three piles to one side.

"But the new schedule came down, and he had overpaid by three, two, and two, so she rebated him the deilist three, two, and two to square accounts with him."

I slid three coppers, two filles, and two shards to my left. "She paid the tax collector two, two, and one." I reached again for the pile representing Madame Rupon and slid two coppers, two fille, and one shard into a third pile.

"Add it up: there's nothing missing." I stood. "I hope the puzzle has amused you."

Toshtai's head inclined almost measurably, then straightened. "Lord Edelfaule did add correctly in the first place, though."

"Of course," I said. "Lord Edelfaule is correct: after the adjustment, the deilist has paid twelve, four, and one; Lord Toshtai has received two, two, and one. When you add those two numbers together, you do get fourteen, six, and two."

"So where *are* the copper and shard?" Edelfaule snarled.

"The numbers you report were entirely right, Lord Edelfaule; your addition was perfect. The only problem is that the sum of what the deilist eventually paid and what Lord Toshtai eventually received is a meaningless one. There were fifteen, six, and three originally. Of those, Lord Toshtai now has two, two, and one," I said, indicating one pile, "the deilist has three, two, and two; Madame Rupon has the rest: ten, two, and none. All balances, and balance—"

"Now, wait." Arefai smiled. "You mean that my brother is as correct as he always is, always must be? But that his correctness is irrelevant as usual?" His smile was genuine, but malicious.

And definitely nothing I wanted to either answer or ignore. I was debating how to avoid it when Lord Toshtai spoke up.

"A pretty puzzle, Kami Dan'Shir," he moved his chin ever so slightly toward the pile of coins. "You will please present the tray and the coin to Madame Rupon with my compliments, and then conduct her and her daughter back to their home." He looked from Arefai to Edelfaule. "Arefai, if it please you, go now to tell the warden of the dungeon that I have increasing faith in Kami Dan'Shir."

He could have simply passed along the order that the two women were to be released to me, but he was deliberately if subtly raising my status. The warden would take the meaning, and so would Edelfaule.

It took Arefai a moment to get it, but then he smiled, rose, and bowed. "At once, father," he said, slipping his scabbard back into his sash as he walked quickly from the room.

Toshtai nodded, again. "A very pretty solution, Kami Dan'Shir. And I am told you made a very pretty shot with an arrow today, despite a minor injury," he said, with a gesture at my scabbed left forearm. "You will join us at dinner tonight, if you are free."

That was no surprise. Toshtai wanted me at dinner for reasons that he didn't want to specify in front of anyone else, nor did he want to give me the status implicit in a private meeting. He had been intending to use the morning's hunt as a pretext—a reward for a brilliant shot that had provided the venison—but this had proved a substitute, or at least a supplement.

"Of course, Lord," I said. It was a dismissal; I gathered up the tray and coins, Edelfaule's eyes on my back all the way.

Interlude:

The Hour of the Ox

EDELFAULE PACED BACK and forth, slowly, through the inner garden. His father was impatient with impatience, and Edelfaule had been told to wait.

So he waited.

Midafternoon was the wrong time of day to be in the inner garden, though. The hour of the ox was a dull and obvious time of day, when the sun, while no longer directly overhead, simply shone down, casting no interesting shadows. Yes, the flowers were pretty, but their colors were too garish, too ordinary, too bourgeois in such direct light. Edelfaule preferred the hour of the dragon, when hints of the soon-to-be-rising sun would slowly give color and meaning to the showers of flowers and sprays of blossoms.

It was much better late at night, on a clear night, when the stars and moon would turn dark greenery into shadow, barely alleviated with hints of color from the hanging lanterns. On more than one occasion, after his father had retired, Edelfaule had brought a favored concubine into the garden, and led her carefully between the plants to a soft and grassy spot before untying her robes and tossing them gently to the side.

Having her in the garden was like having Den Oroshtai itself.

Edelfaule felt at his neck. But Den Oroshtai had troops committed in the Ven, and it would soon be time for Edelfaule to rejoin them. A dangerous thing, that. Patrice in particular would much rather Den Oroshtai fall into the hands of a fool like Edelfaule's brother than Edelfaule himself, and if an accident could be arranged—and such accidents had happened during a battle more often than not—that might well happen.

What would Toshtai do without Edelfaule? Turn the realm over to Arefai and hope for the best?

But, with Arefai married to that ViKay woman, ViKay of the large brown eyes and small red mouth, that would make the lord of Den Oroshtai also the husband of the favored daughter of Lord Orazhi of Glen Derenai. Orazhi was no fool, and Arefai would defer to his wife's father on matters of strategy and alliance.

Once Arefai was safely married, Edelfaule and Lord Demick would have a mutual interest in keeping Edelfaule alive.

His fingers toyed with the thick leaves of a spiny fulminor, enjoying the way the bristles felt smooth as a cat's fur when he stroked it toward the tip.

He had crouched to sniff at a crimson melrose when he heard his father behind him. The old fool.

"Edelfaule," his father said.

He rose, one hand on the hilt of his knife, and nodded. All he had to do was draw, step, and slice. It would be so easy, so very easy, to become lord of Den Oroshtai in one smooth motion.

Except that would never be allowed to stand, and Edelfaule didn't seriously consider it. Dun Lidjun would not follow a patricide; Arefai would not permit him to live. Eliminate them, and there was still the delicate web of partial alliances and subtle affiliations that Toshtai had woven around Den Oroshtai and that were all attached to Toshtai. It would be possible to transplant them to Edelfaule, but that would have to be done slowly and carefully by Toshtai himself.

No; he was his father's heir in name only until and unless that could be changed. At the moment, and for the foreseeable future, Toshtai was not expendable.

Edelfaule had no softness toward the filthy peasants or the middle class and bourgeois, all of them stinking of business and money. He didn't care for his mother or his half-brothers, and while he enjoyed his essences and his concubines, he didn't care for them. No weakness there.

The only weakness was here. In all the world, there were two things that Edelfaule cared for: himself, and Den Oroshtai. The buildings, sturdy and homey; the south wall, where the land spread out below him like a quilt; the garden, where night whispered its pledge of troth to him in the dark.

"Father," he said. "It seems I made an error."

Toshtai's head seemed to nod. "That appears to be so."

It was all that Kami Dan'Shir's fault. Nobody except for the widow and her daughter would have ever known that Edelfaule had made an error, and they wouldn't speak from the grave. The affair would have stood as yet another lesson to the lower classes that they must not try to cheat their nobility; that would have done no harm.

But one thing had done harm. By exposing their innocence, Kami Dan'Shir had lowered Edelfaule in his father's eyes. Unforgivable, unpardonable. He would have to be dealt with.

"Not in your computation," Toshtai went on, "but in your calculation. You were too precipitous, Edelfaule. Where would she flee? She was no traveling perfumer, here today, gone tomorrow, leaving nothing behind but a scent. No need to take action until you were sure. It's every grain as important that the lower classes understand that good conduct will be rewarded as it is that they fear our swords and hands when they behave badly."

"Yes, Father."

"I have no objection to punishing bad service, or theft, or insolence, as I trust I've demonstrated today, but it is bad practice to punish the innocent, eh?"

Edelfaule lowered his head modestly. "Yes, Father. I am sorry."

Toshtai's lips pursed once. "Very well. Let's not mention it again. We have more serious matters to discuss. We leave for Glen Derenai in two days for your brother's wedding."

That was one of Father's cleverer strategems. Edelfaule was the oldest living son and therefore the presumed heir to Den Oroshtai. He had to be, what with Arefai being such a fool. So bind Den Oroshtai and Glen Derenai closer together with a marriage between Arefai and ViKay, but not so threateningly close as one between Edelfaule and ViKay would be. Always tentative, like a musician idly plucking the strings of his zivver while he thought of something else. Toshtai was patient, slowly knitting together a skein of alliances that would, someday, become a garrote around Demick's neck.

Patience was a virtue, and Edelfaule would be patient. He would even things with Kami Dan'Shir, but not now. Kami Dan'Shir was too clearly under Toshtai's protection. For the time being. But that could change.

Timing was everything.

He would wait.

5
Dinner, TaNai, a Puzzle, and Other Mixed Pleasures

IT'S BY NO means unknown for a bourgeois to dine in the Great Hall, but it's not ordinary, either. Dining customs differ from one end of D'Shai to the other, but in no part of the country does convention regularly require our beloved ruling class to put up with the noisome presence of us lesser beings.

The trouble, of course, was where to put me.

The seats of greatest honor are the ones next to Lord Toshtai, and while other positions are in theory all also of honor, the ones next to a bourgeois would be the least so.

The solution was elegant: I was put in the group at the foot of the right arm of the staple-shaped arrangement of tables, with Arefai on one side and Lady Estrer on the other. That made the right arm a perfectly acceptable place to be, nervous as it made me.

The slow playing of the musicians kept us audibly isolated, although I'd heard better than this six-person group. The silverhorn was good, although he really should have had a backup player; the zivver was acceptable if too eager to show off his fast fingerwork; and the watercrystal player was *very* good, with a nice, direct way of hitting her crystals without keeping her fingernails on them for a moment more than necessary. The drummer, though, was a disappointment; he kept hitting at just the end of the beat, not the beginning, following the tempo, being dragged by it instead of driving it. I hate when that happens. The trompon was inoffensive if uninspired, and the bassskin player must have had an ingrown thumbnail, to judge from the way he kept declining to dig in and really bring out the notes.

At least the music kept me from worrying about somebody else misinterpreting something I might say and taking offense.

The three of us were physically isolated from the next group by a huge silver soup tureen in the shape of an inverted turtle shell. It had been raised high above the table on skinny but sturdy silver legs, staying slowly simmering over a dozen sputtering candles.

There was no particular slight in that; the forty-some people spread out on the wall side of the table were broken up into smaller groups by food vessels: one serving tray heavily laden with crispy pork loins that had been stuffed with spicy Shalough sausage; a tureen of murky brown soup with bits of carrots bobbing gently at its roiling, oily surface; a huge onyx vat of chipped ice, indented to hold tiny glass plates, each topped with a small ball of fundleberry sherbet sitting on a circle of rose leaves; the remains of what had been a rack of venison.

I didn't mind the isolation; I would have preferred more. Slantwise across from me, right next to Toshtai, Minch's eyes seemed too often pointed at me.

Lady Estrer's withered hands trembled as she manipulated a sliver of pheasant first to the bowl of green mustard, barely touching it to the thick sauce, then to her dry lips, following it quickly with a tiny mouthful of roasted barley. She chewed with an even rhythm, like a cadence, as though it was a matter of ritual and ceremony, as though eating had nothing to do with hunger or taste.

She looked over at me and snorted. "Kami Dan'Shir, you eat as though this were to be your last meal." Her eyes, staring out of dark pits in a lined face, watched me too closely.

"It could be," I said, after swallowing a large mouthful of the turtle soup to rinse out the taste of the marinated frog hearts in clotted cream. It is not one of my favorite dishes; hot dishes should be hot, cold dishes cold. This sort of lukewarm mush hiding lukewarm snippets of frog didn't even have any spirit to its temperature. "If the rest of the food is like the frog hearts," I added.

Her thin lips curved up. Lady Estrer always likes a little audacity, as long as it's only a little.

"It's a classic dish," she said.

I nodded. "I'm sure that is so, Lady."

She chuckled thinly, then subsided.

Out of the corner of my eye, I could see Arefai grinning as he beckoned to one of the servitors to spoon some more of the horrid green and off-white mixture onto his own plate, right next to his double helping of snails in aspic.

The trompon blasted out an adequate arpeggio as the doors swung open. Stupidly, I looked up for the entrance of the jugglers, but there was no such thing: no Gray Khuzud, balanced naturally on the balls of his feet, no Sala of the Rings, her costume always just about to slip open interestingly or fall from her bare shoulders, no Large Egda, no Eresthais, no Evrem, and there would never be an Enki Duzun. My sister was dead, dead, dead, and the fact that her murderer had died was as cold in my mouth as lukewarm frog hearts.

No: all it was, was Dun Lidjun, escorting a pair of ladies, returning from a quick turn around the gardens. The old soldier brought them to their seats, then quickly reclaimed his own, the path only coincidentally bringing him around behind most of the foreign visitors.

Of course. All is accident.

He dug into a huge mound of the local version of Precious Rice, his eating sticks clicking like dice.

"You were saying something, Kami Dan'Shir?" Lady Estrer asked.

Oh, no. A bourgeois can't afford to have his mouth working away when he doesn't intend to. "I am sure Lady

65

Estrer is correct, but I can't recall what I said; I'm certain it's of no importance."

"Pfah." She lifted a goblet and drained half of it, as quickly as she could pour. "The truth is that you weren't saying anything, that you've been sitting in insolent silence. This, Kami Khuzud, Kami Dan'Shir, or whatever you call yourself now, is a dinner. A dinner is a social event, at which one acts sociably. To act sociably, you make a comment every now and then; I do the same. Perhaps we find a matter to dispute politely, or possibly we find some other person, one not here, whose flaws to discuss in some detail." She made a choppy gesture, a twist of the wrist that brought her hand palm-up. "Your turn."

I opened my mouth, closed it, then opened it again, reddening.

Arefai laughed, which only made me more frustrated, but his laugh was friendly. Thank the Powers for small favors, eh?

When in doubt, try for the truth.

"I'm sorry, Lady Estrer, but all of this is new to me. It's . . . a different life I find myself in, and I'm not used to it, not yet." I held my hands out in front of me, open. "I'm used to fitting in with local customs, but that's in a superficial setting, in terms of keeping out of trouble. In Ourne, I'd know to cross a street sunwise of any of our—of the nobility, no matter the time of day, and in Market Indon I'd know not to step into anyone's shadow, but not to worry should their shadow cross me. I can fulfill a guest's cooking chores in the mountains of Helgramyth, or spend a quiet evening on a chair on the white cliffs of Wisterly, watching the Tetnit watch the Sleeve . . ."

I spent the next minutes explaining myself, trying hard, trying even harder not to offend.

". . . but I'm not used to making polite conversation with my betters in Den Oroshtai."

Lady Estrer's lips pursed in what could have been a smile. "Oh," she finally said.

I don't know what Arefai was smiling about.

HOUR OF THE OCTOPUS

* * *

As I said, dining customs vary slowly from one end of D'Shai to another. In the north—all the way from Helgramyth and Otland to Wyness Tongue—it's considered a matter of impoliteness or immaturity to temporarily leave the table during a meal. In Wisterly, by contrast, the host must keep bringing food until after you have done so, the social fiction being that a sufficiently large meal requires some walking off to aid digestion. (In Wisterly there's an amusing legend about how Lord Flin had his cook grind an emetic root into the soup for the twenty-seventh course that Esterven the Insatiable had begun eating at his table.)

Den Oroshtai, located in the moderate middle of the south, is moderate; it's not obligatory, but it's not considered unusual to absent yourself in the midst of a meal that's likely to last from late in the hour of the octopus well through the snake and into the bear.

In no place is it wise for a bourgeois to draw attention to himself by being either the most present or most absent from table; I looked to Lady Estrer for permission, and at her nod pushed back from the table, then walked quickly toward the door, trying to look invisible.

The door led into a hallway; the hall took me past the guards into the courtyard.

The courtyard was quiet but not silent in the dusk that accompanies the hour of the snake. The snake comes in with the night's death of the sun, and lasts through the onset of true night, only to give way to the hour of the bear in either starlight or black darkness.

Shadows turn from gray to black in the hour of the snake. It's the traditional time for forbidden lovers to find each other, to kiss and caress in the all-concealing shadow of a building or the overhanging branches of a tree, then to slip off into the night if they part, or to steal away together and find their bed for the evening.

I like the hour of the snake.

Above, on the walls of the keep, a trio of young watchmen paced, their eyes turned out toward the night, their triple tenor harmony sending shivers up and down my spine.

"Kami Dan'Shir?"

TaNai was sitting on a stone bench under the bolab tree, her hands folded in her lap. In the dying light, her eyes seemed vague and distant.

"Good evening, TaNai," I said.

We both liked this part of the courtyard, near the corner over by the morningwise wall; while the whole courtyard was in theory free for use of the bourgeois staff so long as we left quietly at the approach of any of our betters, this was less used than more of the heavily worked parts and less likely to subject us to interruption.

She was in the same robes she had worn earlier, but she had belted them less tightly about her waist; mentally, I worked at untying the seven-bend knot over her belly.

I smiled. Silly, silly Kami Khuzud, my sister would have said. What is the rush?

You live here now; you will be in Den Oroshtai for the foreseeable future, probably forever. Take some time; enjoy the moment, the game. Life is to be eaten one bite at a time so that you can enjoy it, not swallowed whole to curdle untasted in the stomach.

"You're smiling," she said. "Is there a reason for that?"

"Several," I said, smiling.

She cocked her head ever so slightly to one side. "Are they secrets?"

"Not at all," I said. "I'm smiling because after being in the noise of a formal dinner, it's a pleasure to be out in the dark and quiet; and I'm smiling because it's a lovely night, with bright stars in the sky, soft smells in the air, and you, sitting in the dark, smiling at me."

The way of the acrobat includes a few sleights, and I'd mastered some of the easier ones. I reached out my right hand toward her ear, and as she followed the motion, I palmed the rose in my left hand.

"No," I said, as she looked toward my empty hand. "It's not there. But I thought . . ."

Her brow furrowed.

"Ah," I said, bringing my left hand up to her other ear. Just as my wrist went past the edge of her eye, I transferred the rose from my palm to my fingers, then pulled my hand back. It's a neat effect that fools the mind on a level both above and below that of logic and reason: you see somebody reaching an empty hand past your ear then immediately pulling it back, no longer empty.

"I *thought* I saw a flower," I said. I sniffed at it once, then handed it to her.

TaNai smiled. "Very pretty, Kami Dan'Shir." She tucked the rose into her belt.

"I'm glad you're here," I said. "The night wouldn't be complete."

She touched a finger to my lips. "Shhh," she said. "You don't have to try so hard."

"Eh?"

"I know, I know," she said, "good bourgeois girls are supposed to mimic their betters, and make a game of it all, to make you take a large step forward while we take two small steps back, to extract flowery phrases and clear commitments while we evade at each step, until we weary of the game and finally fall into your arms or your bed, but I'm not a good bourgeois girl, Kami Dan'Shir. I was born to the middle class, daughter of a quarrymaster, and raised to bourgeois only because Lord Creeslai, Lord Toshtai's oldest son, wanted me as his concubine." Her tongue touched her lips, once; I envied it. "The games he wanted to play had nothing to do with evasion and reluctance, and I grew to like his directness." Her face was sad in the dark. "And when he died, something warm and alive in me died, but that didn't." She rose and took a step toward me. "So don't play with me: ask me. Next time."

Her lips were warm and dry on mine for just a moment, and then she spun away and was quickly gone.

I had absented myself from table long enough; it was time to return to the noise and the awkwardness.

* * *

I took my seat between Arefai and Lady Estrer just in time for the refreshment course of raspberry puffs with mint, hot from the oven, so light in the mouth that they melted on the tongue as quickly as sherbet.

Arefai was just toying with a nice arrangement of mustard crab and fennel. While his father could put away a prodigious amount of provisions, the aptitude or perhaps the desire had not been passed to either of his living sons.

He had opened his mouth to say something when his attention was drawn by something over my shoulder. It was Crosta Natthan; I hadn't seen the old man walk up.

"Lord Toshtai invites you to appear before him," he said. How the chief servitor managed his administrative duties while also serving as Toshtai's personal valet was one of the puzzles I hadn't tried to solve. "Lord Minch has brought a difficult puzzle that he believes you might find interesting."

I stood. Yet another way to go wrong; was I being invited to go around behind the table and sit with Lords Minch and Toshtai, or was this another performance? Assuming for the moment that no matter what I did was wrong—a fair assumption, given the perversity of the world—it was better to be humbly wrong; I stalked across the marble floor, trying to keep my paces slow and confident.

This, at least, was something I had done before; I knew that when all eyes were on you, the slightest nervousness to any motion looked like an out-of-control lurch. Movements in front of an audience must look smooth and confident, or they will stop believing in you, and an acrobat depends on having the audience believe what you're implying. Never mind that my father's drunk act is always done stone-cold sober; they have to let themselves *believe* that he's drunk, that the others of us are surprised and helpless, that the slightest error will result in one or more knives *thunk*ing into his chest or neck.

I stopped in front of Lord Toshtai and bowed at the waist. In front of him on the table sat the wooden box that he had had earlier, during the audience in the morning room.

70

"Lord Minch," he said, "knowing my affection for puzzles, has brought me a difficult one, made by a craftsman of his employ."

He opened the box to reveal a mess of wrought iron, gold chain and wooden balls lying on a bed of purple velvet. Toshtai gestured that I should pick it up. "A simple problem: remove the ring from the . . . rest of it."

Minch sat back, looking ever-so-slightly smug. He was arrayed for the evening in another outfit of red and gray, this time with a loose scarlet dining tunic, cut loosely at the waist, over a blousy pair of gray silk pantaloons. His sword and swordbelt hung from a peg on the side of his chair; he toyed with a tassel on the belt.

I picked up the puzzle.

Superficially difficult, of course, but those can be the easy problems. On one end of it, a wrought-iron triangle had been welded to the end of a golden chain; a silver ring, just barely too small to slip off the end of the triangle, had been threaded on the chain, as had been a marble ball. The other end of the chain was welded to a smaller ring that also enclosed the end of a long, flat, recurved piece of iron, itself suspended by an arrangement of steel rings inside a perpendicular curved piece.

Nothing would slip through, clearly, but if you slipped the ring beside the recurved piece, you could slip it and the triangle through, followed by the ring. Work the ring over one end of the recurved piece, then around the other side, then slide it back here, and through. Then lift the silver ring over the edge there, instead of around, and . . .

It takes longer to describe it than to do it; the silver ring came off in my hand, and the gasps from those at the table triggered old performing reflexes: I tossed the ring high in the air, then caught it behind my back and brought it forward.

I displayed the ring in one hand, the rest of the puzzle in the other fist—no sense in letting anybody see exactly what I had done—then brought my hands together and quickly reversed the process, metal clicking against metal, until the ring again dangled from the end of the chain.

To more than a smattering of applause, I laid the puzzle back in the box.

I've always liked puzzles, and this was a fine one of its type, such as it was. The reason most people will take too long to solve it is that they're looking for some unfair trick—taking a saw to the iron triangle, for example, or bending or stretching something—because, deep down, they don't feel that the problem has a real solution, and aren't willing to work toward that. That's the sort of phony puzzle that somebody might try to use to embarrass somebody, and this, of course, could be mistaken for that.

Giving an insoluble puzzle would be a great insult, and falsely accusing, even indirectly, someone of doing that would also be a great insult, and one that would have to be properly apologized for.

Lord Toshtai knew enough not to lightly accuse Minch of giving him an insoluble puzzle; he would never make such an accusation unless he had seen proof, and not merely suspected that the puzzle was insoluble.

But perhaps someone who didn't enjoy puzzles wouldn't understand that, wouldn't see the important difference between unsolved and insoluble?

Truth: trying to figure out the subtleties of the interplay between members of our beloved ruling class is something that I'd never had either the opportunity or the taste for. An acrobat isn't above it all; he's beside it all.

But I wasn't an acrobat any longer. And I had been too busy thinking it all through to be watching faces.

Lord Minch was not applauding me; his head cocked a bit to one side, his bony face was studiously blank.

The ends of Toshtai's lips twitched upwards, then sagged back to normal. "A fine puzzle, Lord Minch," he said. "I am grateful that you went to all the trouble to bring it to me, and hope that you will allow me to do something in return."

Minch's smile almost seemed genuine. "I can think of nothing," he said.

Toshtai dismissed me with a quick flick of a finger. I forced myself to turn and slowly walk away.

"Except, of course, to be sure to bring your Kami Dan'Shir to the wedding in Glen Derenai; I am sure he will be very entertaining there, as well," Minch said.

I didn't have to see Toshtai nod. "Of course," he said. "It would not have otherwise occurred to me, but ... of course."

I didn't for a moment believe Toshtai's words, and the undercurrent of Minch's tone sent chills running around the circumference of my neck, just about where a sword would separate it from my head.

Just what I needed: another enemy in our beloved ruling class. I had survived one, but I didn't want to have to establish a pattern.

There was a spot outside the keep, over by the south wall, that held fond memories for me. A flat spot of grass edged by an old, crumbling retaining wall, the slope above held at bay by the roots of a huge jimsum tree. There wasn't much of a path to and from it, and the path had largely been overgrown.

It was where NaRee and I had first kissed, and it was where we had, a month ago, a generation ago, lain together for the last time, as it turned out.

I didn't miss her much, not anymore.

I wouldn't miss my own breathing.

The last time I was there, the night had been alive with sounds and smells; there had been the cry of an owl, the whispered music of rustling leaves, the minty scent of a cool wind blowing gently through trees.

But now it was quiet and still, and I couldn't smell anything.

When the moon is full, the hour of the bear is a bleak and pitiless time in the night. The light, no less harsh for its weakness, pours down on everything, reducing all to shades of an unflattering, unloving blue-gray, robbing everything of color. The one-peden fields below, spread out like the squares of a single-bone draughts board, were even and square, if I looked at them from the right perspective, like I was a piece waiting to be played on the board.

And then, because there didn't seem to be anything better to do, and not because my eyes were sagging shut no matter how hard I tried to keep them open, I went back into the keep, staggered up to my rooms and into my bed, and was fully asleep before I was fully horizontal.

6
Travel, a Spot of Archery, Predisposition, and Other Portents of Problems

I GUESS IT's just superstition, but I had a hard time finding an appropriate freden, a throw-weight.

It's something that Gray Khuzud taught us to put in our pouches, as we walked from village to village, from city to city: a small stone or tiny stick or piece of bone perhaps, of no value or usefulness. It shouldn't be too anything: not too large or too small, not too rough or too smooth. Just something ordinary, and dispensable. You tuck it in your pouch—near the top, if you please—and then you forget about it. Just forget about it.

Until.

Until the road gets too long, until your packs are too heavy, until your legs just can't stagger another step, and until each breath burns in your throat as each step shoves sharp knives up through the soles of your feet. Then—and not before; it won't work if you don't wait, for the timing is everything—you reach down into your pouch, and take out the small stone or stick or perhaps piece of bone that you've selected, and you invest it with all the weight and weariness of the road, you imbue it with every bit of exhaustion and fatigue and pain.

And you throw it away, far away, as hard as you can.

Perhaps it's magic that anybody can do, or perhaps there

is something else to it, but when you do that, the road seems to shorten in front of you, if only a little; your legs gain strength, even though it's just enough strength to go on, and perhaps your breath is a little cooler in your throat and your feet ache a trifle less.

It's enough.

I finally found an appropriate freden near the walls of the keep. Just a plain stone, smooth but not polished, about the size of my thumb. I slipped it into my pouch and let it clink against the few coins there.

Back when I was with the troupe, we had a fair amount of equipment to haul with us, although nothing more than we could carry on our backs.

Acrobats must carry their own rigging and their own props, as well as the ordinary sorts of things you need when you're often going to be spending nights between towns, sleeping by or on the road itself. Each night, generally, we'd have to use one or another: either we would make camp outside of civilization, and have to break out the camping gear, leaving the balls, sticks, knives, costumes, lanyard, halyards, and such safely packed, or we would be safely ensconced in a town, in which case we could leave most of the camping gear stowed away, while we'd take out the props and do a show.

Sometimes, rarely, when we played the smaller villages, we would have to use everything: make camp just outside of the village, set up our own equipment, do a performance for which we would be paid in rice, vegetables, and chickens, then cook for ourselves, sleep, and be ready to leave when the hour of the dragon gave way to the hour of the cock.

That was the worst case: everything out, everything used, everything to be properly stowed before we could move on.

But it took, at most, in the worst case, maybe half an hour from the moment we arose to the moment that Large Egda, the most heavily burdened of the troupe, would swing out on the road, a mumbled, half-remembered song on his thick lips.

It's not hard: you wake up, you fold up, you put it in a bag, you put the bag on your back, and you go.

Leaving "promptly in the hour of the cock" seemed to have a different meaning for our beloved ruling class. As far as I could tell, they didn't have a thing to do but empty their bladders and bowels, and as far as I knew their personal attendants could have done that for any of them. But there were clothes to pack, panniers to be loaded up, horses that not only needed to be fed and saddled but apparently would become better mounts if, saddled, they stood in the hot sun for hours.

Narantir was amused. "You haven't traveled with nobility before, I take it?" he asked, his smile broadening. "Or you would long since have given up shouldering your pack."

As an acrobat, I'd carried two bags. The other, the equipment bag, was long gone with the troupe, but the canvas bag in which I carried my own possessions and my share of the cooking and camping gear was on my back, feeling familiar, yet strange. It was too light, and the balance was off.

Such was my life, eh?

I shook my head.

"I've seen them on the road, of course." And gotten out of their way, naturally, even if that meant leaping into scraggly brush along the side of the road rather than chance frightening a noble's horse.

"If you'd ever seen them try to get ready, you'd likely still be in bed."

Other than his ample bulk, the wizard carried only a small leather sack. Either he didn't think that he would need a change of clothes—always a possibility—or he was awfully sure that the procession wouldn't proceed for a while, and didn't see any need to haul his gear around with him.

Well, if you're so smart, why are you awake? I didn't say.

He answered the question anyway. "Because you're not particularly bright, and were likely to be awake right now."

"I didn't know we were such boon companions."

Narantir shrugged. "We are this morning, because Madame Rupon makes the best biscuits in Den Oroshtai, and because I have an appetite for good biscuits this morning, and because it's my guess that there may be some made quite freely available to the wizard accompanying the dan'shir who talked Lord Toshtai out of having her head cut off."

I thought about it for a moment. The way of our beloved ruling class is sometimes easy to figure: they wouldn't wait for me, but since the morningwise road out of town, the road toward Glen Derenai, passed through the Bankstreets, and since Madame Rupon's house was on a Bankstreet corner, there would be no problem for me to wait there, complete with my bag.

It would be fun, though, if I could keep it going long enough, to watch Narantir have to hustle his bulk back up the hill to the keep in order to get his gear. Given Madame Rupon's biscuits, and the apple orchard honey she served them with, this was a decided possibility.

I nodded. "Your biscuits await."

I hadn't tried to count the number of biscuits I'd eaten, and had stopped counting Narantir's at seventeen, as we sat on the front porch at Madame Rupon's, looking out at the street and the day.

I sipped at my hot mug of urmon tea, and before I had set it on the weatherbeaten arm of the chair, FamNa had bustled out through the door, poured another cup, dispensed a smile that I'm sure she thought was ingratiating, and bustled on back, while her mother sat on the other side of the broad porch, close enough to hear, if she was of a mind to eavesdrop, which she likely was.

Narantir rearranged his bulk in the chair facing mine, a smug smile on his scraggle-bearded face. "You see, little Kami Dan'Shir, I sometimes do know what I speak of."

His eyebrows needed combing; they stuck out all helter-skelter, like a cat's vibrissae.

I hid a smile. *Go ahead and feel so superior, wizard.*

"I wouldn't doubt it," I said.

"Well and good." He didn't bother to hide a belch behind his hand. "We'll find good food in Glen Derenai, but I doubt we'll find biscuits of this quality." He frowned. "I suspect that I'll have to urge Tebol to do better from the keep cooks; he has little appetite, and less sense of taste."

"Tebol?"

"The wizard at the keep. An old friend of mine; we apprenticed together."

I had an acquaintance or two in Glen Derenai, but not the local wizard. I shrugged.

It was taking a long time for Lords Toshtai, Edelfaule, Arefai, and Minch and the rest of the noble part of the party to get themselves ready, but the hour of the cock was giving way to the hour of the hare, and they would have to be leaving shortly.

Narantir was too involved in satisfying his appetite to notice how late the morning was getting. My bag sat on the porch; I could join the procession out of town, but it would do me good to watch Narantir have to hurry up the hill back to the keep to get his own gear.

Hmm ... if I was hearing right, there was a distant clomping of hooves off to morningwise.

Just a few more moments, wizard, and we'll see if your bandy legs can churn like a—

His head straightened. "Listen."

"Eh?"

"Do you hear that?"

Off toward sunwise, there was a sound like running, the rapid tattoo of beating feet.

His bare feet taking impossibly swift steps, a Runner rounded the corner and leaned heavily into his turn as he changed direction and headed up the Bankstreets toward the road to the keep. For a moment it looked almost as though he would lose his balance, that he'd leaned too heavily into the turn and would slide away across the flat stones of the street, but appearances are deceiving; the reality is all.

He had raised kazuh, and a kazuh Runner could maintain his pace indefinitely, perhaps forever; I don't know. There are secrets to each of the kazuhin, and while I knew those of the Acrobat and had to learn those of the Dan'Shir, I would never know those of the Runner, anymore than I would know those of the Ruler or Painter.

All I knew was the obvious: he was there, and then, long before the dust marking his passing could settle, he was gone.

Narantir sighed. "There and gone. The morning dispatches received, and others to be dispatched. The Long War but simmers in the south and boils in the Ven while the lords of D'Shai play their endless games of status and superiority, eh?"

I sipped my tea. "Of course that is not so." A shtoi approximation: *You could lose your head for such loose talk, Narantir.* Or: *I agree, but I will not agree openly.* Shtoi is not precise.

What did he think, that I'd keep quiet if asked? And in front of Madame Rupon? She was over on the other side of the porch, yes, but she was neither deaf nor mute.

Narantir ignored my understatement. "What is there to fear?" The wizard smiled. "Madame Rupon? If you please?"

She nodded and walked back into the house.

Eh? I didn't follow at all.

Narantir set the palms of his hands on his chair and pushed himself to his feet just as the lead horse rounded the corner, coming from the direction that the runner had taken.

Arefai was on the lead horse, probably the same fine black mare that he had ridden to the hunt the other day, except that both he and the mare were decked out in silks of black and yellow, fluttering madly in the light breeze.

He nodded at our bow, and smiled. No comment about being late, which was just as well, all things considered.

Close on his heels came a troop of a hundred soldiers of

the Lord Toshtai's personal guard, with old Dun Lidjun, in full armor and regalia, mounted on a coal-black mare at their head. Lances were all properly set into stirrups, their tips graced by garlands of ochre orchids and ruddy roses that wouldn't slow them down much at all, whether they clove through the air or through flesh. Short horn bows were strapped to the odd saddle here and there, although Dun Lidjun's own bow, a long one of horn so translucent as to be almost transparent, was in the boot of his saddle.

Minch's personal guard followed, followed in turn by another detachment of mounted Den Oroshtai soldiers. And then came the palanquins.

Pebbles, wheels, and Bhorlani are forbidden on D'Shaian roads, by order of the Scion. It is worth the lives of an entire peasant's family to leave the tracks of a wheelbarrow across a road—as opposed to a path or trail—separating two paddies, even if owned by the same peasant family. The Scion owns all roads, and does not care for them to be mistreated, not even by our beloved ruling class, and certainly not by the peasantry.

I couldn't actually see him behind the beaded curtains that let in air and light but let none escape, but it didn't take a dan'shir to figure which palanquin was Lord Toshtai's. It was suspended between two huge horses, each probably a third again as large as the other horses. The animals were probably originally of farming stock, but had been caparisoned as though they were the finest of saddle horses, from their intricately braided manes down to their lacquered hooves.

Mixed among the palanquins were a trio of musicians, playing as they walked. The drummer, his instrument a long and narrow one, manipulated the top with only his thumbs, keeping up a marching pace that was acknowledged rather than echoed by a silverhorn and wolute.

Behind the palanquins came the rest of the staff: the head cook and his nine assistants, some carrying pots and pans, others carrying cages filled with squawking chickens and ducks or sad-eyed squirrels, some leading a harnessed pig, chivying along a somber steer, or twitching a milk

Joel Rosenberg

cow into a more rapid gait; the servitors, bearing trays of sweetmeats and striped clay bottles of honeyed wine to offer the occupants of the horses and palanquins; the porters, either carrying huge bags strapped to their strapping backs or pulling reluctant draft donkeys fully laden with boxes and sacks of all shapes and sizes; a team of five hostlers, each leading two spare mounts; a claque of six concubines, exchanging whispers and giggles among themselves and the launderers accompanying them; a brace of woodsmen with their climbing gear, ready to climb trees and cut down the highest, softest pine branches for the base of Lord Toshtai's bed; and, finally, a troop of walking soldiers, their bone armor *clicketyclicketyclick*ing as they walked.

A simple expedition from Den Oroshtai to friendly, almost allied Glen Derenai.

I figured that the end of it all would be a good place for me—if the dan'shir brought up the end, I decided, he was about as far away from Lord Minch and his displeasure as was possible—so I picked up my bag and stepped off the porch.

"Bide a moment," Narantir said.

Puzzled, I turned.

The door opened, and Madame Rupon stood there with a small wicker basket, its contents concealed by the several sheets of greased rice paper that had been tucked around the perimeter.

"Be well on your trip," she said, "and thank you again, Kami Dan'Shir."

I knew I'd missed something, something important. Narantir had just talked treason openly, and as a result Madame Rupon had prepared some food for the road.

The wizard was fingering a smooth piece of glass that I hadn't seen him holding before. He rose, tucking it away in his robes.

He smiled. "Just a little cantrip using the Law of Predisposition," he said. "It doesn't take much magic to make something be itself or do what it wants to do. Works for starting an avalanche, and it's a terrific aphrodisiac for the eager-but-hesitant. I'd use it for sharpening a knife, but a whetstone works better.

"It also can be used to make a simple and loyal middle-class woman hear that somebody has enjoyed her food—something she is predisposed to hear—rather than that he has talked treason, eh?" His grin broadened. "I might even want to use it, some time, to make you make a fool of yourself."

I held back my own smile. It wasn't hard. As soon as he figured out that he was going to have to run to catch up . . .

He jerked his thumb at the basket. "Carry the food, eh?"

"My pleasure," I said, shrugging my bag over one shoulder and taking the basket in the other hand as we walked out onto the road, following the last of the soldiers. One turned to look at the two of us for the longest time, but then he turned away.

"I'll meet you further on," I said. "After all you have to run up to the keep and get your bags."

It would be fun to see. And a bit of revenge. Narantir had enjoyed sticking me with needles the time he'd fixed my broken bones, and he had particularly appreciated his own cleverness in getting me to be the victim, or subject or whatever you want to call it, the time he had run the pathos spell and joined me with a sword.

Now it was time to get a little self-appreciation back.

Narantir shook his head. "Not at all. I woke up early to stow my bags aboard the packhorses." He tapped me on the chest, not lightly. "You see, if your gear is first aboard, then additional horses will be laid on to carry that of the nobles. You must always know your place, Kami Dan'Shir, and know how to fit into it." His smile was gone. "And you must learn who to trifle with . . . successfully, eh? Bring the food."

There wasn't much to amaze me that morning and afternoon as we walked down the road toward the camping ground. I had been walking the roads of D'Shai since I was old enough to walk, and before that I had been carried. It wasn't going to surprise or amuse me that the sun-wise road out of Den Oroshtai passed through paddies of rice and fields of wheat and fulgum before it twisted into the cool green of the Korbi Copse and up into the wooded hills, snaking almost to crests before it dropped down into the valleys, sometimes bridging rivers, sometimes dipping beneath streams at a ford, emerging from the water on the far side.

Yawn.

The first time you walk a road, something new is around the bend, and its newness makes it interesting. Anything will do: a fence, a field, a flower, a flight of fidgetbugs. The second time, it's still entertaining. By perhaps the fifth time, if you've any memory at all, there's the same old thing around the same old bend or over the same old hill, and by the time you've lost count nothing new will either surprise or please. By the thousandth time you've stepped out on the roads of D'Shai, it's all the same, no matter which road you're on. There's nothing to surprise.

Yes, birds sat in the trees: redbirds in the lowland areas, watching unafraid from the green leaves, as though they blended safely in; blackly sleek crows, mocking us from perches on the heavier limbs; the odd sparrow flitting back and forth.

But a bird is a bird.

Trees were trees, whether they were the giant elms that canopied over a flat stretch, shielding us from the heat of the afternoon, turning it all into a cool green tunnel, or whether they were the fertapines that stretched straight up toward the sun, tapering so slowly and elegantly that perspective momentarily betrays you and you think they're actually cylindrical, really reaching up and scraping the clouds as they go by.

But, as I said, trees are trees.

Only three things amazed me.

One was how slowly the procession moved. I guess I should have foreseen it; it's obvious in retrospect that any group that's going to stay together is delayed by the slowest of the party. For the troupe, that had been Evrem the snakehandler, and his preferred pace wasn't really much slower than that of the Eresthais.

Here, the slowest walkers, much slower than the average, were the concubines and the oxen. I'm tempted to try to learn something from that, but I guess I'd better not.

The second thing that amazed me that day was how quickly I had gone soft, lost my edge. It had only been a month or so since the troupe had left, but when we reached the first night's camping ground in the hour of the octopus, I was actually tired. No, not tired: exhausted, and in pain.

The last thing that amazed me was how much I hurt. I had walked the roads of D'Shai barefoot, in sandals, and in heavy peasant boots; it hadn't occurred to me that my new bourgeois boots would rub the inside of my big toe into a mass of blisters.

I didn't have much to do in camp, once the hour of the snake had given way to the hour of the bear. A razor-sharp knife, a basin of tepid water, a cloth, some horrid-smelling Estrani soap, and a surprisingly odorless salve from Narantir had dealt with my blisters. Dinner was over; the chief cook and his top assistants were already in their tents, presumably asleep under the soft red silk that rippled in the light wind. The animal handlers, both hostlers and stablemen, wrestled with their appropriate animals at the far—downwind—end of the huge clearing. Most of the soldiers were asleep, in regular lines and files, in their blankets, while others kept watch out in the night, or sang quietly among themselves.

A nice time of night. Back in Den Oroshtai, I would have been walking in the gardens, hoping to accidentally encounter TaNai trying to accidentally encounter me. It was nice to be able to take things slowly with her, but our time would come, perhaps.

But not now.

Two bonfires had been lit; in their flickering light, Lords Minch and Arefai shot at the target box they had set up at the far end of the clearing. Estrer, Edelfaule, and Toshtai watched, seated on the middle three of the five thrones, while fat Narantir stood behind, occasionally snatching up a sweetmeat from the tray between the two of them.

I was going to see if I could strike up a conversation with one of the servitor girls, but as I started to turn away, Minch's head turned toward me. He made a two-fingered gesture, beckoning me over.

"Lord Arefai and I have been trifling with some target shooting," he said. He hadn't given up on his theme of red and gray in his clothing, although he was wearing hunting clothes, and the red of his thick overshirt was muted almost to the point of brown, while the gray of his pantaloons was mottled with brown blotches; he could easily disappear in the woods.

Arefai grinned. "Trifling, indeed. I've put seven into the box, and three arrows into the night."

Lady Estrer chuckled behind her hand. "Between the two of them, I suspect the night's ready for dressing out and cutting into thick, juicy steaks."

Minch pretended not to hear her. "I would like to see you shoot, after that heart shot of such fame," he said. His thin lips narrowed. "I might even like to shoot with you."

I rubbed at the inside of my left arm, and shook my head. "I'm sure I wouldn't be good competition for Lord Minch," I said.

He smiled thinly as he snapped his fingers; in response, a white-clad serving girl brought a bow.

"After such a shot? A shot worthy of a noble?"

"Lord Minch is too kind."

"I doubt that." He turned his head back to the servitor. "Leathers for Kami Dan'Shir, please—it seems he neglected that the other day." He smiled at me. "I'll leave you at no such disadvantage, Kami Dan'Shir," he said, turning to the servitors. "And my finest arrows."

He turned his palm up and beckoned that I should follow him over to where Arefai stood, leaning on his bow.

"This seems interesting," Arefai said. He nodded to the

servitor standing by the target, indicating that she should remove the arrows.

She did, and, one hand holding up the hem of her white robes, trotted over with them, smiling with apparent genuineness as she handed them to Arefai, then turned to walk back by the target box, where she again took up her lantern to illuminate the target.

I wouldn't have cared to play at shuffled placques with Arefai; it was impossible to tell from his expression that he knew I was an incompetent shot—he didn't even seem too eager, the bluffer's most common error.

"First-time fortune," I said, not quite daring to shrug off the other girl, who was busy tying a shooting leather to my left arm. "The good luck of a novice."

Minch hefted his bow. "Please." His mouth twisted into a pout. "I would shoot with such a good archer. I'll even take the first shot." He shook his slim head once, to clear the hair from his eyes, and set an arrow to the bowstring.

The arrow still pointed down, toward the ground, Minch drew the string back to its full extension, then brought the bow up and loosed, all in one smooth motion.

The target inside the box was of the standard sort: a disk, barely the size of a dinner plate, that could be fastened to any part of the target box, presumably preventing the shooter from registering the edge of the box as a sight.

The servitor down by the target box didn't even flinch when the arrow made a loud *thwock* as it sunk into the target disk that was less than an armslength away from her chest.

"Closer, closer for Kami Dan'Shir," he said. "He can barely see the target." The corners of his thin mouth turned up, and he handed me the bow.

"No," Arefai said, interposing himself between Minch and me.

Minch cocked his head to one side. Lord Toshtai raised a finger.

"No, Father; I don't mean to interfere." Arefai shook his head. "I'm not saying that Kami Dan'Shir shouldn't shoot. But he should shoot with a bow he's more familiar with—he shot the deer with a bow of mine, and an arrow of mine. Let him use those."

They were brought up, and there I was again, with a bow in my hands, and one of Arefai's arrows, with the three golden rings around the shaft that identified it as his.

There's a reason I hated being around our beloved ruling class: they kept making me do things I had no business doing, things that are properly the province of the ruling class. When I was trying to solve Refle's murder, I'd had to face off against Dun Lidjun with a sword (and, no, I didn't change into a kazuh Warrior and win); yesterday, Arefai had made me ride and hunt with him, and now ...

And now here I was, having to shoot against Minch. Next thing I knew, they'd strap armor all over my body, plop me on the back of an uncut stallion, stick my feet in the stirrups and a lance in my hand, and send me out lancing.

I let that thought lie. The moment was bad enough as it was. The girl down by the target wore a placid expression, which meant she didn't understand the situation. I'd be as likely to hit her as the target. More likely, actually: I would be aiming at the target.

I nocked the arrow and brought the bow up, then pulled it back to full extension, mimicking Arefai's form as I sighted down the arrow and held aim on the box for a long moment, long enough that I could hear Minch and Arefai stirring restlessly. An acrobat has to have strong chest and shoulder muscles, stronger than you need to flog the peasantry; I could hold this stance as long as or longer than any of them.

But I wanted to let go, to shoot; after all, it was just a servitor down there, and I—

No.

I didn't have the courage or foolishness to refuse to shoot, but I wasn't going to risk the girl's life. The head of the arrow felt better as it swung ever so slowly, slightly to the left; I'd miss the target box, and have to hope by less than enough to make it obvious what I was doing.

My fingers loosened. The arrow rushed off into the

night, the string slapped the leather over my arm, and there was a loud *thwock*.

I blinked. Something seemed to be sticking out of the left edge of the target plate.

It was possible that I was a worse shot than even I thought. The arrow should have gone high and to the left of the box, vanishing off into the night so that nobody would see by how far I'd missed.

"Nicely shot," Arefai said. "Barely on the target, but that's not bad at all."

"Very nice," Minch said.

He looked over at me, daring me to say something. The trouble was, anything I said could likely be taken as either patronizing or derogatory, except, maybe, *Please don't kill me*, which would have been sincere. But he might take that as sarcastic, and lop my head off.

I chose silence.

Minch nocked another arrow. "I'll go first again," he said, quietly, as though daring me to suggest that there wasn't going to be another round.

He took his time this time, holding back the bowstring until his arm started trembling. The string thrummed at his release, a deep but quiet bass note. This time the arrow *thwock*ed properly, just above and to the right of the center of the target.

Fine. All I had to do was miss now without being too obvious about it, and Minch would be the clear winner.

Arefai handed me another arrow. "Do your best," he said.

Keep it simple, I thought.

Notch into bowstring, then fasten two fingers around the string, letting the waxy string rest against the pads. Take up a proper stance, feet perpendicular to the target, about a shoulderswidth apart.

Fine, so far. I took a deep breath and pulled the bowstring all the way back, and held it.

Nice and slow now. Plenty of time to cheat properly.

A little more to the left this time. Think of the night as

the target. Surely even I couldn't miss the night. Surely I could—

Thwock.

"A *center*," Arefai said. "By the Powers, a beautiful shot! Did you see the way he held the bow until the right aiming point revealed itself, did you see that, Lord Minch?" He clapped me on the shoulder. Hard. "Mag*nif*icent, Kami Dan'Shir."

I saw Narantir tucking a gem into his pocket. And smiling.

That made one of us.

In three days we were in Glen Derenai.

Part Two
GLEN DERENAI

7
Lord Demick, Two Courtesy Calls, Nighttime in Glen Derenai, and Other Milestones

I HATED LORD Demick at first sight. Not that it mattered.

In retrospect, I wish I'd at least caught sight of him when the troupe had played Patrice; it was, after all, part of our regular tour, and I knew that city and its environs well, from Dockwood to Hillford, Bast to Roundtop. I had some friends, in the loose sense, in Patrice, and could easily recollect three good houses for quartering and four pretty girls interested in listening to tales of the road told under a bright moon.

But the Lord of Patrice had no interest in acrobats, and, knowing that, I was already predisposed to dislike him.

Besides, I had heard the stories. Too many of them.

About how he had ordered all white horses in Patrice slaughtered for food because one white horse had thrown his daughter to her death.

About the killing of a hundred peasant families around a small village because one of the minor nobles of Patrice had disappeared near that village.

About how, back before Thornfield was part of Patrice, back when the family of Solway Dell had ruled Thornfield for as many generations as could be remembered, Evan of Solway Dell had sided with Oled and Shalough in a dispute with Patrice over the Near Islands. While leading the forces of Patrice to victory, Demick had been able to capture Evan of Solway Dell before Evan's guards could kill him. It's said that Demick welcomed the bound Evan to Patrice with open arms and a broad friendly smile, and that Evan's death took ten days.

Arguably, as a subject of Lord Toshtai, I would have disliked Demick as his enemy, but in fairness to me, I don't think of myself as so devoted to any member of our beloved ruling class as to hate his enemies . . . or love his friends.

While Den Oroshtai is no dwarf of a domain, it retains some of the tradition of smallness from when the old donjon there was Oroshtai's summer retreat: the Great Hall of Den Oroshtai is large enough to hold an audience for perhaps two hundred people, and the ceiling is only twice my height.

Glen Derenai is, as they say along the shore, another net of fish entirely. (I don't care for the figure of speech myself, but then again, I don't live along the shore.)

Here, the vast floor was divided into nine rectangles, one for each hour of the day, and even the smallest could have contained the Great Hall of Den Oroshtai. The thrones had been set up on a bright carpet in the northwest rectangle, the one floored in rough gray stone that looked like it ought to be as slimy as the skin of an octopus; I'd had to cross over what felt like pedens of snow-white Ottish granite and endless strips of black mahogany edged in gold.

I couldn't even hear the echo of my own footsteps.

The ceiling arched high above, high enough that if the troupe had set up the trapeze near the top, we would have had to be very careful about the placement of the safety net.

I swallowed convulsively. The safety net hadn't done Enki Duzun any good at all. Yet another harm caused by our beloved ruling class.

The three lords were dwarfed by the Great Hall of the keep of Glen Derenai as they sat on three thrones arranged as though at the corners of a square, an empty fourth one to the left of Toshtai. Each had a table at his elbow; servitors came and went, bringing flasks of heated or chilled essence and small plates of dainties.

Each the master of armies, each the ruler of an important domain within D'Shai, each capable of intelligence, cruelty, and subtlety, they sipped and nibbled and chatted amiably, waiting for me.

Perhaps, in another lifetime, Demick would have been the proper complement to Toshtai and Orazhi. The three of them seemed to make up a matched set: fat Toshtai, lean Orazhi, muscular Demick.

I'll take none of each, but I thank you, good shopkeeper.

Where the lord of Den Oroshtai was fat and round easily to the point of magnificence, Orazhi was lean as a running-hound, and Lord Demick of Patrice was built almost like an acrobat, strong muscles under thin, almost transparent skin.

None of their faces betrayed any serious benevolence, but while Toshtai's eyes seemed to exude only a cold intelligence and Orazhi's a neutral beneficence, when he turned his slim head my way Demick's seemed to radiate an active if quiet animosity, as though he was the sort to idly consider which of my teeth to have pulled out next.

"So this is the . . . sole practitioner of the new kazuh you've discovered, eh, Toshtai?" he asked, his eyes on me, not waiting for an answer before he put in a comment: "Impressive." His eyes were the color of fine nebbigin steel and his short-cropped black hair was shot with gray, his face clean-shaven and all angles, a sculpture cut from the most stubborn granite.

Orazhi nodded. "I have been given reason to think so," he said, softly. "By my eyes, as well as my friend's word."

Demick's eyes more nictated than blinked. "I've always taken the position that one should be most careful, most sure before announcing such a major discovery." His smile at Lord Toshtai even seemed genial. "As I'm sure my noble friend is." His hand flopped on the end of his wrists, but that was just for effect; I've seen acrobats with less well developed wrists and hands. "Please—Kami Dan'Shir, is it?—would you be so kind as to show us your abilities?"

"Excuse me?"

His hand flopped again. "Solve for me a puzzle, if you please. Juggle a ball, if that's what you do. Shoot a deer, love a woman, sail a boat, but do something, man, something to show that you—ah," he said, looking past my shoulder, "Lord Minch has just entered the hall to join us, with Lady HaLyn, if my eyes don't betray me."

"Your eyes, Lord, will never betray you," Toshtai said. "But perhaps Kami Dan'Shir can demonstrate his abilities at some later time."

I thought I saw Lord Orazhi muffling a smile.

"We do have a problem with you, Kami Dan'Shir," Orazhi said, turning to me. I tried to read the expression on his face as I tried not to feel at my neck, failing at the first, succeeding at the second. I know how our beloved ruling class likes to solve problems.

"Who shall you pay a courtesy call on?" he went on, smoothing one hand down the front of his roomy robes.

I hadn't realized I had been holding my breath until it came out in a *whoosh*, causing Demick to smile. My underarms were clammy with sweat, and with good reason. The answer to too many questions in D'Shai tends to be "kill him," but that was unlikely to be the answer to this one, regardless of whether the question was real or rhetorical.

An acrobat avoids politics, just as any itinerant has to, resisting the blandishments of any local, no matter the locality. It's a matter of survival: you move from town to town, from domain to domain, and if it becomes even a matter of suspicion that you are partisan of any of the domains, you die. I once saw a head mounted on a spike at the entrance to Wake's Seat; a zivver soloist had been suspected of spying for Swanse, Gray Khuzud had explained.

(To be fair, I later learned more about it: the lord of Wake's Seat had had his wizard administer a truth spell to the zivver player, whose denials had been demonstrated false. I am told that sometimes truth spells even work.)

On the other hand, when you're part of a visiting entourage, some degree of espionage is expected; D'Shai being D'Shai, this practice has been given a name: it's called "paying a courtesy call on a colleague."

A visiting warrior will be shown around, say, training fields and armory by another warrior, quite likely after the training grounds have been carefully swept to avoid any hints of new formations and any improved weapons have been hidden away. The hostlers will be given a tour of the stables, perhaps while the fastest stallion has been sent out to the country to breed. The cooks, of course, will be shown around the kitchens, the assistants having been carefully briefed to avoid working on the bread stuffed with goose liver paté or other secret recipes.

Hence the problem: no dan'shir to show me around, carefully leading me away from the local puzzles.

Lord Orazhi was still looking at me. "Do you have a suggestion?"

I smiled. "Of course, Lord. I'd love to pay a courtesy call on your courtesans."

I had solved that puzzle correctly: instead of calling for the nearest guard to hack off my head for impertinence, Orazhi smiled. Not getting killed is always a good omen.

"The huntsman, I think," he said, considering. "I've heard you're quite a bowman, perhaps you can teach him some things."

I bowed. There would be worse things in the world than going out to the hunting preserve, and away from the nobility.

"And the wizard," he said. "The huntsman this afternoon, the wizard tonight."

Toshtai nodded his assent. "Enjoy yourself, Kami Dan'Shir. I will likely send for you tomorrow."

Minch waited patiently a few paces away, a tall slender woman at his side. Her robes' print repeated a stylized lion on its hind legs, the bright yellows, warm browns, and dark greens setting off Minch's crimson and gray. She eyed me openly, then returned my bow with a slight nod.

I was trying to decide whether or not courtesy called for me to say something when Minch dismissed me with a flick of his wrist.

"Good day to you," Toshtai said, making it clear that my presence was no longer required.

While one white-clad servitor brought up a tray for Minch, another led me away.

As it turned out, I already knew Orazhi's chief huntsman, although I hadn't known that I knew him.

No, that's a bit too complicated. Back when I was with the troupe, when the troupe passed through Glen Derenai, I struck up an acquaintance with JenNa, the daughter of the gamekeeper.

A lovely girl, with straight black hair that hung down to the middle of her back, and eyes that were none the less warm for being blue. I first met her when she was starting to become slender rather than skinny, and we got to know each other somewhat better on my subsequent passes through Glen Derenai.

She wasn't as special to me as my NaRee had been, of course, but JenNa had an easy smile and a musical laugh that echoed down the country lanes as she ran and hid, and she was warm in the dark, her knotted muscles playing under her soft skin that felt different for being so sunbronzed.

She was also long gone, and had been gone the last time I'd been through Glen Derenai; I had heard that she had taken some passing lord's fancy, and he had made her one of his concubines. Not a bad deal for a bourgeois girl, by and large; she would be particularly marriageable if the lord were to release her, or taken care of for life if not.

I wished her well.

She was long gone, but her father, Penkil Ner Condigan, still looked at me the way he used to, back when I would come to call on his daughter. Of course, then I had been calling at the gamekeeper's cottage, not at the door of the chief huntsman's studio in the bourgeois wing of the main donjon of Glen Derenai.

My guide exchanged a few whispers with the servitor on duty on the second floor of the donjon, and they both led me down the long hall, past pastel paintings of spotted fawns frolicking in a cool green bower. A whole herd of the long-legged young deer, their soft pelts a warm and friendly brown, capered all the way down the wall, some with two hooves high in the air, some hunkering down, ready to spring into a sprint, others already chasing each other in an endless game of flee-and-touch, the whole effect occasionally broken by the knob of an invisible door. Everything, from the blue of the painted sky to the cool minty green of the grasses, seemed to glow from a gentle inner light.

It was all bright and cheery enough to ruin even a perfect day.

The servitor stopped in front of a doorknob that was the only sign of a door's presence, then knocked four times against the white tail of a prancing baby deer. I heard no answer, but she pulled on the knob, and the ragged edge of invisible door swung open. I admired the workmanship as I walked by, the way that the door had been cut around the outline of the fawn and the trunk of a drawing of a tree.

She guided me down a short hall to what looked like a workshop: light splashed through the open windows onto a bank of rough-hewn tables. There were longbows in various stages of assembly and disassembly, and a fletching stand holding a single long arrow, plus various and sundry other implements, including an object that looked more like a thread-spinner than anything else.

Over an alcohol flame, a potbellied clear glass flask boiled merrily.

Penkil Ner Condigan was leaning back against a worktable, his thin arms crossed in front of his chest, his slim head tilted ever so slightly to one side. He was a tall man, almost skeletal in his slimness, but while no loose flesh hung beneath his chin, his face seemed to be that of another, a fat man; all the angles were smoothed out by fat.

His shirt bloused above well-scratched black leather trousers, the scabbard of a wide-bladed knife angled on the front of his belt.

"So, Kami Dan'Shir," he said. "You've come to pay a courtesy call on me." Penkil Ner Condigan's deep bass voice trembled as he spoke. I didn't understand his anger; even if I wasn't of his profession, I was now a bourgeois, instead of an acrobat and peasant. He wouldn't have to stoop class to spend time with me.

I nodded. "True enough, Penkil Ner Condigan." I shrugged. "No offense is intended." I spread my hands. "Nobody seems to know exactly where a dan'shir fits in. Myself included."

He visibly struggled for control, and got it. A wan smile spread partway across his lined face. "Very well."

I wasn't going to mention JenNa—that was likely to be a sore point—but courtesy did require that I say something about his family. "I hope that LonDee is well."

He shrugged. "As well as usual. My wife works as assistant to the chief cook in the kitchens below, and likes it enough."

There was a bone carving on the wall next to him, a pale white representation of a pig's face, its mouth held open by a red apple. He pulled the apple from the mouth, listened for a moment, and spoke loudly into the pig: "A tray of sweetmeats to Penkil Ner Condigan's workshop, if you please." He squeezed the apple back into the pig's mouth without waiting for a reply.

I guess I looked surprised. "A speaking tube," he said. "It terminates at the servitor's station on the first floor, below."

He picked up a set of silver tongs. "Tea, first, Kami Dan'Shir; then I will show you around."

Make a square in the dirt, and bisect it from top to bottom with a line that stretches out a short way above and below it: the symbol for hare. If you preface it with the semicircle symbol for time, it means the hour of the hare. If, instead, you thicken the lines, then blow it up to immense proportions as you lay it out on the ground, you have the basic floorplan for the donjon of Glen Derenai. Just lay three others on top of the first one, and you're fine.

There are some irregularities, and more than a few additions: rooms on the first floor that are of double-height, fully open to the second; the turrets at each of the outer corners, the highest one at the southeast corner, holding the wizard's workshop; the bulge in the northern part of the central section that is the Great Hall; two covered servants' ways, seemingly resting on thin air, that bridge the center sections near the middle.

But save the irregularities for later, and grasp the form first. The form left plenty of room for the gardens that bring the keep its fame. The trees, hedges, and flowers of the courtyards were under the direction of the chief gardener, although neither he nor his men were in evidence. Gardeners try to stay invisible.

The livestock in the courtyards were under the care and control of Penkil Ner Condigan.

Pheasants, their tails spread in pride or disdain or whatever birdy reason pheasants have for spreading their tails, walked the inner courtyards among tall trees and carefully manicured hedges. Tiny meer-squirrels gibbered and capered in the trees overhead, occasionally pausing in their endless mindless dance to turn wide eyes at the humans below before scurrying off. In a half-dozen tiny ponds, rainbow-skinned fingerlings broke the surface to suck down unwary insects.

The main path led to the right; we took it, but Penkil Ner Condigan held out a hand.

"Let's try another route," he said, as we reached a break in the high hedges.

Ignoring his frown, I glanced around the corner. At a marble bench under a spreading chestnut tree, a lord and a lady were engaged in a quiet but heated conversation.

I didn't recognize either of them, although I would have liked to have gotten to know the lady better, despite getting only a glance: her robes were pulled tightly at slim waist and nicely rounded hips; her hair, long, black, and glossy, fell almost to her waist. Lovely.

He was a not unhandsome man, with what I would have thought were the shoulders of an acrobat if the sword at his waist hadn't proclaimed him a warrior just as much as his arrogant stance did. He reached out a hand toward her, not stopping when she tried to turn away.

Penkil Ner Condigan pulled me back. "There are some things best not seen," he whispered.

"Very well," I whispered back. "But who are they?"

He shrugged as we continued down the path. "The lady is Lady ViKay; the lord is Esterling, an old friend."

An old friend, indeed. The way he had casually put his hands on her suggested something a bit more intimate than old friends. Or maybe I was just overexercising the right of the dan'shir to draw conclusions.

Penkil Ner Condigan and I stepped to the side of the narrow path at the approach of a pair of nobles, the lord a narrow-faced man in afternoon white with gold trimming along the seams of his tunic, the lady in a matching gown of some light, gauzy material gathered tightly at left shoulder and hip, slit up the right side to midthigh. I have seen worse thighs. Her face was pale and delicate, her mouth pink and full, framed by dark brown hair glossy as fine wood.

"Lord Drack; Lady RuAn," he said, with a bow that I hope I echoed rather than mimicked.

"Lovely day, Penkil Ner Condigan," the man said, accepting the bows with a mild, supercilious nod. Under a shock of thinning gray hair, his skin seemed taut, as though pulled too tightly.

Lady RuAn opened her mouth as though to say something, then closed it.

"No, no, dear, I see no objection to an introduction," he said. "Your companion is . . .?"

"Kami Dan'Shir," I said, bowing again. "I am Lord Toshtai's . . . puzzle solver."

"Here for the wedding to solve puzzles?" Lady RuAn's

eyes rested on mine for a long moment. I'd never seen quite that deep a shade of blue before.

I nodded. "I am here to entertain, should the occasion arise. At Lord Minch's request," I said. *At Lord Minch's request, as carefully manipulated by Lord Toshtai*, I didn't add. I am, after all, a discoverer of truths, not an obligatory revealer of truths.

"Fascinating," Drack said unconvincingly, dismissing us with a nod as he again offered his arm to Lady RuAn and the two of them walked on.

I watched them for a moment, enjoying the sway of her hips under the tight gown. Officially, of course, noble ladies are unapproachable by the likes of acrobats and dan'shirs, but my own experience is that unofficial approaches are just as pleasant.

I thought that I'd just given them a glance, but Penkil Ner Condigan was glaring at me. I gave him a blank look and we continued down the twisting path across the courtyard.

A tiny brown rabbit scurried out from underneath one bush, hopped frantically down the path a few steps, then ducked into another invisible hole in a hedge. I would have wondered what the rush was if a ridgecat, its long ears flattened back against its wide head, hadn't immediately followed. Its claws clicked a rapid tattoo against the stone of the path as it turned, then disappeared around the bend. I could have sworn the ridgecat was wearing a thick leather collar, and wondered how much healing attention whoever had collared the ridgecat had required.

Penkil Ner Condigan shook his head. "I think we need a new ridgecat; I'll have to have words with the keeper."

"Eh?"

"Lord Orazhi likes to have rabbits in his gardens, granted, as well as other animals, but there must always be a balance, eh? And not just for the benefit of the gardener who is always tired of having to plant seven bulbs for each one uneaten." He bent in front of the place where both the rabbit and the cat had emerged. "Lady ViKay's private garden is on the other side," he said, "or I'd have one of the huntsmen do it. Where the family is directly concerned, I like to do things myself." He dropped his leather bag to one side, then dropped to one knee in front of the hole. "Care to lend a hand?"

"I guess that depends on what we're doing," I said as he took out a few turns of thin, exquisitely braided leather rope and set it down beside him.

He had stopped frowning for a moment, but he started it up again. "Ah. I forgot for a moment. Never mind," he said. "I'm just fastening a noose. You wouldn't know anything about that."

"That would depend." I squatted and picked up the rope. It took me almost no time to make a loop and choke-knot, then to hang the loop from the bush so that its bottom bend didn't quite touch the ground. I left a few turns of rope lying on the ground next to the hole, then held out my hand. "Stake, please."

In the wild, a stake is a piece of gathered deadwood, possibly with a point whittled carefully enough to look unwhittled. Penkil Ner Condigan's was an ornately engraved brass staple with long legs and a wide crown. One turn of the rope around the crown and a quick push of the sharp points into the soft green grass, and it fastened the rope to the ground tightly enough to hold a struggling rabbit.

"Odds are small," I said, "that it'll break its neck when the noose pulls it off its feet. If not, I wouldn't want to bet that that fancy rope of yours will choke it. Slides too easily on itself," I said.

He pursed his lips. "You would suggest?"

"Simple twine, Penkil Ner Condigan," I said.

"Oh."

"The tendency of the bourgeois is to prefer the complex over the elegant."

His eyes twinkled. "I take it you've done this before."

I shook my head. "I can't imagine how you would think that, Penkil Ner Condigan," I said.

He looked for a moment as though he actually was going to smile, but instead beckoned me on. "You wouldn't mind helping me fasten a few of those around the gardens?"

I spread my hands. "Just a part of the traditional courtesy call between a huntsman and a dan'shir, no?"

Then he did smile.

Unblinking, three hairy owls watched me from their cages near the window.

The beer tasted of vinegar and rodent; I coughed once, twice, three times. I wasn't used to it, or to the way that my head was swimming.

"... stupid."

"Dumb."

"Moronic."

"Clodwitted."

"Dull."

"Listless."

"Slow."

"Overdue."

"Ooo." Tebol shook his head. "I can't think of one that begins with an oo. Your point, Narantir."

The fat magician smiled. I drank some more and coughed some more. Narantir slapped me on the back, harder than strictly necessary, stopping only when Tebol raised a slim finger.

"The beer in Den Oroshtai is weak, and breeds weak tastes," Tebol said. "Unfortunate."

"Tragic," Narantir suggested.

"Catastrophic," Tebol said.

Narantir nodded. "Mmm ... cataclysmic."

"Enh." Tebol sipped his beer and thought about it for a moment. "Calamitous."

"Fine. Sad," Narantir said.

"Well ... let it be." Tebol raised an eyebrow. "Disastrous."

"Err ... sorrowful?"

" 'Sorrowful'?" Tebol shook his head. "I let 'sad' go by, but that's a bit much."

"Perhaps." Narantir reached out his unwashed hands

and took another deep-fried tentacle from the bowl on the table. "You have a play?"

Tebol smiled. "Somber?"

Narantir didn't return the smile. "Ah: I should have challenged. Your point." He offered me the bowl, but I declined. I'm not overfastidious, I would hope, but I had the feeling that Narantir hadn't washed his hands or brushed under his nails since the Tenancy. Wizards are like that, most of them.

Tebol was an exception. His gray robes were tailored to his modest frame, belted tightly about his waist and neatly hemmed at the calves; his hair had been freshly trimmed, each hair to the same length, so that it seemed layered all around his head. His nails were square-cut, and his hands scrubbed pink, as though cleanliness mattered to him. Although you never know with wizards. Despite the apparent fastidiousness, it didn't seem to bother him to be eating out of the same bowl as Narantir.

"The tentacles are palatable," said Narantir.

"Luscious?"

"Certainly. Scrumptious."

"Savory."

"I'll challenge."

"Hmmm . . . your point."

I took my mug of beer and went to the window.

Everything is different; everything is the same. In both Den Oroshtai and Glen Derenai—and everywhere else— the wizard's workshop was kept well away from other things. Nobody likes to be around a working wizard. Forget any danger; the smell is enough to drive you away.

While Narantir's had been tucked away in the dungeon, Tebol's workshop was pushed up and away: the Glen Derenai wizard lived and worked in the turret built into the outer wall.

Below, guards in the livery of Lord Orazhi walked the inner parapets, each foursome of local guards accompanied by a mixed foursome, one each from a visiting lord.

All is illusion, all is deception; Lord Orazhi had made sure that his own guards were walking the parapets on the outer curtain walls, and inside the courtyard, even at this late hour, a hundred of them pretended to take their ease, a small choir harmonizing on a gentle lullaby. The mother of the lord of Glen Derenai in fact *did* give birth to an idiot son, but she drowned him in a washbasin, and it was his brother Orazhi who ruled Glen Derenai; proper security would be maintained.

Further below, in the main gardens off the Great Hall, a reception was in progress.

Custom undoubtedly prescribed who was giving it, and for whom; all I knew was that clusters of members of our beloved ruling class were engaged in conversation and dance beneath smoking, flickering torches. Only traces of music filtered up this high: the distant tinkling of chimes, a flare of silverhorn or thump of a drum.

Tebol was at my shoulder. "You're silent for one paying a courtesy call, Kami Dan'Shir," he said.

"Way of the Dan'Shir, Tebol ha-Mahrir," I said.

His smile was neither friendly nor hostile. "And what *is* the Way of the Dan'Shir, Eldest Son Discoverer-of-Truths?"

I pursed my lips. "I'm trying to decide that, Rainy Sunrise User of Magic," I said, formal as he was. "It's not easy."

"Many things are not easy." He drained his mug with one huge swallow, then gestured that I should do the same. "Drinking enough to be ready for the tour is one."

"I don't understand why we have to drink so much," I said.

Narantir looked at me as though I was stupid. "Because it's part of the spell," he said.

Oh.

Tebol laughed drunkenly. "Because if we were sober, we wouldn't want to do this. Because if they were sober, the owls wouldn't let us."

"If we're really going to do it."

"Indeterminate, as well as pathetic," Tebol said. "One never knows. Drink."

"Consume."

"Mmm . . . your point."

Acrobats don't tend to drink much, and I'd never cared for beer. But I was noticing that the taste improved, or at least got less offensive, with every mug. By the time I had another six or so mugs, it would probably taste good.

"What do you mean, indeterminate?"

"Tentative, unsure, ambiguous, doubtful, uncertain, problematical, undetermined, equivocal, unclear," Tebol said.

I decided I liked Tebol, but also that I'd like him better if it was politic to hit him with a stick a few times. "I am no wiser."

"The spell depends on indeterminacy. Which is why we lock the door."

"And what happens if the door opens while . . ." I waved my hands, vaguely, which was only fair, given that I was vague about what we were going to do. ". . . whatever is going on is going on? Is that indeterminate, too?"

Tebol shrugged. "Well, yes and no. Whoever stands in the door would be able to tell if our bodies are still here, which would make it determinate, yes?"

"Well, yes."

"There are some things man is not meant to know." He smiled. "There are three solutions. If our bodies are here, then we cannot be elsewhere; the spell would fail, and we would wake up. If our bodies are not here, then we must be elsewhere; the spell would fail, and we would be lost in the ether."

I have no philosophical objection to being the catcher and letting somebody else show off. "And the third solution?"

"Ah." It was Narantir's turn to smile. "The third possibility: our bodies are neither here nor not-here, because all is illusion."

"And what would happen?"

"The universe would then end, of course." Narantir drained his mug, and refilled it, slopping half more at than in the bowl in the largest owl's cage. He was weaving, barely able to stand.

Tebol had cleared a space on his largest workbench, spread a black felt cloth on it, and assembled a collection of devices. Some were familiar, like the knife, bell, watron, pen, and brush. Others were completely strange, like a tangle of wires wrapped around and running through something that looked like a shriveled cucumber. There were pots of various foul-smelling paints and pastes, and a wet bone ball.

"Feathers," he said. "We each need a feather." Weaving, he approached the cages. When he snaked out a hand to pull a feather from the tail of the first bird, the fast-moving beak barely missed; the second and third birds didn't even come close. Maybe he wasn't as drunk as he seemed, or maybe he wasn't as drunk as the birds.

"This ought to do it," said Narantir as he slipped a fifth bar over the door, then tied his belt even more tightly about his waist before slipping out of the top of his robes.

Half-naked, he was even uglier than clothed. His huge, hairless chest and belly were covered with scars and lesions, one whole series of parallel scars running up his left forearm.

Tebol had stripped to nothing but a lotai, wrapped tightly about waist, buttocks, and loins. His chest and upper body, too, were covered with scores of scars and cuts, again with a whole series of parallel scars on the left forearm. All were minor injuries, certainly, but it looked like somebody had regularly spent time whittling away at the wizards.

He caught my expression and smiled broadly. "Amazing how often a bit of fresh wizard's blood is needed in a spell, eh?" he said, picking up a sharp knife. Suddenly, without warning, he sliced at his forearm with a practiced stroke that left a red cut in parallel with the old scars.

A thin stream of blood ran down Tebol's bent arm; by the time it began to drip from his elbow, he had a crystal chalice underneath to catch the flow. The cup filled quickly, almost brimming until Tebol muttered a quiet syllable as he touched a wand first to a pot of some horrid white mess, then to the wound, instantly staunching the flow.

"I take it you have done this before," I said.

Narantir smiled. "The dan'shir not only sees, but he observes," he said, while Tebol took up a brush and began to paint complex runes on his chest and belly, dipping the brush first into one horrid-smelling pot, then another. His movements were swift and sure.

At Narantir's gesture, I removed my tunic. Tebol's paints were cold and awful against my skin. He went to the window and unlocked the cages, although not opening them, ignoring the drunken hooting of the owls.

Tebol sat down in a corner of the room, while Narantir stretched his bulk out on the floor.

Tebol muttered a few syllables and the paints flashed into cold flame in front of my eyes, momentarily blinding me.

First was the pain. All was red agony, as my arms jammed themselves back hard behind my back and my body leaned forward at the waist in a way that should have sent me off-balance, but somehow didn't. My fingers had grown immense, but indistinct; if they hadn't hurt, I would have said they felt almost numb, as though I was wearing deep feathery gloves.

The universe had grown around me; the bars of my cage now arced far above my head. I turned my head almost all the way around, looking first at the cage on my breeze-ward side, and then at the one on my lee side. I guess I could have looked back by the door, where the three bodies either lay or didn't, but I either didn't think of it or couldn't.

It hurt, but the hurt began to fade, then was washed away in a hunger. The only thing I could think about was how hungry I was, and how bright and clear the night was outside.

It is, isn't it?

I know I didn't hear it as words, not exactly, but that's the only way I can remember it.

Yes.

I had always thought of darkness as a single black color, but here that wasn't true; it was broken into scores of shades from black to white, from the dark satiny blackness of the sky between the stars, to the rich, deep gray of the fields to windward, or the glossy, oily gray of the fish-ponds in the gardens. The night was broken by hot white flares, so bright they should have hurt my eyes, but didn't.

I took wing, working my shoulder muscles hard, climbing in a tight circle into the night sky, high above the walls of the castle.

Wait, didn't quite sound behind me. *This is new to you; you might make a mistake.*

I didn't wait. The night was calling. I stretched out into a shallow glide, wheeling across the sky while the two others climbed up toward me.

There were stupid humans below on the grass, chasing the prey away, involving themselves in their overly complicated lives instead of properly searching for prey or resting to digest. Eaters of carrion, taking bits of dead, burned flesh from servitors, a mocking parody of the way a mother would feed her chicks.

Hmmm. Still, off in the darkness, thinking himself hidden in the shadows at the edge of the lighted portion of the garden, a fat mouse waited, eyeing some crumbs dropped on the moss a quick dash away. If I came up behind him, it wouldn't matter whether he did or didn't make a dash for the food; I'd be on the same path as he was and, skimming over the ground, could snatch him up before he would get a squeak out.

The approach was the tricky part; I swooped over the walls to the west and set myself into a steep glide, picking up speed as I stooped. There wasn't a straight path to the mouse, not exactly; I would have to duck under low branches, rise high enough to clear the hedge, then put myself into a final approach, snatch him either out of his hiding place or on the run, then climb quickly enough to clear the serving table beyond.

I dove, wind rushing past me in a loud but constant whisper that my feathers muffled. The mouse was but a tiny spot below me, something far too small for human eyes to notice or human mind to care about, but I could see his beady little eyes and watch the nervous twitch of his whiskered snout.

I pulled myself down, under the branches, then cupped my wings to gain barely enough altitude to clear the hedge. No need to flap more; I was going fastfastfast, talons outstretched to grab and hold, only needing feather touches to—

The ta*roo* of another owl was almost in my ear; I pulled up, hard, climbing into the night, while a stick of some sort *whoosh*ed under me, just barely missing my feet as I wheeled high into the sky.

Below my feet, the warrior looked up in irritation at having missed what should have been an easy kill, while another was busy fastening string to bow. It only occurred to me later that the thing that saved me was the fact that there were so many out-domain lords around, making it both polite and politic to get permission before nocking an arrow.

Both of the other owls were at my side, one of them plumper than the other.

Go a-hunting where it's safe, the thin one said, *if you have to go hunting at all.*

Birds don't smile, or the fat owl would have smiled. *I'll show you where to find a nice, fat mouse, out in the fields, where it's safe to hunt.*

He did.

Look: I am not at all certain that the wizards were telling me the truth about the indeterminacy; wizards have been known to lie. Wizards have been known to create illusions, as well, and illusions are hard to see through when you're drunk. On the other hand, they're not Helpful Owen of tale and legend who knows all, answers freely, but always lies; that would be too easy.

On yet another hand, something happened during the night. I don't know what, not for sure. The only thing I do know is that I woke up with a horrible headache, and a horribly queasy stomach, and half a dead mouse on the floor near my mouth.

I didn't throw up. I didn't want to see what I would throw up.

Narantir's thick face was too near mine. "Wake up, Kami Dan'Shir," he said. "Lord Arefai invites you to join him for the morning hunt with his bride's father."

He splashed some water in my face.

Great. Now I was scared, hung over, more than vaguely nauseated, and wet.

8
ViKay, a Hunt, an Attempted Deception, and Other Reasons to Kill

EVERYBODY HAS A function in life. Even our beloved ruling class.

Peasants raise wheat, rice, cotton, pigs, and milking cows; members of our beloved ruling class eat bread and steamed rice, wear clothes of cotton and leather, and drink milk. Ranchers raise beef cows and horses; members of our beloved ruling class eat beef and ride horses. Cobblers make shoes; members of our beloved ruling class wear shoes. Acrobats and musicians create beauty with sight and sound; members of our beloved ruling class sit on their tender buttocks and watch. All of the lower classes raise sons and daughters; members of our beloved ruling class have them clean their stables or tend to their rooms and persons.

I just don't know what the rest of us would do without our beloved ruling class to consume what we produce. I do know, though, that I wouldn't mind finding out, or at least I wouldn't mind not finding out later than just after sunrise.

With a hangover.

The dew hadn't left the grasses, and the birds had already started their mindless chirping about how pretty the day was, as though anybody cares what a bird's opinion is.

The sun was too bright, and standing as we were outside of the east gate, there was no shade; no trees are allowed to grow near the outside walls of D'Shaian castles. A stiff, damp breeze blew from sunwise, hard enough to whip dust into my eyes. Damp, sticky dust. The wind also brought the stink of the dozen or so horses that waited with their handlers a short way down the road. I guess that a few horses voiding themselves would have interfered with the ceremony.

I hate the hour of the cock. If I had my way, I'd go to bed just before the departure of the lion, and rise with the coming of the horse.

"Good day, Kami Dan'Shir," Arefai said, as he knelt over his gear.

"Good day, Lord."

He was stylish even at this offensive hour, dressed in the finest of deer-hunting gear. The pleats of his tunic were sharp enough to shave with, and the leather thigh pads of his trousers were polished to a sheen bright enough to shave in. The corners of his beard had been freshly trimmed, and his hair was still damp from a morning bath. As he checked over his quiver of arrows, eyeing the fletching here, checking the sharpness of a broadhead there, he looked so fresh and bright and clean that it made me want to retch.

I suppressed it; I'm not completely sure that Lord Arefai would have considered my voiding my stomach all over him to be an entirely friendly act. From the way Lord Minch was looking at me, I am sure he would have wanted to find out; I had the feeling he was almost as unfond of Arefai as he was of me.

"Good morning, Kami Dan'Shir," Toshtai said.

"And to you, Lord Toshtai." Toshtai's huge tunic was cut unstylishly full, and he was wearing leather trousers instead of the more fashionable leather-inlaid ones. I guess he already had to kill so many cows for one pair of trousers that he didn't want to empty Den Oroshtai's barns for a new set of hunting chaps.

If he had had an expression, I would have guessed he

was frowning at the thought of having to be up and around, a real sword and hunting knife belted about his waist, with nothing but an intricately carved spear to lean on—if you didn't count old Dun Lidjun, and Toshtai only leaned on Dun Lidjun metaphorically.

But he didn't have an expression on his face, so I didn't guess.

Dun Lidjun looked fresh and vigorous in his hunting tunic and trousers of heavy blued cotton, inlaid with leather patches of chest, elbows, knees, thighs, and seat. A note of discord: his limp gray hair was tied back with a red ribbon, the sort of thing that could have been a lady's token.

He stood near Toshtai, leaning on his longbow, although I had the definite sensation that if the bow were to disappear, Dun Lidjun wouldn't stagger for a moment. His narrow, gray eyes rested on mine for a moment, then moved on, a death sentence passing me by.

Edelfaule, as usual, looked like an underinflated version of his father, from the rawn-yellow tunic to the old-fashioned hunting trousers, even to the way he leaned on his spear.

He snapped his fingers at the nearest of the servitors. "Weren't you listening to my father a few moments ago? He said that Kami Dan'Shir was to hunt with us today."

I soon had a totally useless bow in my hands and a quiver strapped around my waist, as well. Everybody else was checking out his gear, so I pulled out an arrow, trying to look like I knew what I was looking for.

Demick, perhaps even more stylish than Arefai—his clothes were hemmed with silver thread, which seemed to be all the fashion along the coast—was watching me closely.

Arefai raised his eyebrows, then nodded. "I see you've seen what we've done."

Other than the usual? Other than putting me in a situation where I don't belong, with members of our beloved ruling class looking at me as though they're deciding when instead of what?

I spread my hands. "I am not fresh, wet and bloody, from the womb, Lord," I said, bluffing.

Orazhi was watching me impassively, and Demick with a flat stare.

Demick caught my eye. "I wonder if you would tell us . . ." he started.

Oh, no. I didn't expect him to try me out. There would have to be a way of declining gracefully, but how was I to be expected to think of it with a dozen of them looking down at me?

"Impressive," Toshtai said, interrupting. "I would not have thought you would see such small markings with such a quick glance." He turned to Demick. "My apologies, Lord; you were saying?"

Small markings, he had said. *There* it was. A burn mark near the notch on the shaft: three tiny circles set in a small triangle. I forced my eyes away.

"I was saying, Lord," Demick said, clearly keeping his voice impassive and emotionless with some effort, "that I, too, am impressed." His look at me was not friendly.

"I am touched, Lord," I said, with a quick bow. "The three balls symbolize my former profession, of course," I said, taking three arrowheads from the pouch and putting them into an impromptu juggle before putting them away.

Toshtai actually smiled then; the corners of his mouth moved visibly up.

It had all gone on over Arefai's head, but Edelfaule gave out what looked like a quick smile. Which only stood to reason. If Demick had exposed my bluff, it would have reflected badly on Toshtai, and Edelfaule was certainly going to be more protective of the interests of Toshtai and Den Oroshtai than of Demick and Patrice.

"Juggling," Lord Minch said. "Isn't juggling part of acrobatacy, and is that not a peasant thing?"

I smiled in agreement. "It surely is, Lord Minch. Acrobats are peasants, and they do juggle to entertain their betters. Dan'shirs also juggle, to help themselves concentrate." As the Historical Master Dan'Shir and to date the only dan'shir, I figured I was safe from authoritative refutation.

"Hmm. One wouldn't think that a practice would be shared between classes," Minch said.

"No, Lord, one wouldn't. Unless one noticed that, say, peasants walk, a practice they share with the middle class, the bourgeoisie, and the nobility."

That hadn't gone beyond Arefai; his smile was overly broad. "By Spennymore's tepid testicles, Kami Dan'Shir is right. I have seen lords walk, many a time, and never thought to think them lowering themselves thereby."

Minch didn't quite glare.

We waited in front of the main gate of the keep, a hypocritical hunting party: Arefai, Toshtai, Edelfaule, Minch, Demick, Orazhi, Esterling, and ten or so other lords I didn't know by name, accompanied by ten times that many servants, if you include me, which you ought to.

Or, perhaps, you ought to include me in the hunting party: I had a bow, too.

Yes, we all were armed with bows and arrows, and soon we would ride out in search of prey, but first there was a drama to be enacted.

Off in the distance, within the castle grounds, far beyond where the huge doors of the main gate stood open, a party emerged from the south door of the donjon. The women were all in white robes decorated with black, green, red, and pale yellow, symbolizing birth, growth, blood and beginnings, although no two of the robes were quite the same; some were cut low, some high, some were decorated with embroideries of animals, others with abstract designs.

It all made me quite queasy as they made their way toward us.

But then the group parted, and there she was, in a simple robe of pale yellow belted at the waist, the color either symbolizing a beginning or making a tribute to Lord Toshtai, who often wore the same shade.

ViKay was tall and graceful, her body slim but not boyish. Her face was delicate without seeming fragile, her lips

119

full and rich and parted in an easy smile. A thin gold chain encircled her neck, securing a small bone placque just below the hollow of her throat. Her long black hair, shiny in the bright sunlight, was twisted into a complicated knot at the back of her neck, secured with three long bone needles.

On the night of their wedding, I would envy Arefai as he removed those needles, then worked at the knot at her waist.

"My lords," she said, her voice lower and warmer than I had expected. "I come to wish you a good morning." She turned and met the eyes, one by one, including mine. I can't say for sure, but it felt like the corners of her mouth barely turned upward when her eyes rested on mine.

They were deep eyes, warm and brown. All bowed toward her. I didn't mind bowing toward those eyes.

"Daughter," Orazhi said affectionately, although formally, "I have invited these lords to accompany me on the hunt, to test their worth, to prove their merit. It is my hope that you will look with favor on the victor of the hunt."

It seemed somewhat more than barely possible that the victor would be Arefai, given that custom called for all the other hunters to let him take both the first and last quarry, and for nobody to make a better kill than his first. It would be a major solecism for anybody else to outdo Arefai, the sort that would lead to a challenge. A nasty way to commit suicide, actually; it would be an insult not only to Arefai but to his family, and that meant that the challenger would have to face every warrior of Den Oroshtai in turn.

There is the legend of Lord Ulane, who—in a somewhat different context—challenged the son of the lord of Rewsby Grove, and found himself taking on all the men of Rewsby Grove one by one, but, frankly, I don't believe it; I've been through Rewsby Grove, and it's a tumbledown ruin, not worth anybody's fighting for.

"Lady," Lord Arefai said, his voice taking on a formal lilt that I hadn't heard from him before, "I go, as our ancestors have always gone, in search of game for the table, hoping that my search will prove fruitful, that my eye will be sharp, and my arm strong and accurate."

I didn't think that would be a problem, all things considered. I didn't know of my own observation, mind you, that there were deer in the forest beyond, but I would have been astonished if there weren't, and wouldn't at all been surprised to learn of a dozen of them, hobbled and blindfolded, waiting in the woods. Our beloved ruling class does not like to come back empty-handed from the hunt, and the chief huntsman was absent, no doubt assuring that there would be game in our path.

The wind brought me a scent of patchouli and lime as she reached into the bosom of her robes and pulled out a piece of red silk. I'm sure it's called a scarf, although it was far too light and sheer to keep out any wind. A stiff breeze would have torn it.

"A token," Lady ViKay said, "for the most successful of the hunters."

Two servants appeared at her elbow, one with a silver salver, another with a teak tripod. Without looking down, she set the scarf down on the salver just as the first servant managed to set the salver on the tripod. I was expecting the breeze to blow the silken scrap away, but one of the servants had already thought of that, and immediately set a highly polished onyx weight on top of the silk.

Under the shiny bone-white stone, the crimson silk fluttered in the breeze like a pinned butterfly.

Arefai looked over the group carefully, his eyes resting on mine for too long.

I don't mind a bit of acting, but this was ridiculous. I wasn't going to shoot his deer, embarrass him, and commit suicide, all in one stroke. The only reason I had been credited with the kill back in Den Oroshtai had been because Arefai was using my arrows—which he knew. The contest with Lord Minch had been fixed by Narantir's predisposition spell, cantrip, incantation, or whatever it was—which he should have known.

I had no illusions about my abilities as a bowman, and no intention of finding some now. I would shoot low and wide and late, thank you very much, and let the spells fall where they may.

His eyes swept past me, and I could breathe again.

The horses were waiting for us at the bottom of the hill.

Hunting in Glen Derenai turned out to be different from hunting in Den Oroshtai.

Where the hunting trails in Den Oroshtai were paved, those in Glen Derenai were dirt paths, sometimes barely broad enough for a single horse and rider, sometimes wide enough for half a dozen to ride abreast. Where the hunting trails in Den Oroshtai cut mainly through dark woods, occasionally skirting a meadow or glen, those in Glen Derenai stretched out alongside fields, over unfarmed hills, and down next to streambeds shining in the sun. Strips of forest separated plowed fields from meadows, but the paths tended to cut across the strips, instead of running along inside them.

It was all a much more open, much brighter, much more golden than green thing to hunt in Glen Derenai.

It was, however, equally painful: bouncing on the back of a horse hurts. There's a sleight to the way you move your hips and back, and I didn't have it. Everybody else did; except when they stood in their stirrups, it looked like the bottoms of all the lords were glued to their saddles. Even Toshtai, looking far too large for his suffering saddle horse, didn't bounce up and down as he rode.

Riding through grasses that brushed my knee, we topped a hill. I finally caught a glimpse of the sea—Eter Kabreel, the Closed Sea, the body of water that separates D'Shai from the mainland north of Bhorlan.

We quickly rode downslope, and the sea disappeared, but I still had to repress a shudder. There's something about the Eter Kabreel that always bothers me. I don't know what it is, honestly, and I probably never will.

It's not unfamiliarity; I spent my first seventeen years as an itinerant, and I've seen large bodies of water before; it's not like I'm a peasant, away from my paddy and hut for the first time.

I've seen the waters of D'Shai, from the friendly gray and blue waters of the Eter Shalough that separate the Ven from the rest of D'Shai, where sailboats both large and small follow the zigzag trade route north and south, to the Eter Enothien, the Open Sea that laps on the morningwise coast of the Ven, Helgramyth, and Otland, and the waters that go on forever from there.

And I have seen the icy lakes up in Helgramyth, so clean and blue that it looks like they never have been sullied by man.

I have walked from north to south and sunwise to morningwise in D'Shai, from Wyness Tongue in the north to Flinder Bay in the south, from the most morningwise coast of the Ven to Lower Midwich, and south from there to Wisterly, where the Tetnit stands guarding the Sleeve, that narrow body of water that separates D'Shai from Bhorlan and the Bhorlani.

I have seen the waters, and have drunk and swum in most, but something about the slate gray water of the Closed Sea always chills me, no matter how bright and hot the day.

Arefai, riding beside me, caught my shudder. "What is it, Kami Dan'Shir?"

I shook my head. I couldn't admit that it was just a glimpse of the distant sea that bothered me. Truth has nothing to do with what I will or won't confess to, after all.

"Nothing much, Lord," I said. "I just had a flare of kazuh." I pursed my lips and tried to look intelligent. "A feeling that there is . . . some subtle danger, some subtle threat."

Given that I was riding with a party of a dozen D'Shaian nobles, some of whom had long been making war on each other, the chances of that being the case were roughly the same as of there being a flea somewhere in a pack of wild dogs, of there being some bark on one of the trees yonder, or of an aged concubine coming unvirginal to one's bed.

Nevertheless, Arefai looked impressed. "I will stay alert."

"Very good, Lord."

Far ahead of us, Lord Orazhi, almost at the crest of the hill, raised a hand and dropped lightly from his horse.

"Quarry ahead," Arefai whispered, as all the horses slowed.

We dismounted and moved forward, the high grass coming more than waist-high, sometimes tickling my nose. It was good to be back on solid ground again, although I was having some trouble keeping my balance; it seemed that I had gotten used to the rocking of the swaying animal.

Without a word, Lord Esterling and another young noble whose name I didn't know gathered the horses, leading them downslope. Esterling glared at me for a moment—the idea of serving a bourgeois didn't please him, apparently—but gave me enough time to untie my gear from the saddle before he added my horse to his string; the idea of leaving the horse in my awkward hands probably bothered him more.

I took my time stringing my bow, although I probably could have done it quickly. I was getting good at this.

Arefai and I made our way up to the top of the hill in a half-crouch. I didn't and don't know much about hunting, but I did notice that the wind was blowing toward us, which would tend to carry both smells and sounds away from whatever was in front of us.

We topped the hill and looked down.

Down below us, a stream had carved a shallow valley as it wound its way from the distant snow-rimmed Sorkle Mountains, to fall off the black cliffs and splash into the Eter Kabreel.

Three deer stood by the side of the stream, drinking: two females and a large male, a rack of antlers crowning his erect head. I didn't have a lot of experience to compare them to other such, but either the male was unusually huge or the females were tiny.

"The buck is a worthy shot," Minch said, quietly, quickly reaching for an arrow. There was something strange about the way he was fumbling at his quiver, instead of smoothly drawing and nocking the arrow the way Arefai did. Even so, he pulled an arrow and nocked it at the same time that Arefai did.

Arefai drew his string back.

Minch drew his own string, and fired.

Arefai's eyes grew wide.

My kazuh flared.

In retrospect, both the problem and the solution were obvious.

It would be a coarse and obvious solecism for Minch to outshoot Arefai; it would be equally coarse and obvious for Arefai to falsely accuse Minch of having done so.

Unless Minch outshot Arefai *without* outshooting him. Unless he did it right in front of our eyes but could, nevertheless, credibly deny the plain evidence.

That was what he had done.

An acrobat has to be able to move quickly: before Arefai's arrow had quite come up, I reached out a hand and plucked his string from his fingers, firing his arrow down into the tall grasses just as Minch's shot spunged into the chest of the buck below.

"Brilliant shot, Lord Arefai," I shouted. "Stunning."

His eyebrows shot up and his nostrils flared wide, and for a moment I didn't know how it would go.

Minch solved the problem for me.

"What did you say, you filthy little bourgeois?" he said, squaring off against me, one hand on his bow, the other on the hilt of his sword. "You interrupt the hunt with your—"

"Minch." Arefai dropped his bow to one side and took two quick steps toward Minch. "I have had enough insolent—"

No, no, no, I wanted to scream. *Let it go.*

The purpose of the whole thing was to provoke Arefai into making an inexcusable attack on Minch, be it a physical attack or just an accusation. But I was only a dan'shir, not a warrior, and I had no chance of stopping a pair of swordsmen.

Moving quickly but silently, Dun Lidjun stepped between the two of them, his face flat and impassive, like the surface of a moonlit pond. One open palm faced Arefai as Dun Lidjun turned to face Minch.

Dun Lidjun's gesture had silenced Arefai, stopping him in his tracks. The old man made no motion toward his sword, but Minch's hand jerked away from the hilt of his own blade as though it were on fire. That wasn't part of anybody's scheme, for Minch to draw on Dun Lidjun and be hacked to death in self-defense.

Nobody said anything for the longest time. We stood, motionless as a mural.

"A brilliant shot, indeed," I finally threw into the silence.

"Yes," somebody else said, "a fine shot, Lord Arefai."

Dun Lidjun's voice was low. "I've seen none finer, Lord Arefai," he said, his eyes never leaving Minch's.

"No offense intended, Lord Arefai," Minch mumbled. "A good shot, indeed." His expression was dutifully passive, but he hadn't given up, not yet.

Demick didn't say anything, but Orazhi gave a low laugh.

"My old eyes deceive me, Kami Dan'Shir," Lord Orazhi said. "Foolish eyes that they are, for a moment—and I say this in self-mockery, you understand, commenting on the weakness of my eyes and foolishness of my mind, and nothing more, you see—it almost looked as though it was Lord Minch who had shot, and not Lord Arefai."

Perhaps my eyes flashed my thanks, although I tried to keep my face calm.

"With respect, Lord," I said, "you are correct: your eyes were mistaken." It's safe to contradict a member of our beloved ruling class when that's what he has as much as told you he wants you to do. "You'll see that it is one of Lord Arefai's arrows that has pierced the heart of the buck, and not one of Lord Minch's."

I was trying to decide how Minch had set it up, how far he had gone, when I realized it didn't matter, not at this level of hypocrisy.

"I am sure that is so." Orazhi beckoned to a huntsman. "The arrow, and quickly."

"Lord Minch, might I see your quiver?" I said, holding out a hand.

He looked from me to Dun Lidjun and then back to me.

"Here. Take it," he said, unbuckling it from his waist. It dropped to the ground; he spun on the ball of his foot and stalked back toward the horses.

I fell to one knee and picked up the quiver. "You see, Lord Orazhi," I said, as I dumped the arrows out on the ground, "all of these have the markings of Lord Minch, and none of Lord Arefai. There was no unfortunate blunder in which Lord Minch got Lord Arefai's quiver."

Which was unfortunate. If he had been carrying more of Arefai's arrows, that would have brought the whole matter out in the open, or as out in the open as things were going to get. Which would have settled Minch. To pick a fight with a visiting lord is a solecism, but being caught that way would have put the solecism squarely on Minch's head, which would quickly have been rolling about the ground.

Now, I don't know much about swordfighting, but it was clear to me that Arefai was certain that he was the better swordsman, and I would have been willing to bet that he was right, particularly since I'd be betting Arefai's life, and not my own.

The huntsman, half out of breath, trotted up with the arrow held high in his hands. At Lord Orazhi's nod, he handed it to me. The slim arrow was redly darkened from head to fletching. I rubbed my thumb along the shaft, near the nock point, revealing three gold bands.

"Lord Arefai's arrow," I said. "Nicely shot, Lord Arefai. Would you not say so, Lord Demick?"

Demick smiled too easily. "I would be happy to say so," he said.

There is a nasty game that they play over in Agami, in some of the smaller domains near the foot of Mount Ashen.

A peasant, usually—although sometimes it's a bourgeois or a middle class, if there's somebody in particular that the local lord wants to punish—is turned loose along hunting paths, given a start before the members of our beloved ruling class start after him or her. There is, in theory, a goal that the victim can reach in safety—a bridge, a stream, a field, a town, but it's likely that somebody so impertinent as to defeat a lord's sport isn't going to enjoy the experience.

Yes, him or her; there's two versions of the game. One is merely a rougher version of what members of our beloved ruling class do with peasant girls anyway; the other is a hunt for a human quarry. Manhunters take a single tooth from their dead victims; I've seen lords with a whole necklace about their noble throats.

From the way that Lords Minch and Demick kept looking at me as we rode down the road toward the fields of wildflowers beyond, I knew how the quarry felt.

A low stone fence cut the meadow ahead, stretching across the rolling ground from horizon to horizon. It looked low, that is, but as we approached, it seemed to keep growing, until it was clear it was at least waist-high.

"Excuse me, Lord?" I asked Arefai.

"Yes, Kami Dan'Shir?"

"Where is the gate?"

"Gate?"

Yes, yes, you brain-feeble idiot, the gate. The gate that we open, so that we can walk the horses through to the other side of the fence.

"No gate?"

He gave his reins kind of a twitch. "Oh, we don't need a gate. We'll just jump." His smile was, I think, supposed to look casually reassuring instead of moronically optimistic. "Just kick your horse toward the fence; he will take it by himself."

Lord Orazhi kicked his horse into a canter and took the fence easily, as though this sort of insanity was something that he did every day, pulling up his horse a short way beyond and waiting for the next rider, Lord Toshtai. Even carrying his considerable bulk, Lord Toshtai's large white horse had no trouble with the jump, although I think it may have resented his heft—do horses actually grunt, or was I just hearing things? Edelfaule was next, then it was Arefai's turn. As though he was trying to persuade me how easy it all was, he took the leap in grand style, to clear the fence by, so it seemed, easily half again its height.

Very well, I decided. This couldn't be as hard as it seemed, and while there had to be a gate somewhere, I couldn't not try, not with Lord Demick behind me, ready to use my reticence to somehow cause Lord Toshtai to lose status.

So I kicked my heels against the hard side of my horse, and he (she? it? I hadn't looked, I realized) went from a bouncy walk to an even more bouncy canter as he or she or it followed the others to the fence.

Just at the last moment, when I was absolutely certain that the horse was going to crash into the low stone wall, the wall fell away below us as the horse leaped it, far higher than I thought it should have, as though something had startled it at the last instant.

There was a moment there that felt every bit as good as flight. The ground wasn't as far below, of course, but I was in control. I, little Kami Khuzud, had managed to jump a horse across a fence.

Arefai was right, I decided.

This wasn't bad.

Then the horse landed hard, tearing me from the saddle. The ground came up and hit me, harder, on the side.

It was just as well I hadn't had breakfast, all things considered.

9

The Deep Personal Concern of Our Beloved Ruling Class, the Gentle Touch of Wizards, and Other Lies

"I THINK IT safe to move him, eh, Tebol?" Narantir's thick, whisker-rimmed lips split in a smile; one of the many things I hate about Narantir is how much he enjoys his work, particularly when that work involves me being hurt.

I didn't remember the others leaving, and that bothered me. Not that I would have expected members of our beloved ruling class to loiter to see to the welfare of a lowly bourgeois.

But there was fuzz around the edge of my brain. And I hurt, badly.

"Best to be sure," the slimmer man said. Tebol pushed the end of a long straight rod into the ground next to me; it looked more like a spear than anything else. He knelt on the grass and tied the tops of two canvas sacks, each large enough for a body, to a long, thin board, then lifted the board into the air, the bags dangling below.

They clicked and clattered, like dice. Or bones.

"Bones," I said. It hurt to talk. It hurt not to talk.

"Be silent," Narantir said. "And don't move. If you move nothing wrong, you'll hurt nothing more; if you say nothing, you'll say nothing stupid."

"Minch? The others?"

Narantir sniffed. "All gone. They saw no need to stay

around and watch after a damaged bourgeois, not that I blame them."

"Narantir . . ." Tebol raised a finger. "A bit of fairness, a touch of honesty, a trace of truthfulness would go well. Arefai wanted to remain to see after you, but Narantir and I told him it wasn't necessary. You took quite a clobbering, and were muttering things. You could have said something that he might have had to take exception to." The slim wizard pulled rolls of wires from his magician's bag, and talked while he worked. "Nice bit of inference on the arrow, by the way. Clever of you. Almost as clever of Minch, though."

"Demick," Narantir put in. "Minch doesn't have the wit."

Tebol shrugged. "So it would seem. But someone has enough wit to see that trying to get Arefai to dishonor himself is the best chance at stopping the wedding, and Minch was, at least, the one who put his neck in the way. Rather nicely done, whoever had the idea in the first place."

I snorted. It hurt to snort. What sort of worm tries to trick another into making a true-but-disprovable accusation?

Narantir's snort was louder than mine. "Don't be so quick to despise Minch. By the standards of the nobility, he hasn't done anything dishonorable—he's just ridden himself hard near the thin edge of dishonor, trying to lure Toshtai or Arefai to jump after him, miss, and disgrace himself. But lie still and let Tebol work." Not ungentle fingers pushed my head back. "Are you ready to test the bones?" Narantir asked.

"Just a moment . . . there. Ready."

Bones, I thought.

I knew how this worked; I had been through this before with Narantir. Law of Similarity. One bag contained a skeleton, its bones intact; another contained a skeleton with each bone carefully broken. They would connect each of my possibly broken bones to the corresponding bones of the skeletons with bright wires that terminated in sharp, painful needles that Narantir would stick into my flesh until it touched the bone.

They then would apply the Law of Similarity; like to like. Phlogiston—whatever that was—would flow from unbroken bone to unbroken, or from broken to broken. A few hundred stabs with needles, and they would know just what was and wasn't broken. And I'd be spotted with hundreds of tiny sores that would heal indecently slowly. Therapeutic magic is never for the comfort of the patient.

I was surprised when Tebol balanced the beam holding the bags on the spearpoint. It bowed a trifle, then started to slip off until Tebol adjusted the center.

His magician's bag provided a covered ramekin, a clean brush, and a pair of silver scissors; he uncovered the ramekin, revealing a dark goo, then dipped the brush and touched it to each of the ten pulse points, first cutting through the clothing over my elbows, armpits, and crotch.

The goo was green and somewhat translucent. I tried to hold my breath against the stench I was certain it gave off, but finally had to breathe in. It really didn't smell bad. The odor was thick and sickly sweet, to be sure, but held overtones of perook, patchouli, and eucalyptus that would have been very agreeable under other circumstances, and were even kind of pleasant now. Maybe even a bit of mint?

Tebol muttered a few words I didn't quite catch, and made a gesture with his long, aristocratic fingers that looked more like somebody flicking away a fly than anything else. The goo flashed momentarily, painlessly into a silent green flame and the balanced bags pivoted neatly on the spearpoint, one swinging toward me, one away.

"Amazing," Narantir said. "Nothing broken."

"No bones," Tebol corrected, running the little finger of his left hand up the side of my calf. It twitched, as though from palsy. "But there's torn muscle and tendon in here," he said, dipping a finger into an inkpot and touching it lightly to my flesh in two places. "And ... here."

Narantir's brow furrowed. "How?"

"Eh?"

"You know. How did you determine that? I see nothing there to resonate with torn muscle or tendon."

Tebol smiled. "Ah. You like it?"

Narantir's mouth twisted. "Please."

Tebol's smile broadened. "I shouldn't, but . . . since it's you—I cut a tiny bit of muscle and tendon in here," he said, raising his left little finger, "and slid a small piece of squid quill into the cut so that it can't rejoin. It resonates to cut muscle and torn tendon, yes? Like to like, no?"

"And to squid," Narantir said, with a low grumble.

Tebol shrugged. "I don't think that's what we have here." He pulled what looked like a bowstring from his bag. "A simple matter, really," he said, turning back to me. "We substitute a bit of calf tendon for your own, and just let the muscles heal naturally. First, we have to persuade the tendon that it really belongs to you, and to do that we make you similar to a calf for a few hours."

Narantir smiled. "We'll have you crawl about on all fours and graze on the grass. Three or four hours of that, and you'll be more than sufficiently similar."

"You do insist on him doing things the hard way, eh, old friend?"

"You've invented a better way?"

Tebol produced a wide-mouthed clay bottle from his bag. He handed it to me; it was cold to the touch, dew beading its sides. "Drink this," he said, uncorking it with a twist.

The bottle held some sort of white, milky fluid.

"What is it?"

Tebol shrugged, as though to dismiss an obviously stupid question. "Milk."

10
Dining, a Missed Party, and
Another Surprise

WHEN SHE KNOCKED on the door, I was resting in my room, lying stretched out on a pile of blankets next to the low window, my back propped up against the same sort of soft cushions that elevated my healing leg. A small salver of food slivers sat at my left hand; a large mug of milk at my right.

I was getting awfully tired of milk.

Below, in the courtyard, the evening's party was well into its second hour. Beneath flickering smoky torches, a full hundred of our beloved ruling class exchanged insincere compliments and heavily coded insults, while servitors passed among them with trays of fruits and sweetmeats, bottles of cold juices and heated essences.

The knock was somehow both peremptory and tentative; before I could answer, the door swung open, and she stood framed in the light from the hall lamp. Wisps of her hair had broken free from the knot at the back of her neck; their silken ends touched at her cheek and chin.

"Lady ViKay," I said, starting to rise. Pain is merely inconvenient; failing to show respect for a member of our beloved ruling class can easily be worse. Much worse.

"Please, Kami Dan'Shir," she said, closing the door behind her as I started to rise, "be still."

She had dressed for the evening in only vaguely formal robes that closed on her right side, loose at the rise of her bosom, pulled in tight at her slim waist, joined with a tie over her right hip, leaving her right leg bare almost to the hip. A daring style, but noble women may be daring without risking anything.

Particularly in front of a damaged bourgeois.

In contrast to the complex hairstyle of the morning, her long black hair, shiny as teak, had been twisted into a simple knot, secured only with a piece of red silk that dangled at the nape of her neck.

She knelt next to me, her head cocked to one side. "I came to thank you for what you did today," she said, taking her time before selecting a sliver of jellied liver from the tray between us. "Lord Arefai is sometimes too . . . brash." The sliver vanished behind sharp white teeth.

Lord Arefai is an idiot who would throw his head at an enemy's spearpoint, I didn't say.

"You're welcome, of course, Lady," I did say.

She gestured at the tray. "You were eating. Please don't stop because of me." Her smile seemed warm. "It wouldn't be gracious for me to stop you doing anything, and I hope you have found and will find us quite gracious here in Glen Derenai." She tucked her robes in around her legs, perhaps accidentally revealing more long smooth thigh than intended.

Or perhaps not. Teasing the animals is a habit women of our beloved ruling class can safely acquire. Her bare thigh was only a handsbreadth away from my left hand, close enough that I could almost feel the warmth of her flesh. I could have reached out and parted her robes, if I was overwhelmingly interested in too closely witnessing an execution in Glen Derenai.

Below, pairs of noblemen and their ladies had squared off to dance on the wooden tiles scattered across the grass in a pattern something like the squares of a single-bone draughts board, but with some squares missing. I often think of our beloved ruling class as having a few squares missing.

I bit into a slice of beef. It wasn't gristly, but it was tough and flavorful, cut from the rump or round, not the loin that was the portion of the nobility.

"You tear into that like . . ."

"Like a peasant, Lady?" I tried.

"I was going to say like someone who has not eaten for days. Please take no offense."

She still didn't quite know how to take what I'd said, so I forced a smile. "No offense taken; I've been an acrobat most of my life, and we all know that acrobats are part of the peasant class."

"Oh . . ." She picked up my mug, took a sip, made a face, and quickly set it down. I guess she had been expecting some white essence, not milk. "I've always thought that a silly classification," she said. "But the ways of the Scion are His own, yes?"

"Yes."

She reached behind the nape of her neck with both hands, perhaps unintentionally emphasizing the swell of her breasts as she unfastened the red silk from her hair. She tossed her head to let her long hair fall about her shoulders. Unrolled, the red silk was filmy and diaphanous.

"This was promised to the most successful of the hunters," she said, laying its cool softness across my hand. "It seems that you, Kami Dan'Shir, brought back the dignity of Minch."

"And a bit of Demick's, as well," I said, then instantly regretted it. A dan'shir doesn't always have to drop truths all over the floor like a beginning juggler.

She arched a fine eyebrow.

I folded the silk neatly and set it aside. "I thank you for this, Lady." Her eyebrow was still arched. Well, there wasn't a way around it. "The assault on Lord Arefai's reputation was both subtle and clever."

"Not as clever as the defense," she said, one side of her mouth lifting.

I waved it away. That wasn't the point. "But Minch

isn't either, not at that level. Demick is both." I shrugged. "I'm sure that Lord Toshtai took it that way—"

"He said as much?" She leaned forward.

Lady, if Lord Toshtai were to start sharing confidences with me, I'd hardly be indiscreet with them, no matter how much of your lovely breast you're willing to show me.

I raised a finger. "Just this once, Lady, I will tell you: no. Lord Toshtai and I haven't spoken since my . . . accident this afternoon," I said, hoping she didn't notice the catch in my voice. I wasn't at all sure that the fall was accidental. It wouldn't have taken much to distract my horse at the critical moment, and Demick was the sort who could easily look far enough ahead at the advantages of holding a sharp throwing stone concealed in his palm.

It was likely Demick who was behind both my fall and Arefai's close call. It was likely Demick, but not necessarily Demick; the difference was important. I could think of four others with a motivation to embarrass Arefai (which is what the afternoon had threatened), others with reasons to humiliate Minch (which is what happened, after all), and even one with a cause to make me look clever.

Two of the latter, if I included myself. I mean, I hadn't had anything to do with setting up Minch, but I would have been willing to do far more than humiliate somebody I didn't even like in return for such warm brown eyes resting on mine. They were wide, filled with something; admiration, perhaps? Or something warmer and more personal.

It didn't matter.

Yes, surely I would have, I could have kicked a vicious dog in return for that look, whatever it meant.

I shook my head to clear it. Her eyes had a way of fogging my mind. This was getting dangerous and I needed it clear as she leaned toward me, face raised to be kissed. Her hair smelled of lemon and sunshine, of sweet roses and peppery morningsuns. Her eyes, still resting on mine, were wide open.

There was only one reasonable thing to do, after all. I couldn't afford offending her. Soon she would be Arefai's wife, and it would be far too dangerous for me to have my protector's new wife angry with me. In the shorter run, if she were to raise an outcry, it would be me who would be the one in sudden, serious, fatal trouble, and never mind that I was still badly battered, barely able to stand, incapable of attacking her.

All of that occurred to me, even then, but it didn't matter.

What did matter was that her eyes were warm and alive, and she smelled of lemon and sunshine, of lush sweet roses and peppery morningsuns, that her tongue was warm and wet and alive in my mouth, tasting of both sweet laughter and bitter tears, that beneath her robes, surprisingly strong muscles played under her silken skin, that later, the first time that her breathing went ragged and her husky whispers hoarse, her legs locked tightly about my waist until the world went all vague and dreamy for me too.

That was all that mattered. Then.

When I woke, she was gone.

Interlude:

The Hour of the Lion

THERE WAS NO point in wondering why his father had summoned him, Arefai decided for the hundred-thousandth time. Matching wits with Lord Toshtai was a contest he couldn't win.

As Aunt Estrer would often say—in private, thankfully—"Your fool neck always rests on his chopping block, so you might as well let the emphasis be on *rest* instead of *chop*." It wasn't just that Father was the lord, and therefore the final arbiter. That was part of it, but only part of it. More of it was that Father was smarter than Arefai was, perhaps cleverer even than Aunt Estrer, almost as clever as Edelfaule thought himself, and that was that.

Arefai would wait; he was patient. He settled himself more firmly into the cushion of the dark room that Toshtai had selected for himself.

That was another of the many things that Arefai didn't understand about his father. Most people preferred their rooms bright and airy, white walls almost glowing in the light of the sun or a well-placed lantern. The walls of the room Toshtai had chosen were black as coal dust, soaking up every splash of light from the single lantern set on the knee-height table that separated him from Estrer and Arefai. When Arefai squinted just right, it looked as though the three of them were seated on a splash of bright carpet in an endless sea of night.

"I've always liked Snow Blood at this time of the evening," Aunt Estrer said, tossing back a thumb-sized earthenware flask of the precious white essence as though it were the heated milk that Arefai and she often drank before bedtime. The old woman's hair, a thin gray that denied it had ever been raven black, was pulled back even more tightly than usual, as though to proclaim her control and discipline.

Lord Toshtai took the pointed hint and manipulated the filigreed silver serving tongs to take the heating flask from its simmering water bath and refill her drinking flask. "I'm so glad it is to your taste. As I trust it is to yours, my son?"

Arefai took a tiny sip. Snow Blood was too cloyingly sweet for him, something his father knew; in any case, when dealing with Lord Toshtai, Arefai wanted his head clear. As clear as possible; Toshtai had the sleight of making Arefai's brain feel it was coated in thick wool.

"Of course, Father," he said.

Toshtai turned to Estrer.

"It's a surprise that you can join us this evening," Toshtai said.

Even Arefai understood the implication. It was both unwise and unsafe to surprise Toshtai without delighting him, and the presence of a sharp-tongued old woman at a private conference with his son was unlikely to delight him.

"I should hope so." She didn't quaver under implied reproach. "You've so rarely called upon me for advice that I'm dumbfounded you recognize this withered face." She settled back into her cushions, smoothing one gnarled hand down the front of her faded robes. Once they had shown a flock of bright, and fiery redbirds perched on the limb of an oak in full autumn colors: the red of fresh blood and the orange of sunfire contrasting with the warm but restrained browns of the tree bark. But the years had faded them all into muted pastels that somehow still held a hint of their former fire and passion.

"There are few other pleasures available to me in the last years of my life," she said. "This old body is one constant ache, and of no interest to anyone other than me, and to me only as an inconvenience. I can barely taste the finest of food, and have to swill cod liver oil in order to be able to pass it without pain. I doubt that I'll have to put up with this much longer, sick old woman that I am."

The corners of Toshtai's lips turned up slightly. "I have heard this before," he said.

She sniffed. "Then I beg that you order one of your swaggering bullyboy warriors to execute me, Lord, if you think I'm senile and useless." She tugged the top of her robes open, revealing her thin neck, its folds of flesh hanging loose. "But have it be one of the less clumsy, if it please you. This is my neck; it is not a tree trunk to require a dozen crude chops."

Toshtai raised a flipper of a hand. "Hardly my point. I was recalling having heard similar complaints for many, many years now, back to when Arefai was still soiling his swaddling clothes. You are a long time dying, old woman. Which is perhaps just as well, for that means your mind is still available to my idiot son here."

Well, that was that: Toshtai was furious. He was too angry to address Arefai directly, but he was furious.

Toshtai's eyes were passionless as they met Arefai's. "To challenge someone like Minch, where you can only lose for winning, and lose for losing, is the act of a fool. You were saved only by the speed of Dun Lidjun's hand and the wit of Kami Dan'Shir."

"But that's only part of it. Write it out for the boy, every stroke and dot," Estrer said. "Or I will. It's not his fault; you had him trained for war, not for politics."

Toshtai dismissed that with a tiny chopping motion of his hand. "It's all the same; only the tools differ." He turned back to Arefai. "Arefai, Arefai, think next time before you challenge. If Minch had beaten you—"

Arefai wouldn't have thought of interrupting, but

Toshtai apparently caught something in his expression. The lord of Den Oroshtai slammed his hamlike fist down on the low table, sending flasks and serving plates dancing and clicking.

"*Don't* you tell me that cannot happen. Minch is a fine kazuh swordsman, and if his inner strength exceeds yours on a given day, it'll be you who gets opened from left shoulder to right hip." He calmed himself with a visible effort. "As I was saying, as your aunt insists that I say bluntly: if Minch had beaten you, the only way to cement Den Oroshtai to Glen Derenai would have been to marry ViKay to your brother Edelfaule, a man she does not care for and her father does not trust."

Estrer snickered. "A likely prospect, indeed. When peasants bathe! And the rest?"

Toshtai's lips turned up at the edges. "Alternately, if you had killed Minch, it would have cast shame upon Lord Orazhi—what sort of host is he, that his son-in-law-to-be would challenge then kill another of his guests?"

"I should have let him challenge me, then."

Estrer rolled her eyes. "Don't swear to keep your pole in your robes until *that* happens, or your new bride will be turning to peasants and vegetables for her satisfaction. You think Demick would allow you to cast yourself in the role of the preserver of the peace of Glen Derenai?" She took a pair of sweetmeats from the tray and popped them in her mouth, chewing quickly, like a peasant, then washing them down with a long pull from her flask. She pursed her lips. "Very nice. Almost as nice as your move in keeping that Kami Dan'Shir close to my nephew here. A clever one, that Kami Dan'Shir, if not particularly loyal."

Toshtai arched an eyebrow. "Oh? Why would you accuse him of disloyalty?"

"Accuse? I don't accuse. I often observe, I frequently note, I declare far too often, and I state constantly, but I don't accuse."

Toshtai snorted. "Very well. And what is it that you note about a flaw in Kami Dan'Shir's loyalty?"

"And why should he be loyal? Just because you've

taken him from the comfort of his family, providing no substitute?"

Toshtai smoothed one hand down the front of his robes. "There are many ways to look at things." He turned to Arefai. "All of them suggest that you need a better mind. Kami Dan'Shir has one. Spend time around his. Brush up against his thoughts, his way of thinking. Some of it may rub off."

Estrer laughed. "Your game is deeper than that."

Your game is deeper than that. "It's obvious—" Arefai stopped himself. No, it was all wrong. It wasn't going to work. Arefai just couldn't do it, and Toshtai wouldn't listen.

Or perhaps he would: "Go on," Toshtai said, leaning forward ever so slightly.

Arefai swallowed. "I was going to say, Father, that it's obvious you want me to spend time around him because my sword and arm can quite probably protect him while his mind can quite probably protect me, no?"

"Well." Toshtai grunted. "Perhaps you aren't a complete simpleton after all."

Estrer's eyes were shining with pride.

Arefai wasn't unhappy about it, either. It would have been better if he had done it with his own wit, but nonetheless he had impressed his father by putting in the observation Estrer had told him to make at just the moment that Estrer had signaled him to make it. He wasn't really stupid, she had explained. It wasn't his fault that he was more direct, less subtle than the likes of Toshtai and herself.

But indirectness and subtlety could be learned, she had said. They were simply aspects of timing.

And timing was, she had explained, everything.

11

Breakfast, Placques, Gold, Narantir, an Apple and a Knife, a Flock of Birds, and Other Gains and Losses

MORNING DAWNED—AS it has the habit of doing every day—with me confused—as I seemed to be almost every day.

You would think I would get used to it after a while.

I would have been tempted to think the previous night a dream if it wasn't for a vague hint of perfume in the air, a red silk scarf on the floor near my bed. Perhaps even that wouldn't have persuaded me if I hadn't noticed various marks on my body here and there that hadn't been made by falling off a horse. I mean, I could write off the pain from scratches on my back as having been from the ground, but I don't really think I could have persuaded even the most credulous that my horse had rubbed rouge against my left shoulder and right thigh, or left teeth marks under my right nipple.

And I couldn't have persuaded myself that an old, familiar feeling of luxurious lassitude came from a good night's sleep. That was how I felt—how I had felt—after a night with my NaRee.

I washed myself quickly in the washbasin over by the door, eyeing myself in the mirror.

I didn't like it. The sharp-eyed fellow looking back seemed to me to be somebody who had spent the night with the betrothed of the closest thing he had to a friend among our beloved ruling class, but maybe it wasn't quite tattooed all over his face.

Very well, ViKay: why?

It's not my way, not particularly, to be so ungrateful as to question the motives of an attractive, willing woman. Well, no, that is a lie: it *is* my way to question the motives of anybody and everybody for doing anything and everything, but only within reason. It hadn't seemed reasonable last night, what with ViKay warm in my arms and silken in my bed, but it was now morning, and I was suspicious.

It was possible that her only reasons were gratitude and passion. Anything was possible, I guessed.

I walked to the window. Below, where last night our beloved ruling class had frolicked, the lawn was littered with the detritus of the reception: uneaten food dropped here and there, pebbles scattered from the paths and onto the lush greenness of the lawn, an occasional flower picked here, a fern crushed by a careless footstep there. While two old, arthritic maids stooped to load trash into their baskets, a six-man team of gardeners, their bronzed torsos already slick with sweat from working under the low sun, busied themselves with the bushes and flowers, scissors and rakes flashing and clicking in the sun. A pick-pick here, a snip-snip of scissors there, a pat-pat of a hand over there, a splash-splash of water somewhere else, and a refuse-strewn, slightly worn garden was quickly becoming a typical piece of convenient lush loveliness.

I would have stayed and watched them work, but a distant savory smell and my own hunger drove me into the hall.

There are advantages to living the way the upper classes do. There must have been a servant posted outside my door, waiting for sounds of my rising. Outside, in the hall, under a two-life tapestry of sweating peasants working in a field, a breakfast tray had been left on a hall table. The rich smell of the bread made my mouth water, and hunger cramps almost doubled me over.

I brought the tray in quickly. The two fist-sized loaves

were fresh, still warm from the oven. Under the silver dome, an arrangement of cold asparagus, sliced boiled eggs, and garlicky slivers of squid waited with several sauces that they shared with a small plate rimmed by a dozen paper-thin pieces of raw beef lying on a thin coat of golden mustard sauce.

Not a bourgeois meal; whoever was running the kitchen here had apparently found it more convenient to issue me a noble breakfast.

I tore into it, not taking the time to savor the way that the tarragon butter set off the crunchiness of the asparagus, barely noticing that the squid had been taken from the heat at the precise tender time between rubbery raw flesh would become rubbery overcooked. It practically melted in my mouth, but I could have eaten it anyway. The beef slices were light but rich, the way thinly sliced beef always is, and the slices of egg only served to convey dollops of a rich brown demiglace sauce to my mouth. The bread wiped up what was left.

Refreshed with a quick use of the thundermug and a less abrupt towel bath, I dressed and was ready to head out into the day. It was still early yet, not quite into the hour of the hare.

But Arefai was waiting for me out in the hall. Sprawled in an armchair that hadn't been there before, he was toying with a few sweetmeats on the platter balanced on the arm of the chair, a steaming cup of urmon tea on a hallstand. This morning, his color scheme was off-white, from the cream-colored taband binding his damp hair back, down through a wan sieved pigskin tunic, down to heavy silk trousers gathered tightly at waist and bloused at the ankles over lambskin boots.

He lolled at ease, considering the tapestry across the hall from him. It was worth a second look.

"Very pretty," he said. "Notice how the shadings make the sweat drops on that broadfaced man come alive? I would swear that they're ready to run down the side of the tapestry." He took another sip of tea and set the cup down.

"I didn't know you had such an eye for art, Lord," I said.

He brushed it away. "Just repeating something my aunt pointed out to me the other day. Not that it doesn't seem so, once she pointed to it. She's both persuasive and observant." His smile was genuine, and affectionate. "I don't doubt that you've noticed that about Aunt Estrer."

"It had occurred to me."

"In any event, we are off wrongly: a good day to you, Kami Dan'Shir," he said, rising smoothly, not swiftly, not, thank the Powers, the way one would rise to kill the impossibly impertinent bourgeois who had spent the night with his woman.

"And to you, of course, Lord Arefai." I waited patiently. Another thing I didn't understand: he had wanted to talk to me, but instead of interrupting me, Arefai had simply waited until I had finished my breakfast.

So why am I being treated as though I matter, Lord Arefai? Because I had your woman last night while you slept?

Somehow, I doubted that.

"I . . ." he stopped, then started. "I didn't have the chance to thank you properly, or publicly, yesterday."

It took me a moment to realize what he was talking about. Minch's trap.

He went on: "I ask that you permit me to remedy the failing."

"No thanks are due, Lord Arefai." That was true enough. I'd happily trade a quick-flash-of-insight-keeping-Arefai-out-of-trouble for a night with ViKay . . . without thinking he need throw any thanks into the bargain.

Then again, were we engaged in some after-the-fact bargaining for the favors of his intended, I suspect he would have insisted I include, say, half of my liver.

"Those of us in the lower classes live but to serve," I said, careful to keep anything resembling a hint of a trace of an inkling of sarcasm out of my voice.

He tilted his head to one side, then nodded, accepting what I'd said at face value. "Lady ViKay has invited

150

Lords Demick, Debray, Minch, and Everlea for a game of placques this morning. I carry her invitation, and my own: Would you join us?"

I'd much rather juggle knives, I didn't say. I'm safe juggling knives.

"It would be my pleasure," I said.

Sitting on an elbow-height marble table, my cup was barely three-quarters full as a white-clad servitor refilled it with a gracious dip of the silver teapot, while another wielded a tiny silver hook to remove the old, soggy sweetleaf from the teacup. Idly, I crumpled a fresh sweetleaf and tossed it in, then considered ViKay's profile over the edge of the cup as I sipped.

"Yours to play," she said to Minch. Perhaps as a preview of the wedding, she was all in red and orange today, from the bare dusting of rouge that kissed her cheekbones to the flame-colored polish coating her long fingernails. Her gown was enough loose wrappings of a diaphanous crimson silk that it only hinted at the curves beneath, but I remembered.

I shouldn't have worried about her; our beloved ruling class learns young to keep their thoughts to themselves. Her occasional glance my way was neither furtive nor overly bold, nor was it any different from the way she looked at any of the young lords gathered around the placques table or waiting their turns under a nearby jimsum tree. For all I knew, she had gone from my bed to one of theirs.

Well, actually, that seemed unlikely, all things considered.

I bit into a cherry tart. There are worse ways to spend a morning than under scented trees playing at placques.

Back in the troupe, every now and then we used to play a game of placques around the campfire during the evening, after dinner, after practice, usually me and Enki Duzun against Sala and Gray Khuzud, although sometimes Fhilt or one of the Eresthais would play. We would spread out a blanket, pile clothes at the four corners to screen our hands from view, and shuffle our cheap bone set of placques by the simple expedient of shaking their bag, then each of us drawing our nine just by reaching in. It took some doing, to prop up the battered old placques so that only your partner, sitting opposite, could see them, but that was acceptable.

Here, we sat around a table that looked like the crossroads of two walled streets. Each player's viewing area was protected by chin-high diagonal translucent rice paper screens drawn upwards from the surface of the table itself. Instead of the cheap lacquered bone, short symbols for beast and season inscribed in ideograms, each of the placques in front of me had been carefully painted: the summer hare stood crouched in summer-tall grasses, clearly ready to run at the slightest challenge; the spring cock was frozen in midstrut before a budding bush; the spring octopus sat improbably straight on the banks of a swollen river; the autumn bear stood tall on its hind legs, looking out over the hills that were naked of leaves, waiting for the winter's snow.

The summer dragon, of course, was just a summer landscape, tall wheat bending beneath what could have been the wind instead of a dragon's chill breath. There is much magic in dragons; few magicians with any sense often deal with dragon magic, and no nonmagicians with any sense ever do.

"I should have another victor here," Minch said, for the severalth time.

Wrong, I didn't say.

I could see Minch's hands fumble behind the paper, but that was only to be expected. If I had the pattern of this racking figured out—and I did; this was by far too simple—he had trapped himself into leading from his own rack instead of from his partner's. Just a matter of not taking pains to play it out ahead of time.

The order of rank of the beasts is the same as the hours of the day: dragon, lion, bear, snake, octopus, ox, horse, hare, cock. He had only summer placques left: the lion, snake, and ox, with me left with the dragon and hare in front of me opposite the cock, horse, and bear in front of Arefai. My other placque was only the cock of spring, but it was the sole spring placque left.

Finally, he tipped over a placque. It hit the marble surface with the familiar *tik*, and a quick push slid it to the center. The ox of summer. Not good enough. I beat it with Arefai's summer bear, then slid my own summer hare to the center when Minch called for the winter cock from Lady ViKay. Arefai carefully stacked the placques to one side.

The rest were mine. I had Arefai play the summer bear to my dragon, and finished with the simple little cock of spring.

"Brilliantly played, Kami Dan'Shir," Arefai said, no doubt endearing me further to Minch.

Well, it was good enough. There were no other spring placques left out.

Really, much of placques is a simple game: you simply have to learn how to count to nine, and then decide to count to nine in each of the four major seasons. When one opponent fails to follow season, you know how many placques of that season he originally held. Add that to the number in that season you held, add in the number your partner held, and subtract from nine, and you know how that season was originally divided.

It gets more complicated if you play merchant placques, which includes both the minor seasons and adds chickens, mares, cows, she-bears and lionesses, but only merchants like things so complicated, what with almost eighty pieces out. To play at standard placques, all you have to do is count to nine.

Arefai beckoned the serving girl with the waxboard over. "I count twenty-eight in front of the brilliant Kami Dan'Shir, and . . ." He rose, to look down into Minch's playing area.

Eight, I didn't interrupt and say. *There are thirty-six placques. I have twenty-eight. Minch has eight. Thirty-six minus twenty-eight is eight.*

". . . eight in front of Lord Minch."

The serving girl removed the piles from in front of us and set them down on the shuffling table. Her long fingers moved blurringly fast as she moved the pieces of cold marble over the silk-covered table, so fast that the clicking of the placques sounded like an even drumroll.

As though by magic, when she straightened, the stone tablets had been divided into four groups. ViKay pointed at the one nearest her, Arefai selected his, Minch his, leaving one for me.

When she placed the rack gently in front of me, I sipped at my hot tea while considering the layout. Five summers, two springs, and a single winter and autumn. A nice summery rack, actually, topped by the lion and dragon. The trouble was that I had nothing better than an ox in any of the other seasons, and it was ViKay's turn to lead. I gave a mental shrug as I put the spring cock and autumn hare facedown on the table and slid them toward Minch, then reached for the placques that ViKay had set in front of me.

Dragon of winter and bear of summer. A friendly pass. Far too friendly a pass.

I set my placques in their rack facing Arefai and leaned back. Unsurprisingly, out came the lion of winter from ViKay.

Arefai counted it out several times before he called for the winter dragon from me. With what was in my rack and with three good placques in his own rack, he couldn't help but sweep in all the placques.

Minch glared at me, like it was my fault. Well, I guess I could have slid him valuable pieces instead of worthless ones, but that's not the way the game is supposed to be played. The idea is not to slip good ones to your opponent.

Not that ViKay cared, apparently.

Why she bothered wasn't apparent to me until we completed the game.

"Score of eight hundred twenty-eight to five hundred seventy-six," the servitor announced. "Two hundred and fifty-two to Lord Arefai and Lor—to Lord Arefai and Kami Dan'Shir."

Minch towered over me. "Shall we call it an even

three?" he said, laying down three oblong golden coins on the table.

I could practically hear the twang of my anus clenching. Nothing had been said about money. Nothing had been said about gambling. What if I'd lost?

He moved slowly, with almost exquisite gentleness, as though the thing in the world that most frightened him at the moment was being thought abrupt. More likely he was afraid of leaving himself open for an insinuation that he could not lose with grace.

Arefai gravely accepted the same payment from ViKay, and nodded his thanks.

It was easy not to laugh, because laughing would get me killed. It's probably the oldest form of swindle. The Stranger, it's called. Put together any game where it's all-against-one and you'll find endless opportunities to manipulate the situation to the benefit of the all and against the one.

It was easy not to laugh, because it was all I could do not to vomit. I mean, the game of placques has an elegance and grace that's all its own, an iron symmetry in the distribution of beasts and seasons. On the other hand . . . Lord Toshtai was not ungenerous with his new dan'shir, but my stipend was two silver bice every fortnight. Three years' earnings sat on the table in front of me. I wondered what the penalty would have been when I had been unable to pay, if we'd lost. I know what it is among peasants, and I doubted it would have been much gentler among our beloved ruling class.

ViKay looked at me somberly over the top of her screen. "I believe that Lords Everlea and Debray play next," she said, no hint in her voice of any feeling more intense than the pleasant smile on her face.

Arefai nodded. "It has been pleasant that fortune so smiled on us," he said.

Minch just nodded; perhaps his jaw muscles twitched fractionally, but mainly he just nodded.

Arefai and I rose. When peasants wager at contests of skill, it is the winner who stays until he loses, be the game placques, single-bone draughts, wrestling, or Kimmi-on-the-pig. I'm not sure whether our beloved ruling class does it differently just to differentiate themselves, or for another reason, but I've never claimed to understand them.

ViKay and Minch would stay in an attempt to recoup their losses. This time, they won.

Eventually, the game ended.

"Brilliantly done, Kami Dan'Shir," Arefai said. "It seems that the Way of the Dan'Shir includes the ability to play a fearsome game of placques, eh?"

Yes, yes, I'm a genius, now let me get out of here with my winnings and more importantly my skin intact.

"I was fortunate," I said, trying to sound sincere.

He laughed, and his laugh was picked up first by ViKay and then Debray and Everlea. Minch didn't even try to force a smile.

"Very well," Arefai said. "Be that way. We shall see you at the wedding night reception at the hour of the bear." I guess I let some of my distaste at the idea show, because he dismissed what he thought my concerns were with a gesture. "No, it's not just nobles. You'll find most of the . . . more honored bourgeoisie there as well, joining us in the celebration." He grinned. "Particularly the local robers, who, so I hear, tire of spending most of their time gifting my ViKay with their best work."

ViKay raised an eyebrow. "I will have you know, Lord Arefai," she said, "that the only articles of clothing I have accepted as a gift are my wedding robes."

Arefai chuckled. It was an easy laugh, and it made him hard to dislike. "Very well," he said, offering her his arm as he turned to the rest of us. "We will see you in the hour of the bear."

I sat in the garden by myself, looking down at the dozen golden coins in the palm of my hand, each decorated on the face with the sunrise seal of the Scion, and on the back with the likeness of a spread-winged springbug, a reminder that all wealth is ephemeral. I didn't understand any of it, not really. The troupe could tour for a decade and never accumulate this much gold, but I had it in my hand for having spent a morning counting to nine and accepting the cheating help of Arefai's bride-to-be.

Well, if nothing else, I owed ViKay. I didn't doubt she would someday collect, and I wondered what form the repayment would be.

And, in fact, there were forms of repayment that wouldn't bother me at all.

In the meantime, my pouch was heavy with gold, and my stomach was light with the lack of food. The wizards tended to eat well; perhaps it was time for another courtesy call on Tebol.

I found the two magicians high in Tebol's tower, door open and windows unshuttered to let much-needed air and light into the dank and shadowed workshop. The two of them were bent over a worktable holding something that looked like the insides of a small animal and smelled every bit as bad.

"The Final Day comes. The end of the universe," Tebol said. "See that lesion on the liver? Combine it with the growth on the gizzard and the stain on the sacrum, and what else could it mean?"

"Nothing," Narantir said. "Fascinating."

The Final Day. The end of the universe?

I cleared my throat. "How . . . how soon?"

They turned. Narantir's gray robes had been splashed with something gray, greasy and disgusting, but Tebol was still neat as a pin. It didn't take a dan'shir to decide that the spattered leather apron hanging from a nearby hook was what had kept his tailored gray robes spotless.

Tebol dipped his hands into a washbasin, rubbing them briskly in the soapy water before drying them on a towel. "How soon what?"

I spread my hands. "The end of the universe. The Final Day."

The end of all that has ever been, or will ever be. I hadn't really believed in it, not until now, but the two of

157

them sounded so quietly certain of it that I couldn't help believing.

"Oh, this," Tebol made a dismissive waving gesture with his damp hands, then helped me to a seat. "It's nothing. Take it easy, lad. Sit back and if you feel faint, lean over and put your head down between your legs. Deep breathing." Smooth, sure fingers felt at two of my pulses, and then at the back of my neck. "I think he still is in shock from yesterday, Narantir. And look here, on his back," he said, pulling at my tunic. "We missed some scratches from his fall. Have you any salted salamander salve?"

Narantir grunted. "He'll heal."

"Let's get some lunch," Tebol said. "I have a friend in the kitchens."

"But the entrails—" I protested.

Narantir smiled. "That should teach you not to approach a wizard's workshop unannounced. Among the least bad things that can happen is a fright."

"Just a fright? But—"

"Those?" Narantir dismissed my concern with a flip of his hand. "Those are just mock entrails."

"And what good are mock entrails?" I asked.

"Pleasure reading," he said.

There was a spot in the gardens that I made note of: a small rise, well-screened from view from the plaza below by the pink and white flowered branches of a gnarled tur tree. The grassy knoll was rimmed by an irregular stone fence, flat and level enough to support a basket of food and two clay bottles of wine, that rose to the chest level of a sitting dan'shir. Hmmm . . . make that a *leaning* dan'shir; the stones were cold but pleasant against my back as I leaned back and took another mouthful of the sweet, straw-colored wine. It tasted of spring and flowers, and smelled vaguely but pleasantly of freshly scythed grass.

I rubbed a thumb against a bump in the cold stone. From this distance, or lack thereof, the bumps and hollows in the wall seemed random, as though the stone was unworked. From across the knoll, when the noon sun had hit it all just right from above, the shadows had turned the wall surface into a shadow drawing of the naked torsos of a dozen sweating muscular men, their arms linked, holding back the soil.

Sometimes it doesn't pay to get too close, to get too caught up in details.

"The trouble with the nobility," Narantir said from around a mouthful of mutton, "is that they don't have enough to do." He slurped at his goblet, managing to get most of the fluid into his mouth, just barely staining the front of his robes.

Tebol raised a slim finger. "That's close enough to treason for one luncheon, Narantir," he said. "Shtoi is no longer good enough?"

"Among ourselves we need shtoi?" Narantir gestured around him. "It's said that even the walls have ears, but I've never heard it said of the grasses or the bushes or the breeze."

Tebol didn't answer. He had half of a juicy beefroll in his hands, but was managing to take it in small bites without fouling himself at all.

Me, I was enjoying a meatroll by the simple expedient of popping the whole thing into my mouth. Well-aged beef wrapped around crispy fried turnip cake that was almost too hot, the whole thing flavored with eye-watering pepper and savory garlic—there are worse ways to spend an afternoon than munching on such, and many worse ways than to spend an afternoon munching on such and washing it down with pale straw-colored wine.

"Then say it," Tebol said.

Narantir shrugged. "Look at yon game-players," he said, waving his hand toward where we had seen a claque of nobles gathered around the same placques table that, combined with skillful play and coarse cheating, had enriched my purse that morning. "Were Lord Debray, say," he said, choosing one of the younger nobles, a boy of about fifteen, "an apprentice acrobat, what would he be doing at this hour?"

I had thought his question was just rhetorical, but both he and Tebol waited patiently for an answer. I swallowed heavily, wasting the taste of the meatroll.

"Sweating under the hot sun," I said. "Either on the road between towns or at practice."

"To little purpose, granted," Narantir said, conceding his own point, "but at least to some purpose."

"Each to his own, wizard." I picked up a hard-boiled egg and tossed it lightly between my hands. "It takes effort to make it all look easy, and that's part of the craft of it."

I caught the egg in my right hand, then looped it high in the air, high enough that I could snag an apple from the basket and add it to the juggling. Juggling two things is trivially easy, unless you're doing it with just one hand, which is what I had to do as I reached for a heavy knife. My right hand continuing to juggle the egg and the apple, I gave the knife a few preliminary tosses with my left hand, then threw it high in the air, spinning it *hard*.

From then on it was a matter of timing: catch the knife, spin it again, even harder, faster, then throw the apple up into the spinning blade. Do it wrong and the knife and pieces of apple will go off in all directions, only splattering you with sticky fruit if you're lucky.

But time it right, throw everything with the proper tempo and sufficient authority, and the blade will cleave right through the apple without appreciably slowing, and you can reach into the whirring disk of steel and snatch out a knife by the hilt, and then properly shower an egg, a knife, and two halves of apple.

I did it right, then ended with a flourish that left the egg arcing high overhead, while the knife stood quivering in the ground between the two wizards, with me carefully setting half an apple down on each of their plates, then cupping my palms together just in time to catch the egg.

I cracked the shell with a knuckle.

Tebol's mouth was split in a broad grin, and he tapped two fingers sharply against his wrist in applause, while even Narantir's scowl was relieved by an expression that could have been a smile, perhaps.

"Plaudits, Kami Dan'Shir," Tebol said. "I've never seen it done better."

"Or to as little point as most of the nobility live."

Tebol's lips twisted. "You make too much of it all, Narantir. Consider the tree, eh?"

Narantir nodded. "There is that."

I had to ask. " 'Consider the tree'?"

Narantir turned his stained palm upwards. "Look at it. Consider it," he said, gesturing toward a gnarled savorfruit tree, its diamond-shaped leaves whispering gently in the breeze. "The tree maintains. The birds on its branches, they—"

"There aren't any birds on its branches."

The wizard glared at me for the longest moment, then without a further word, reached into his pouch and pulled out a small bundle of feathers, wrapped tightly with a leather thong. He started to untie the bundle, then shook his head and hefted it in his palm.

"Wait," Tebol said, taking the feather packet from Narantir for a moment and then carefully extracting a half dozen feathers before returning the bundle to the fat wizard. "Let us leave that one out of it, shall we?"

"We can do without the roc, I suppose." Narantir sighed, then gestured several times over the packet before throwing it high into the leaves of the savorfruit tree. I guess it caught on a small twig or something, but it looked like it was just hanging there, next to the leaves.

Birds swarmed into the tree from all different directions, chirping and tweeting and squawking in an arrangement that could only have been orchestrated by the tone-deaf. Crows called out their disdain in counterpoint to the blue warblers, who tilted back their heads to spill out incredible arpeggios, while robins sang and a single brayhawk screamed.

Tebol had a clay bird in his hands and was manipulating the beak. He raised the model to his lips and whispered a quiet word.

161

The singing and squawking and screaming of the birds cut out all at once, as hundreds of beady, birdy eyes looked down on us.

"As I was saying," Narantir said. "Consider the tree. It maintains. The birds may find purchase in its branches. Some of them may eat of its fruit and others may take from it dead twigs to build their nests. But which has more dignity? The lower-class tree that lives but to live, to produce, or the noble birds, who exist only to squawk and bray?" One feather clutched between his fingers, he raised his right hand and gestured with his left.

The packet of feathers fell to bounce firmly off the head of Tebol's clay sculpture, then *thwock*ed firmly into Narantir's palm, sending hundreds of birds flying in all directions, save directly over us.

"As I said," Narantir said. "Consider the tree." He bit into a meatroll.

"And consider that not only former acrobats can use broad gestures to make a point?" I asked.

He just smiled.

12

A Reception, an Encounter, a Noise in the Night, and Other Calculations and Miscalculations

To THE DISTANT blare of silverhorns and the deep *thrumm* of a bassskin from the musicians at the far end of the Great Hall, Lord Orazhi received me with a smile on his thin face, perhaps a sad one. It was hard to tell.

"Good evening, Historical Master Dan'Shir," he said, accepting my bow with the slightest of noble nods. "A pleasure to have you present this evening." His black-and-silver robes, belted tightly across his thin waist, were decorated with a simple pattern of silken white flowers. Next to him, Lord Toshtai, in yellow belted with brown, loomed like an enormous belted egg yolk.

Two haughty silverhorns picked up a four-note theme from the chimer, then lazily passed it to the baritone waterpipe, which liquidly, lazily toyed with it for only a moment before the zivver and a bassskin snatched it away.

Behind Lord Toshtai, old Dun Lidjun, his robes the color of summer straw, stood watching the world with eyes that neither rested nor flitted.

"And a good evening to you, Lord Orazhi, and you, Lord Toshtai, and you, Lord Dun Lidjun. I am, of course, honored, Lord Orazhi," I said, bowing low.

I was about to complete the courtesy by dropping to my knees on the parquet floor, but Lord Orazhi ordered me to desist with a quick gesture that Lord Toshtai seconded with a nod. Old Dun Lidjun's expression was the usual death sentence, waiting to be carried out against someone, although I never quite got the impression that just anybody would do.

I caught Edelfaule glaring at me from half across the room, while in another corner both Demick and Minch, surrounded by courtiers and courtesans, eyed me levelly. Minch raised his hand to his lips and spoke briefly behind it. If he hadn't crooked his fingers quite so much, I likely could have read his lips enough to extract the gist of it, but I probably didn't need anything else to worry about.

"I take it you have recovered from your fall?" Lord Toshtai asked.

I had thought that to be just for the sake of form, but he looked at me directly when I didn't answer. Not with any hint of threat or menace on his broad, fat face, but with attention, perhaps, as though the rest of the universe could wait until Lord Toshtai had been answered by Kami Dan'Shir.

"Almost recovered, Lord Toshtai," I said. "A few scratches here and there, the odd bruise, but nothing of any consequence."

Lord Orazhi's thin lips pursed for a moment, then relaxed. "I've given word to my head servitor to see to any special needs you may have. Don't be afraid to be . . . bold in your requests." He made an idle gesture toward a nearby servitor, and I found myself with a flask of some orange essence in my hands, the flask so cold that water was beading on its sides.

I started to tilt it back.

"I've also asked my daughter to make sure your needs are taken care of," he said.

I couldn't help it. I choked, but managed to suppress enough of the choking reflex to avoid splattering the two lords with the orange essence, and, immediately thereafter, my own guts.

"I beg your pardon, Lord Orazhi," I said. "I'm not used

to such fine essence," I managed to croak out. "When I see an orange essence, it's not a fine Sun Tears that comes to mind, but more likely some Hare Sweat."

"Understood, forgiven, and forgotten." He dismissed it. "As I was saying, my daughter is a fine hostess, and I hope she'll keep up the traditions in Den Oroshtai."

Well, so do I, sort of. And I do thank you for your daughter having taken care of my needs, dangerous as that was.

Not that I thought for a moment that that's what had gone on. ViKay's motives could have been anything, and it was as likely to do me little good to speculate on their nature as it was unlikely that I could prevent myself from speculating.

Unlikely that I could prevent myself from speculating? I mulled that thought over several times and decided that I had been spending decidedly too much time around our beloved ruling class. Regular people don't think that way.

Lord Orazhi nodded in friendly dismissal, as did Lord Toshtai.

Old Dun Lidjun was at my elbow as I moved across the room.

"I take it you haven't paid courtesy to Lords Minch and Demick this eve," he said, gently steering me in their direction. Old Dun Lidjun would gently lead a lamb to its butcher, I suspect. To make matters worse, Edelfaule had joined Minch and Demick, his cruel eyes not, for the moment, on me. I would have rather tickled a bear's tonsils.

There had to be another alternative. Over by the south wall, under a tapestry of a herd of deer caught in midfrolic, ViKay and Arefai were surrounded by a cluster of nobles and ladies, an island of relative safety in a sea of touchy nobility. Old Lady Estrer was ensconced on a padded chair high on a platform—more of a podium, really—far enough away to stay out of the conversation, but close enough to keep a cynical eye on her nephew and his future wife.

What I needed was, say, TaNai spotting the panic in my eyes and rushing up to improvise a previous commitment, but I wasn't going to get that. I tried to think of something.

"I haven't presented myself to Lord Arefai either," I said. "I wouldn't want to insult him and his wife-to-be."

I knew I'd won a respite when Dun Lidjun scowled. "Oh, very well, let's go over and talk to the boy."

Arefai grabbed my hands before I could bow properly. "Kami Dan'Shir!" he said. "It's good of you to join us this evening." The tone was of equal-to-equal, which I could see out of the corner of my eye wasn't lost on the rest of the crowd. Save a lord's honor, and he might even be grateful. More surprising things had happened.

ViKay's smile was a duplicate of Arefai's. "I'll even forgive you for beating me so badly at placques this morning."

"I am touched, Lady," I said, without a hint of suicidal sarcasm. I began to relax. Arefai was still oozing gratitude, and he would keep me involved in conversation long enough for Dun Lidjun to become tired of hanging about at my elbow. I could then make my apologies and slip off to my room to wait until either sleep or ViKay joined me.

Arefai beckoned over to where Minch, Demick, and Edelfaule were ignoring us. "Here, Edelfaule, if you please, Kami Dan'Shir has arrived."

The thin lord made his way through the crowd, Deren der Drumud at his side. Deren der Drumud's eyes never left old Dun Lidjun, although the old warrior neither seemed to watch him nor ignore him. I'd like to know how he did that.

"Ah," Edelfaule said, "the clever Kami Dan'Shir." The flask of green essence didn't tremble in his hand, but perhaps his speech had just a trace of slur. Or perhaps not. "Enjoying rubbing up against your betters this evening?"

Arefai rolled his eyes. "Brother, if I didn't know better, I'd think that an insult against not only Kami Dan'Shir, but those who invited him here this evening." He licked his lips, once. "I wouldn't want anyone here to think a member of Lord Toshtai's family would insult not only his host but Lord Toshtai himself, and I know that my elder brother would not dishonor the family so," he said, an edge in his voice.

The idiot. I had gotten the message, honestly: Arefai was going out of his way to befriend me, for whatever reason. There was no reason to rub his brother's nose against, well, me.

Minch chuckled. "I can't imagine that that would be so. How could anyone think that any noble from Den Oroshtai would insult a *bourgeois*? Were that to happen—and I assure you I think it impossible—the next thing you would find Den Oroshtai nobility out affronting the middle class and committing indignities on the peasantry."

Behind his shoulder, Deren der Drumud grinned too broadly, then laughed too loudly, defying anybody to take offense at that.

I wasn't going to, honestly.

Off in the distance, the bassskin rumbled something insistent that could have been a contradiction, I suppose.

"Lord Minch is quite right," Penkil Ner Condigan's own bass rumble came from behind me.

I half-turned.

Penkil Ner Condigan wore a bone-white shirt over earthy brown trousers today. Long and lean, he loomed half a head taller than anybody around him. His puffy cheeks and several chins were fresh from a careful shaving, but the fat man's face and head on that gaunt body still bothered me.

"I doubt that any noble from either Den Oroshtai or Glen Derenai would invite bourgeois, middle class, or peasant only to insult them," he said. "It's one thing for a lord to ride down a few middle-class girls or to trifle at a game of slap-the-peasant. It would be quite another thing entirely to invite a member of a lower class into one's home only to insult him or to invite one's noble guests to insult them. I'm sure that it would not be done by any noble of Glen Derenai, or of Den Oroshtai, or of Patrice," Penkil Ner Condigan continued, bowing low toward ViKay, Arefai, and Demick in turn.

Minch's lips were white. "I didn't hear you mention Merth's Bridge in that recitation," he said.

"Ah." Penkil Ner Condigan nodded. "My apologies for the error. Of course, I could not imagine a noble of Merth's Bridge acting so boorishly," he said, no trace of sarcasm in his voice or expression.

I had never heard a shtoi insult phrased better, and I couldn't imagine a weaker reason for insulting Minch than the huntsman had. After all, I wasn't really of his profession; the only reason that I had paid a courtesy call on him—or the wizards—was that the nobles hadn't had anybody more appropriate to choose.

Dun Lidjun threw back his head and laughed, almost offensively loud. "No," the old man said, "I am sure no noble of any sort would behave so boorishly. And certainly not one from Merth's Bridge."

I barely caught Lady Estrer's slightest movement of her head, and if I hadn't been watching for it, I wouldn't have thought that Arefai had either, but he broke into chuckles as well.

"Penkil Ner Condigan," he said, in between chortles, "you are a funny fellow."

As if to confirm, the silverhorns and zivver split off into an arpeggio that reminded me of a young girl's laughter. If old Lady Estrer hadn't been looking so pleased with herself, I would have thought it arranged, not coincidental, but the withered old woman would surely have managed to keep the satisfaction off her face if she had arranged for the music to supplement Arefai's chuckling.

Edelfaule wasn't going to be the only lord from Den Oroshtai not so amused, and his own somewhat forced chuckles were picked up by the surrounding nobility in general, those of us of lower class carefully keeping our faces blank, and—presumably; I know I was—wishing for the cloak of invisibility that Spennymore supposedly wraps himself in before his nighttime prowling.

Minch got control of himself only with visible difficulty. I was beginning to think that Lord Demick had chosen the wrong device for creating trouble here. Minch's temper ran just too high, and while he no doubt was able to compensate for that on the dueling field, he would have to be far more clever than he was if he wanted to find himself facing Arefai instead of Dun Lidjun.

Dun Lidjun was still standing next to me.

"Lord Dun Lidjun," I murmured, "pardon the frankness, but do you think you would have any problem beating Minch?"

Dun Lidjun didn't appear to hear. He just laughed some more.

"A funnier suggestion I have never heard," he said, raising his glass.

I found myself in the garden at midnight, just after the hour of the bear gave way to the hour of the lion.

The musicians were still playing in the Great Hall, but all I could hear was the occasional tinkle of the chimer, or a glissade of notes from the silverhorns; the rest was drowned out by the distance, and the whisper of the wind, and the rustling of the leaves in the trees.

The small rise where I had lunched with the wizards was empty, and liable to remain empty, so long as I made enough quiet noise to keep lovers from trysting there. The only light was from the uncaring stars above, and below, where through the trees I could see the occasional flicker of the torches lining the courtyard, snapping and popping in the wind.

The wind picked up, carrying with it a cold smell hinting of a storm to come.

When you don't know what to do, juggle. I don't swear that it's the solution for every problem, mind, but it doesn't hurt anything, and it can let your head clear. I hadn't gone up to my rooms for my bag, but that didn't matter: a half dozen walnuts from the grass would do.

Catch-throw, catch-throw, catch-throw, catch-throw, and invisible blades were still approaching my exposed neck from any direction. Juggle, juggle, juggle, and the politics of our beloved ruling class were beyond my experience and ability to deal with, and . . .

Voices came from below. I juggled softly, catching each walnut shell gently before sending the next one looping on its way.

"No, no, no, Esterling," ViKay said, "I have met you this last time, but that is all." Her voice was light but low, pitched to carry only a little way. If the wind had not been blowing it toward me, or if I hadn't stopped in my juggling to go to the retaining wall and listen more closely, I could barely have heard it.

I couldn't hear the other voice rumble, but the only reason I had no doubt that it was Lord Esterling was because ViKay had identified him as such.

The conversation went on, his low rumble insisting, her voice resisting. I thought about making noise, or about interfering, and decided against it. I know it doesn't sound gallant or heroic, but I was more concerned about my being caught listening than I was with ViKay's safety. Then again, her safety wasn't really at issue. Given that they were in the courtyard of her father's keep, all she would have to do would be to raise her voice, and a score of armsmen would be all over Esterling.

Besides, I'm neither a gallant nor a hero; that's for our beloved ruling class, not us bourgeois types. Let Toshtai make me a noble, and then he can expect me to rescue his son's wife-to-be, I thought, keeping my snort silent.

Then again ... what if she wouldn't raise her voice? What if she couldn't, or ...

It was easy to confront them without confronting them: I tossed a walnut in a high loop that ended with a sharp *crack* on the path below.

The voices cut off immediately, and I could hear a set of heavy footsteps departing quickly, but not running, and then another, lighter set going off in a different direction.

Well, I had learned something. Either ViKay had been involved with Esterling, or he wanted her to be, or ViKay wanted somebody, perhaps me, to think either of the former.

No, that was too complicated, even for our beloved ruling class. I was making it complicated where it was simple: ViKay and Esterling had been lovers, and she was unwilling to continue that any longer, with her marriage upcoming and, just perhaps, her needs being met elsewhere. Esterling had protested, and would now leave her be. Or, even if not, we'd still be done with the wedding and be back in Den Oroshtai in just a matter of days.

The wind died down, but not before bringing me a heavy scent of cold roses.

Enough for one night. Enough juggling, enough wondering, and most particularly enough of our beloved ruling class.

I went searching for my bed and found it.

My dreams were of drowning, of trying to bring my head above the surface of the water by gripping my feet in my hands and pulling up on my toes. It always seemed to be about to work, but then it wouldn't. It was enough to make me scream.

And, in fact I was screaming, in pain and in terror.

I was awake and there was a scream, but it wasn't mine. It was coming from across the courtyard somewhere. The sensible thing to do would be to go back to sleep and not have heard it. That which is not heard is not, after all.

I threw on my clothes and was out in the hallway before I even thought about it.

Old Dun Lidjun was already out in the hall, belting his robes awkwardly with one hand, the other occupied with his naked blade. Two younger warriors, struggling into their belts, tried to keep up with the old man.

"Where?" he said, beckoning at me to follow as he ran down the hall toward the wing where Lord Toshtai slept. His gray hair, usually bound back in a warrior's queue, hung loose about his shoulders; he tossed his head to clear it from his eyes.

I didn't know who he was asking, but all I could say was "I don't know."

The guards at the entrance to Lord Toshtai's suite were on their feet and alert as we arrived at the same time that the huge oak doors swung open to reveal Lord Toshtai and his two sons, each of them clearly just arisen from sleep, Toshtai still in his huge yellow silk sleeping caftan.

"Sheath your blade, Dun Lidjun," Lord Toshtai said. "We are all safe; and more trouble can come from a naked blade in a strange keep than I'd care to think of." Seeing that Dun Lidjun didn't have a scabbard with him, he beckoned for the old man to hand him the sword, then snapped his hands for his own, scabbarded sword—the big one, not the miniature he normally tucked in his sash. "Here. You help Kami Dan'Shir see what has happened, but don't draw the blade unless necessary, and don't annoy Lord Orazhi's people."

Arefai, dressed only in belted pantaloons and boots, slipped his own scabbard into his belt.

"May I go too, Father?" he asked, running his hands through sleep-mussed hair.

Lord Toshtai nodded.

"Be still," Dun Lidjun hissed to all of us. "And keep your hands empty, and in plain view." We crossed the courtyard quickly; Arefai had thought the scream came from across, in the other wing.

Dun Lidjun nodded tightly at the Glen Derenai warriors at the entrance to the other wing.

"Lord Toshtai has sent us to investigate," Arefai said, then silenced himself at a glance from old Dun Lidjun.

"We come with good intentions to offer our help, superfluous though it is, well though we know that the safety of the keep will always be well trusted in the strong hands of the warriors of Glen Derenai and of Lord Orazhi," Dun Lidjun said. I wasn't really surprised that the old man could slip into formal speech without exaggerating it into an insult.

The guard captain, his mouth tensed into two parallel lines, nodded tightly. "The third floor," he said.

Nopad Postet, a hairy bear of a man, was the senior of the Glen Derenai warriors gathered on the third floor. He beckoned us through the crowd of warriors and concubines and servitors gathered in the hall. One of the servitors, a slim woman balancing a domed tray on her shoulder, staggered for a moment, then righted herself and got out of the way.

"Lord Minch's room," Nopad Postet said. "He doesn't answer, and . . ."

And it would be a great discourtesy to enter the rooms of a guest lord uninvited.

Deren der Drumud shrugged. "I'm not at all sure that it came from here, and I know better than to interfere with my lord Minch's play."

"Play?" Arefai's exclamation sprayed the back of my neck with spittle. "If that's the way he plays, with screams that disturb the spirits of the keep, then to the dungpile with this play of his."

Without looking in Arefai's direction, Dun Lidjun gripped the sleeve of Arefai's robe, once, tightly, then released it. He turned to me. "Lord Toshtai instructed me to help you investigate." He looked levelly at Nopad Postet. "The warriors of Lord Orazhi have no objection?"

Nopad Postet clearly didn't like it, but he wasn't about to argue with the marshall of Den Oroshtai, not without specific orders from his own lord.

"Has anyone a key?" I asked.

There was no answer. I strongly suspected that one of the servitors milling about behind the warriors did, but I didn't blame them for not getting involved.

Well, there's no point in craving the feeling of the bar in your hands when you're tumbling end over end through the air. It will come or not.

"Get me in there, Lord Dun Lidjun," I said.

The old man handed his scabbarded sword to one of the Glen Derenai warriors, then ran the tips of his withered fingers down the side of the door. He closed his eyes for a moment, and then moved so quickly I couldn't even follow the motion. One moment he was just standing there, considering, his hands held loosely in front of him; the next, the door was exploding out of the way, the one remaining hinge screaming the way metal does when it's stretched too hard, too fast.

I stepped into the room.

The scream had been Lord Minch, and I couldn't blame him. He was standing up against the near wall, pinned to it by an arrow through his chest. His hands, now limp by his side, were darkened with blood to the elbows, and a dark stain ran down his white sleeping robes to the floor, where a shimmering black pool shone too glossy in the dark of the room.

Out of the corner of my eye, I could see a rip in the paper windowscreen on the opposite wall.

If I hadn't known better, I would have thought that somebody had been through the room before me: over by the window, clothes and implements were scattered under the weaponstand. Minch's own bow and arrows were off in one corner, as though thrown there.

A bit of temper at being outwitted yesterday, eh, Minch?

I had thought that he was dead, and that there was no hurry, but then he groaned, and his body shifted.

"Somebody get the wizards," I said.

"Shall we get him down?" Dun Lidjun raised an eyebrow as he looked at me, as though asking my permission. Why me? Just because Lord Toshtai had told me to investigate? Did that really mean so much to the old warrior?

I didn't know what he was asking permission for, but I nodded.

Dun Lidjun reached out and drew his sword—Lord Toshtai's sword, actually—then slipped it between Minch and the wall. One quick slash cut the arrow shaft, and Minch was falling away from the wall.

I caught him as he slumped.

Now, I never liked Minch, but I also didn't like the way his breathing went all ragged and desperate as he died in my arms. It reminded me of the way my sister had died, and I didn't much like the memory of that.

I stood and looked down at the body. The front of my shirt was wet with blood, and the floor was covered with it. I never realized that there was so much blood in a body.

The next thing I remember was looking up at the three lords: Demick, Toshtai, and Orazhi. It was all I could do not to wipe my hands on my shirt, but that would only have made them bloodier.

"It seems we have a puzzle for you, Historical Master Dan'Shir," Demick said.

"Yes," Toshtai said, "you must find out who murdered Minch. Narantir will be at your disposal."

Orazhi nodded. "All of Glen Derenai is at your disposal, Kami Dan'Shir. You must find the murderer. And quickly, before the wedding."

My gaze was drawn to the same place that all three of theirs was.

To the fletching of the shaft of the arrow projecting from Minch's chest.

"Yes," Demick said. "It could be rather . . . embarrassing otherwise."

And to the three gold bands just forward of that fletching. The three gold bands that announced, for all the world to see, that Arefai had just murdered Minch.

13
A Flare of Kazuh, the Beginning of an Investigation, a Broad Smile, and Other Penalties and Rewards

THREE GOLD BANDS . . .

The bait of a trap, the poisoned whey left for a rat. No, I was neither going to eat the bait nor going to ignore it. We D'Shaians are not an unhypocritical people. "That which is not seen is not" is a saying that we both mean and don't mean at all. There is power in ignoring the obvious, but more in acknowledging it, and still more in threatening to do so.

My kazuh flared, pointing the way. I didn't know enough, not now, to give me the solution, but at least for a moment, the path I would walk toward it shone clear and bright in my mind.

"Of course," I said. "I'll need the wizards—"

"Done," Lord Orazhi said, as Lord Toshtai nodded.

"—and two others to help me investigate," I said, deliberately not addressing anyone in particular. "Lord Dun Lidjun for one."

Lord Toshtai caught my eye. "And why would that be?"

"Another murderer, Lord Toshtai, managed—even before he murdered my sister—to find me and beat me half to death. I have no reason to believe that the coward who murdered Lord Minch by stealth would be more gentle. It's not that I am concerned with being beaten to death, you understand; I live but to serve. It's just that I can't find and expose the cowardly murderer of Lord Minch if I'm lying on a slab with my skull split open."

Lord Toshtai's eyes might have twinkled ever so slightly as he nodded at Dun Lidjun.

The old warrior faced me, his back straight. "I am at your disposal, Historical Master Eldest Son Discoverer-of-Truths."

Lord Orazhi spoke up, "All of Glen Derenai, from the highest to the lowest, is at your command, Kami Dan'Shir. Expose the murderer, no matter what his station might be." His voice held no trace of a quiver or trembling, but his lips were almost white. "Show me, show all the one who murdered a noble guest under my roof." He fought for control, and got it. "From a dungfooted gardener to my own person, you are to ask for any help you require, and it is yours." He raised his voice. "By my command! Kami Dan'Shir speaks with my voice; his commands are my commands; and his words are no gentler than mine will be."

I bowed.

Demick's smile was mocking. "You reach far beyond your station for assistance, Kami Dan'Shir. I'm pleased that Lord Dun Lidjun is so willing to stoop to help." He rubbed a thumb against the side of his jaw, as though idly considering whether or not that lowered Dun Lidjun.

"True enough." Dun Lidjun's voice was flat. "I'd swim through vomit and dig in dung if that would help find the cowardly murderer of Lord Minch," he said, each word a tick on a drumhead.

Demick's smile didn't fade. "Of course you would. Of course any of us would," he said, taking a scrap of blue silk from his sleeve and sniffing at it, as though to refresh himself. His unblinking eyes turned toward me. "And I take it the other . . . assistant you require will be Lord Arefai?"

I bowed deeply. "No, Lord Demick." I knelt next to the body, willing Arefai to keep his mouth shut. No protestation of innocence would do him any good, not now.

I put my finger to the shaft. "I doubt that anybody's noticed it, but this arrow has three gold bands on it. Lord Arefai's marking."

"Oh, yes," Demick said. "Now that you mention it . . . I had thought the arrow looked familiar."

"Which leads me to conclude," I said, "that the murderer wants us to think that Lord Arefai did it."

Or that it is Arefai, and that he's both clever and clumsy enough to portray himself as so clumsy and half-clever.

I was going to let it all go unsaid, but Demick's smile mocked me too loudly. I could take that, but I couldn't let him be the one to spread it all out in the open. Now was the time to deal with that, and to deal with it bluntly.

"Or," I said, "one could conclude that the murderer is Lord Arefai, pointing a clumsy finger at himself. 'Surely,' we all would say, 'surely Arefai would not murder Lord Minch in such a fashion that left him accused but not proven either innocent or guilty.'

"But then we might decide that Lord Arefai is precisely clever enough to do that, and we might never know, leaving a raincloud over his marriage to Lady ViKay. I'll need somebody far too clever to believe such a foolish idea, so that when Lord Arefai is properly cleared of this murder, his reputation will be left clean, as well. I'll need someone whose honor is above suspicion, but who isn't fealty-bound to the father of the obvious suspect."

"And who is this epitome of honor and sagacity?" Demick asked.

I let my smile grow broad, and waited a beat. "Why, you are, Lord Demick. I request and require your assistance in investigating Lord Minch's murder."

I wished that it had been Demick who had been playing at placques with me that morning.

I would have wagered anything that his expression would have been just as flat and controlled, his hint of a smile still every bit as merry and self-satisfied in paying off as it was when he bowed gently, and said, "Then I am, of course, completely at your disposal, Historical Master Eldest Son Discoverer-of-Truths."

179

14
Chicken, Conspiracies, Demick's Cooperation, and Other Things on Which to Chew

FRAMED NICELY IN the wizard's window, the morning sky had clouded over, threatening a coming storm. I would have spat at the sky and told it to stick its threats up its back passage, but I doubt that would have done much good; I'm not a wizard, after all.

I don't respond well to threats, I wanted to say, except that I didn't see any need to tell a lie for practice so early in the morning. I respond very well indeed to threats.

Tebol's face was split in a broad grin that looked like it didn't quite fit on his thin face, but Narantir was unamused.

"Not only do I have to work with you at my elbow, knocking over pots and vessels at awkward moments, but now, in addition, I have Lord Toshtai's hoary killer *and* the Lord of Patrice also to deal with?" The fat wizard reached under his robes to scratch at his crotch.

I shrugged and reached for another piece of chicken before he could handle it. I'm by no means the most fastidious person in the world, but I'd rather not eat food that's been fondled by Narantir. "Them also," I said. "Them too, as well, likewise, *and* in addition." I patted his arm. "Trust me; I'm the Historical Master Dan'Shir."

The centerpiece of breakfast in the wizard's tower was

cold chicken, some sort of honey-lemon glaze baked to the skin. It crunched beneath my teeth; I took another swallow of the straw-colored drayflower wine that had cleared the last traces of morning mouth.

That's the nice thing about a clear morning: it reminds you that the sun always rises, every day a new day, a new rebirth. A new hole to stick your head through, wondering if there's an axe descending toward your neck.

Tebol tilted his head to one side, evaluating me. "You seem, perhaps, relaxed? Happy?"

"Neither." There wasn't any harm in explaining part of it, not really. "But at least I'm doing something that . . . that I'm in charge of. Ever since I stopped being Kami Khuzud and became Kami Dan'Shir, I've been told where to go, what to do. Now, at least for now, I'm in charge of something. Of my life."

"Where do we start?" Narantir asked. "The outer wing? The room from where the shot was fired?"

"Certainly," I said, "if you can tell which room the shot was fired from, leaving alone for a moment how the killer knew to fire through that screen at that moment."

Narantir shrugged. "I would have thought it obvious. The screen was translucent. A lit lamp hung on the wall in Minch's room: his shadow played on the light, and Arefai—"

"The killer," I said. "The unknown killer, if you please, and even if you don't please."

The wizard considered me for a long time. "You know, Kami Dan'Shir, there are even more painful ways to check for broken bones than I've used on you. Perhaps we will discuss those ways next time you come to me with a broken bone."

Tebol tilted his head to one side. "What makes you think there will be another time?"

Narantir snorted. "Anyone with a mouth so loose to talk thusly to the likes of me will be lucky if the worst that happens is an occasional broken bone." He turned back to me. "You don't like my explanation."

"No, I like it fine, but I don't believe it. Minch was

pinned to the wall, all the way across the room, and the lamp was hung above him and to his left. Unless you're going to have me believe that the arrow picked him up and carried him across the room, he was shot where he stood, and whatever dim shadow he cast wouldn't have been on the windowshade, but on the floor."

It was possible, but barely, that while the killer had watched from across the courtyard, Minch had just carried the lantern toward the window, long enough for the killer to aim at his shadow, then brought it back to hang it up against the wall, and that a blind shot at that moment had eventually killed him, but it didn't sound likely.

I mean, imagine Minch's reaction when the arrow *spung*ed into the wall next to him ...

Could that be it? Could it be that an attempt simply to provoke Minch into action had gone horribly wrong?

Anything was possible, including my head rolling around in the dust. I shook my head. "I don't know how it happened; we'll have to find out."

"So we begin with Minch's room, eh?"

"Very good. And magically?"

"With relevance?"

"Probably. Can you tell which bow fired the arrow?"

He shook his head. "That's somewhere between unlikely and impossible."

"Eh?" Tebol's brow was furrowed. "Try irrelevance instead."

"I beg your pardon."

"Beg more humbly, if you please, friend Narantir. Collect all the bows in the castle, and try each. Those that have never fired that arrow will be absolutely irrelevant to it—"

"—assuming we can control for the fact that arrows are *designed* to be shot from bows, and therefore every arrow is relevant to every bow—" Narantir put in, then washed a bite of chicken down with a deep swallow of wine.

"—and if you find one that isn't absolutely irrelevant, you have the bow."

I shook my head. "No, I can't afford that. Arefai."

Narantir drained his mug and poured himself more wine. "I don't understand."

Tebol's brow furrowed. "Nor I."

"More for me, too," I said, holding out my mug. "We're not going to find the bow that did it, nor would it do us any good if we did. What we'd find is that Arefai's bow isn't irrelevant to that arrow. Or worse, that it *did* fire the arrow, because the killer borrowed it and then returned it."

"And, at all costs, we must not find that Arefai's the killer," Tebol said, his voice pitched so that I couldn't tell whether he was speaking frankly or in shtoi.

I decided to take his words as unnuanced, and nodded. "If it isn't Arefai's, the actual bow that fired the arrow has been chopped into little bits and burned, or spirited out of the castle by now. I don't need more evidence against Arefai; that won't do any good at all."

Again Narantir snorted. "And who would such evidence serve? Anyone in this castle is fealty-bound to one of the lords or is one of the lords himself. What good would it do to, say, find that one of Lord Orazhi's armsmen murdered Minch?"

"None," I said. "There's only one person in the castle who it would do good to find evidence on." I held up a thumb. "Arefai and Edelfaule are out; if it were either of them, it would shame Lord Toshtai beyond imagining. Ditto for anybody else in Lord Toshtai's party. I can't imagine that my way will be improved by shaming Lord Toshtai." Adding a finger, "The same for Lord Orazhi. If it's one of his people," like, perhaps, his daughter, "the very least that would happen would be to delay the wedding and interfere with the Den Oroshtai and Glen Derenai alliance."

There were other candidates, certainly. Esterling came immediately to mind; he clearly still wanted Vikay. There were likely others of ViKay's lovers about—I could tell from close personal observation that ViKay was more than casually familiar with the male anatomy—and, frankly, I could easily see how any one of them would happily have wiped out a blot like Minch in return for the possibility of another night with her.

But to implicate ViKay would be more than slightly dangerous. To blame anybody else from either Den Oroshtai or Glen Derenai would be almost as bad.

An old story is told of ancient Lord Rekson, lord of the Agami regions, about how, when a runner brought him the news of the defeat of the Three Armies at Presteen, he insisted that his wizard discover the implications of the defeat by reading the runner's entrails. One of the inferences I've always taken from that story is that bringing bad news to a member of our beloved ruling class is not an entirely safe proposition; even during times of stomach distress, I've always felt that my entrails are entirely happy where and how they are, not lying on the ground and getting all dirty.

"Demick," Tebol said, pronouncing the syllables with relish. "You really think it was Demick."

I shook my head. "I don't think it was Demick. I *hope* it was Demick. I *assume* it was Demick. It had better have been Demick. And I'm going to somehow have to be able to prove that it was Demick, with him watching me closely."

Tebol said, "And I thought that the time Narantir got drunk enough to start drawing dragon symbols was the closest I was going to come to seeing a suicidal madman at work."

I took a final bite of chicken, stood, and rinsed my hands in the fingerbowl before I walked to the door.

Dun Lidjun was outside the door, sitting on the small platform crowning the long stone staircase, his scabbard across his knees, toying with a plate of chicken. He hadn't eaten much, but he had managed to eat something without staining either his fingers, shirt, or beard.

"Ready to get to work, Lord Dun Lidjun?"

He nodded. "First we send for Demick, eh?" He smiled. "It begins."

"That it does."

He tilted his head to one side. "I do hope you know

what you're doing, Kami Dan'Shir," he said. "It could be
. . . inconvenient if you do not."

"The worst they can do is kill me," I said.

Dun Lidjun shook his head. "No, the worst they can do
is to kill you *slowly*."

The first thing to do was to sniff for spells.

Tebol had insisted on accompanying us, to act as
Narantir's assistant. I wondered out loud if a wizard could
put some sort of spell on an arrow that would make it seek
the heart of any enemy. I guessed not, though, or one
surely would have heard of it.

"If I ever develop such a spell," Narantir said, "I'll be
sure to place your order for a dozen such."

The rooms were guarded by a half dozen of Lord
Orazhi's scowling warriors, who let us in without objection, but without any simulation of friendliness.

I wouldn't have minded if they'd kept us out in the hall
longer. The wall was decorated in a fine Mesthai mural,
this one of the Cycle of Sleep. I could tell from the worn
spot on the rug that the face that got the most attention
from passersby was the chubby-cheeked baby sleeping
peacefully, his lips and chin still wet with his mother's
milk. It was nice, but not my favorite. I particularly liked
the face of the old man, restless and unsatisfied by what
they call in the north the wolf's rest, the sleep that does
not refresh. I could have spent hours staring at that one, or
at the carving of the boy caught in a nightmare that he
can't wake up from, or at the old woman, her limp hair
pulled back severely, allowing herself just a short nap before resuming her labors.

But that wasn't what I was here for. I pulled my eyes
away. "I'll light the lamp," I said.

"Never mind." Narantir reached down and opened a
pouch at his waist. Light flared brightly, casting his face
into shadow. He pulled out a brightly glowing gem. I
would have guessed it to be a diamond, but I've never
seen a diamond as large, or one that glowed at all, much
less so brightly that it was hard to look at.

"This should work well here," he said, as he set the gem in the lantern's niche. The curved mirror lining the niche took the white light and scattered it across the room.

It was going to be a mess, no matter what I tried. But it was worth a try, anyway.

Deren der Drumud, the much-mourned Minch's chief guard, insisted on helping, and of course Demick's own chief guard, an overmuscled type with the unlikely name of Verden Verdunt, had to accompany Demick. What with castle servitors constantly coming and going with trays of sweets and cups of hot tea for the nobles, it was all I could do to pretend some sort of concentration.

Minch's body was below, somewhere in the dungeon. "We'll have to examine the body later," I said to Narantir. "Can you . . . do something to prevent it from being tampered with?"

He snorted. "Any of one hundred and twelve things."

"One hundred twenty-three," Tebol said. "At last count." He raised an admonishing finger. "You haven't been keeping up with your studies."

Narantir snorted again. "And how could I, out in the hinterlands in Den Oroshtai? And why should I, even if I could? I don't trust neoteric spells, and I don't care for them. The modern styles are different from when I was young; much of the new magic is too baroque and complex for the likes of me. I like magic that *does* something, and doesn't sit around congratulating itself with how stylish it is."

"True enough." Tebol's smile was noncommittal.

"And loud and never-ending protestations to the contrary, I've often found Jen Poraycis far more concerned with how prettily the spells are constructed than with what they actually do—"

"Narantir," he said, raising a finger almost to lips, "I'm in agreement; cease persuading me. You're trying to make steak become beef. Still, I think you'll like my new contribution to the genre." His fingers traced symbols through the air. "The warnings aside—"

"Simple contagion; all that does is chill the heart of somebody who approaches."

"Which should slow them down," he said, "but then we add *this*," he said, finishing off with a short series of gestures that ended with him brushing away a puff of breath with his fingertips.

"Now, *that* I like," Narantir said. "Let them complete the spell, and—"

"Precisely."

The fat wizard nodded. "Go ahead, then; I'll manage things here." He chuckled and shook his head as Tebol bowed his way out of the room. "Elegant, that is elegant! Applause, Tebol."

Demick was far too poised to show weakness by asking, but part of my job is to ask questions.

"Is this one of those things that only wizards can understand, or can you explain it?" I asked.

Narantir chuckled. "No, it's simple enough even for the likes of you."

I forced a smile. "Then it must be simple indeed."

Narantir's grin broadened. "Indeed. Tebol is now engaged in setting up a dragon spell around the corpse."

I swallowed, hard. Everybody knows that dragon magic is too dangerous to deal with, so much so that even the most temporal of artists will paint a dragon only by indirection—the grass bending before its icy breath, a huge impression in wet sand, a mass of fog concealing a dark, hulking shape.

Narantir raised his index finger. I'd seen cleaner nails. "The beautiful part is that he leaves a critical . . . stroke out of the spell. Anyone who is not . . . made unsimilar to that stroke will complete the spell as they approach. And then . . ." His hands came together with a sound that should have been a clap, but was a *snap*, like teeth on teeth. "Which breaks the indition, dismissing the dragon." He nodded. "Impressive, no?"

"Fascinating," Lord Demick said, looming over me as I knelt in front of the bloodstain that marked where Minch had died. It would have been convenient if I could have found the words "Demick murdered me" traced in Minch's blood, but ...

Well, no, it wouldn't be convenient for everyone. It would push Den Oroshtai and Patrice toward a more direct war.

On the other hand, I'm not everyone. A dan'shir doesn't have to play in the battles that liven up the lives of men of our beloved ruling class.

"Narantir, could you tell which hand wrote a note?"

"Oh, easily. Writing's always relevant to the hand, often to the pen. Only sometimes to the brush; brushes don't have much personality of their own."

Of course, if I wrapped Minch's dead fingers around a pen ...

... I wouldn't be able to write at all, much less lucidly, much less try to imitate the Eastern scrawl that Minch had. Well, so much for that idea.

The arrowhead was still buried in the wall where the shaft had pinned Minch. Which gave me an idea. "Any thread in your bag, Narantir?"

Wordless, he tossed me a ball of thread.

"Hmm ... you didn't roll this yourself," I said.

Narantir's brows raised. "True, and I usually do. Dan'shir magic?"

"Something like that." Actually, it wasn't complicated; the ball was rolled far too neatly for it to have been Narantir.

I tied one end of the thread to the end of the shaft, and walked across the room, paying out thread as I went. "Lord Demick," I said, "would you be kind enough to sight down the thread. What do you see?"

He leaned his head over. "Your hand. And behind it a lovely windowscreen."

True enough. The paper, so thin as to almost glow even in the light of an overcast sky, held an ink sketch of a cock crowing its hour. I usually prefer art that has more detail, but somehow the bold strokes of a brush brought strength and vigor to the bold bird tilting back its beak to pronounce the day properly begun.

"And the hole in the windowscreen," he added.

The hole was two-thirds of the way up on the right side of the windowscreen, the outer edges of the tear just missing the cock's beak. Which was just as well. Killing Minch was one thing, but to defile the painting would be a much worse crime.

I knelt on the floor and looked up at Narantir. "Chalk?"

Narantir tossed me a small chunk; I marked off where the screen's feet were, just in case I had to do this again. I threw the chalk back to the wizard and tied the end of the thread around my index finger. "Now, nothing's been touched since last night," I said, as I pulled back the screen, holding my finger over where the hole had been. "And what do you see as you sight down the thread?"

"Hmmm . . ." Demick frowned. "Directly over your finger, I see the window to a room on the second floor, across the courtyard. If I am correct, it's a room occupied by myself." His smile was self-assured.

Later, I told myself. Now was not the time.

I put the screen back where it had been and rewound Narantir's thread. Fine; I had the spot where the arrow had been fired from, and perhaps I had an inkling of the why, but I didn't have the how.

I walked to the corner of the room, where Minch's weapons lay. His sword was properly scabbarded, but instead of being set on the swordstand next to the door, it was just lying on the floor.

Verden Verdunt, Demick's guard, glowered down at it. "Shameful way to treat a good weapon." He started to reach for it, desisting when Dun Lidjun interposed himself.

"If you please, Raging Sunflower," the old man said, holding up a hand, "not until Kami Dan'Shir has examined it."

The big man looked more irritated than puzzled, although Demick's nod stilled him.

"Not to offend, Lord Verden Verdunt," I said, "but it's always details. Not long ago, the mark of a sword's break against a doorframe helped me find the murderer of my sister."

Narantir's ugly face almost split in a grin, but he didn't say anything. What I'd said wasn't true; I'd already known who the murderer was, and the plans involving using the markings of the sword's break never quite came together.

The hilt of this sword was of highly polished black wood, bound with leather strips that fit into indentations in the wood. It seemed to afford a good grip, but that wasn't something I know a lot about. I slid the blade partway out of the scabbard. The bright steel was beautifully polished, the fine black tracery on its surface almost too small to see.

I handed it to Dun Lidjun. "What do you think, Lord Dun Lidjun?"

"Far too fine a blade for the likes of Minch," he said, an audible sniff as punctuation. "An Old Lithburn, or perhaps an early Middle Lithburn." He raised an eyebrow, asking permission. I was always impressed with old Dun Lidjun, and how well he did everything, even asking permission; I wouldn't have thought of saying no.

He produced a tiny knife—I didn't see where it came from, although I was looking for the motion—and cut at the inset leather in the swordhilt, then pried the hilt away from the sword.

"Ah. Old Lithburn," he said, tapping the point of his knife against the markings on the tang. "I wouldn't be surprised if its name is in the Scion's registry." He fitted the hilt back around the tang and gave the leather a few turns around it, temporarily fixing it in place. Somewhere in the process, he got rid of the small knife. I wish I knew how he did that.

"I'm but little wiser," I said.

Dun Lidjun's dry lips pursed. "Lord Toshtai's favorite sword, the one he gifted me with the use of last night, is a fine blue Greater Frosuffold; this is easily its equal. This is the sword of a major lord, the master of a domain, far too fine for a minor noble of Merth's Bridge, no matter how wealthy the Agami lords they are bound to might be."

He balanced the scabbard level on his palms for a moment, then set it gently on the arms of the swordstand by the window.

Demick looked from Dun Lidjun to the sword, and to me.

"Lord?" I asked. "I know you wouldn't want to contradict Lord Dun Lidjun, but if there's something you'd like to add . . ."

Say, that you bribed Minch to risk his life in embarrassing Arefai and stopping the wedding with the sort of sword that he could only dream of possessing. That would be a nice start.

Demick's expression didn't change as he blinked, twice. "No; Lord Dun Lidjun is correct. But it happens, every now and then, that one can own a sword too fine." His smile was only vaguely insulting. "Particularly a minor lord such as Lord Minch," he said.

The bow was unstrung, but the string hung from one end of it. I handed it to Dun Lidjun next. "A nice piece, but I've seen better," he said, handing it to Demick. "I have better."

"Rather better," Demick said.

Dun Lidjun gestured at the pile of arrows across the floor. "The arrows are unspectacular."

"Oh?" I said, selecting one. "You see nothing surprising about this?" I held it up. It had no arrowhead on it; the point was flat and blunt.

Verden Verdunt snickered, and Demick shook his head.

"An arrow without a head isn't any more unusual than a formerly insolent peasant without a head," the Patricien lord said, letting only the content carry his scorn for my ignorance. "One often removes a head," he said, with just a slight pause, "of an arrow to repair or replace it with another.

"A good arrow is like a woman; each one is different, no matter how much someone who knows nothing about arrows nor women will think them all the same. Some arrows prefer heavier heads, some prefer lighter, or broader." He gestured at the pile. "Likely you'll find a favored arrow or two with damaged fletching, waiting repair; it's the same thing at that end, too."

Verden Verdunt picked up one of the arrows; Dun Lidjun was going to say something, but stopped when I shook my head. I had already looked them over.

Verden Verdunt hefted the arrow in his hand. "Unspectacular," he said. "Balance is all wrong." He balanced it in his palm and swung his arm, throwing it at the nearby wall, aiming roughly for the bloody spot where Minch had been pinned. It clattered to the floor; Verden Verdunt picked it up and wrapped his fist around the shaft, sticking it in only with difficulty.

"What are you doing, if I may ask, Lord Verden Verdunt?"

He shrugged. "Just seeing how soft the walls are, how easily an arrow can sink into one. Except for the balance, this one shouldn't have been a problem. All wrong, but then again we know there was something wrong with Minch's balance," he said, smiling to himself, as though over a private joke.

No matter.

I moved over to the wardrobe in the corner, and ran my finger down, looking for the catch. Like mine, it was Agami larken woodwork, each side made of hundreds of smaller pieces carefully fit together, but this was not nearly as nice a piece of work as mine. Fealty-bound as Merth's Bridge was to the Agami lords, it was likely more plain than Minch was used to. I doubt that he had taken offense, though; a wonderful Mesthai Cycle of Joy smiled down from the wall above, its hundred carven faces expressing joy in a thousand ways.

Too good for the likes of Minch? Perhaps.

Our beloved ruling class likes things complicated. If it had been up to me, there would have been some sort of prefix attached to designations. Maybe feathers, that would be nice. A minor noble, fealty-bound to the lord of a minor domain, might be called a one-feather lord, and wear it in his hair like a low-class courtesan does. Of course, by the time one got past minor lords of minor domains and minor lords fealty-bound to medium domains and medium lords of medium domains up to the whole cast of nobility of a major domain, you'd find lords like Toshtai, Orazhi, and Demick decked out like pheasants, so maybe that isn't a good idea.

Besides, I'm not entirely sure how they all compared. Who was more important? The sole lord of a minor domain like, say, Conner's Heath, or a fealty-bound lord like Dun Lidjun, the marshall of all the forces of a medium-sized but strategically substantial domain like Den Oroshtai?

Well, I wasn't going to sort that out, not today. I was barely going to sort through the clothing. I mean, I don't spend a lot of time going through nobles' wardrobes, no matter what it may seem like, but I was quickly getting the impression that the late lamented Minch could have kept himself busy doing nothing but changing his undergarments.

"Anything of interest, Kami Dan'Shir?" Demick asked, politely.

"Nothing that I can see, Lord," I said.

"Then what is next?"

"The body," I said.

Demick nodded. "It's down in the dungeon, so I am told, with good Tebol. Shall we meet you there?" he asked, not waiting for an answer as he stalked out of the room, Verden Verdunt and Deren der Drumud at his heels.

I folded my hands across my chest as I looked at the door close behind them. I was missing something, perhaps something important.

Dun Lidjun eyed me quizzically. "You seem to see a problem?"

"Lord Demick's being far too cooperative." I shook my head. "Or perhaps not." I had the feeling that I was being led, and not just by the facts as presented. I don't mind being led, as long as it's not to the chopping block.

"Demick," he said. "Demick was directing Minch, seeking to use him to throw young Arefai off—to disconcert him, cause him to shame his house and father."

194

You figured that out all by yourself, Dun Lidjun? That wasn't the issue, now that Minch was dead.

Unless . . . "We'll see."

"About what?"

I took a chance. "With all respect, Lord Dun Lidjun, I am to handle this as I see fit. Let me do that, Lord, without having to face my placques before I have them sorted."

His face was impassive. "As you will," he said.

It's your neck, he didn't have to say.

Narantir looked over at me. "You're being clever again," he said. "I don't like it when you think you're clever." Dirty fingers played in his beard.

Dun Lidjun was idly holding the arrow Verden Verdunt had been playing with. "I wouldn't know about that, Narantir. Perhaps Kami Dan'Shir's cleverness is leading in the correct direction." He turned to me. "May I?"

I didn't have the slightest idea what the old warrior was asking permission for, but that didn't matter.

"Of course, Lord Dun Lidjun."

His face grew flat instantly, and he stood for a moment, the arrow held lightly at the balance point between two fingers. And then he whirled his arm, once experimentally, then spun.

Not just the arm holding the arrow—his whole body spun around once, always in balance, as his arm whirled. He released the arrow as he and his arm came around.

It *thunk*ed into the wall between the speaking tube and the stub of the arrow that had killed Lord Minch, burying its head completely.

"Soft wall," he said.

Just once, I'd like to see a dry, cheery dungeon, its whitewashed walls scattering the bright morning sunlight streaming in through broad windows, a steady crossdraft breeze of fresh air carrying away the dampness and musty smells. They could even put bars on the windows, if they'd like.

But no, all dungeons are the same. The shaft of the arrow tenting the blanket that was covering it, Minch's body lay on a slab in a cheerless cube of a room, dark, dank, and gloomy, the darkness barely challenged by a sputtering overhead lantern, the dankness relieved only by the horrid fecal smell of the dead, the gloom not at all mitigated by anything whatsoever. I wondered for a moment if they always kept a lantern lit here, or if the almost prescient servitors of the keep had lit it and fled, just ahead of Demick and the two huge warriors, but then I decided I had more important things to wonder about.

At my gesture, Narantir pulled the brightly glowing gem from his pouch and set it in a tiny crevice near the juncture of stone walls and the huge slab of stone that was the cubicle's ceiling.

"Still bright," he said.

Tebol smiled, as though sharing a private wizards' joke.

I took the lantern down from the peg and turned to the body under the blanket. Idiotic idea, as though a dead person would need to be kept warm. I pulled down the blanket and looked into his dead face.

Truth to tell, or at least truth to think, I'd never much cared for Minch. We had taken an instant dislike to each other, and I would not dress in white to mourn his death, but there was something pitiful in the way he lay stretched out on the slab, his eyes open and vacant, staring blindly at the ceiling, his sagging mouth unable to protest his being handled by the lower classes, his limp hands helpless to shoo away the flies that were gathering in the blood covering most of his chest and robes.

"Well," Demick said, as though he hadn't a care, which was probably the case, "what are you learning from this examination, Historical Master Dan'Shir?" Once again, he brought a scented silk to his face, as though the smell of it could drive away the stink of death.

"I'm not sure, Lord." That sounded so much better than *Not a wretched thing, Demick*, and was probably somewhat safer.

I held the lantern close to the shaft of the arrow. It would have been convenient to find that the paint on the three gold bands was running or tacky, which would have argued that it was an attempt to blame Arefai, but the paint was dry and smooth to my touch, which only goes to show that murderers aren't concerned with Kami Dan'Shir's convenience, something I would probably have surmised.

The arrow had entered Minch's chest cleanly, halfway between two ribs, which argued for either great bowmanship or great luck. Then again, I can't imagine that if an arrow struck a rib it would simply bounce off; most likely it would be deflected upward or downward into the chest in any case. A dan'shir can easily see things that won't do any good.

Minch's hands were covered with sticky blood, but ... "Narantir, would you get me a pail of water and some rags?"

"Do I look like a servitor?"

"No," I said, "you look like a wizard who has been asked to aid my investigation."

With a snort, he gathered his robes about his bulk and left the room, leaving Tebol behind to hide a smile behind a hand. The thin wizard inhaled too sharply, then reached into his black leather wizard's bag, pulling out a long stubby cone, about the size of a fist. "Have you an objection to me dealing with the stench, or do you like it this way?"

"Please," I said.

Tebol produced a flame between two fingers, whether through magic or artifice I couldn't say, and touched it to the end of the cone, which flared gratifyingly. Tebol pursed his thin lips and blew out the flame, leaving the end to smoulder. He waved his hands in the thin smoke, and almost instantly the horrid fecal reek vanished in a wave of patchouli, myrrh, orangitta, and pepper.

"Law of Predisposition," he said. "Incense is predisposed to overpower other smells, and with a little magical help, it does so ever so much better." He grinned. "One school says that's all you zuhrir users do when you raise kazuh—apply the Law of Predisposition."

Dun Lidjun seemed amused. " 'All'?" he asked. "That would be so little then?"

I wasn't sure how Tebol was going to take that, and was thinking of something distracting to say when Narantir returned, bearing a wooden pail and a pile of rags, which he set down on the slab next to Minch's body.

Demick and the two hulking warriors watched closely while I washed the blood from Minch's arms. Minch's fingers were stiff, but when I pried them open and washed the horrid pasty clots away, the palms were lacerated.

Dun Lidjun bent his head over the palms. "I've seen that before," he said, his eyes growing vague and distant, as though he was suddenly looking at something far away. "You see it in battle. Somebody takes an arrow through the chest or gut, and he tries to pull it loose, as though that will help, instead of tearing out more of your insides." His voice was flat, passionless; Dun Lidjun would share his feelings only at his choice. "Nock point of an arrow's usually fairly sharply cut, and if you manage to pry a bit of fletching partly loose, you can cut yourself on the sliver of quill." If anything, his voice became more flat and colorless. "I once encountered the body of a good friend of mine, half an arrowshaft in his chest, his hands sprouting splinters like a porcupine." He looked up at me. "I don't see any use out of this, Kami Dan'Shir. We know Minch was killed by an arrow."

Demick's smile was a degree short of insult. "So it would appear."

I nodded. "Yes, we do. But I've seen enough. I will need some assistance with more of this, at the hour of the snake, perhaps? Just after sundown; just before dinner, say?"

"Verden Verdunt and I are, of course, at your disposal," Demick said. "Where shall we meet you?"

"In your chambers, across the courtyard, if that pleases you, Lord. I've something of an experiment to run."

"Oh?"

Let him sweat, let him worry. Dun Lidjun was at my side, and while both Deren der Drumud and Verden

Verdunt were huge men, if Demick ordered them into action, I would wager my life that the old warrior would leave the three of them in pieces on the floor.

"Oh, yes, Lord Demick," I said. "I'll be inviting Lord Toshtai and Lord Orazhi to watch the experiment."

He smiled, confidently. "Then I am certain it will be very interesting for us all. In the interim, we will wish you a good day," he said, letting Deren der Drumud precede him, and Verden Verdunt gently close the door behind him, leaving Dun Lidjun, me, and the two wizards alone with the body, and with the smells of patchouli, myrrh, orangitta, and pepper that washed the stink of death from my nose, if not my mind.

I took a last look at the body. "Let's go; we have some preparations to make."

Interlude:

The Hour of the Octopus

THE HEAT OF the tub and the cold of the air were strong sensations, but ViKay preferred her sensations strong. The bathwater, hot enough to coddle an egg, absolutely reeked of honey, orange, and roses, with a slight overtone of vinegar: it was just the way ViKay liked it.

Later, she would rinse off with plain cold water and then raw alcohol, and then dry herself off, so that only gentle hints of the scents would cling to her, but that was for later, to present the appearance of moderation. That appearance was her concession to others: for her, hot and strong was right.

Just the right time of day for a bath, too: the hour of the octopus, when afternoon moved toward sunset, and when the breezes were strong enough to make the air above the huge oaken bathtub painfully cold.

She reached out a fingernail lacquered the color of honey and tapped once, twice, three times at the small silver bell that hung from the edge of the tub; almost immediately, three serving girls waddled in, each bearing a pail of steaming water from the boiling kettle outside.

Averting their eyes from her, each in turn smoothly poured the contents of her pail into the bathtub, then scurried out, as though afraid. They had cause.

ViKay was not particularly harsh with her servitors, certainly not as a matter of practice. She never ordered any of them beaten for a moment of clumsiness, even including the time that ungainly Fren ver Dreben had spilled olive-grape soup all over one of her oldest and finest gowns. Accidents happened. One simply had to accept that a seamstress would occasionally stick you while pinning up some fabric; it was unavoidable that a dresser would, from time to time, let a grain or two of powder fall into the eye instead of on the lid; every so often, it was unavoidable that one's intended would kill a meddlesome troublemaker. None would be commented upon; all would be forgiven.

However, there were two matters that ViKay was adamant on.

Gossip was the minor one; gossip about her was forbidden. Her comings and goings were never, ever to be a matter of discussion. Servitors were simply to be sure that a proper breakfast awaited outside whichever room she was in, and if that meant leaving an extra breakfast here or there, so-be-it. They were to do it, but not talk about it. One maid of hers had, once, made that mistake; she was buried beneath a pigsty.

The major matter was this: ViKay was not to be disturbed in the bath.

ViKay bathed once every day, during the hour of the octopus. During the eight other hours, awake or asleep, she was at the disposal of her lord father, of the Scion, of the realm. All the hours of dressing and dining, of the play that was not play, of the smiling and bowing, of the giggling and pretending to be helplessly pursued . . . all that was theirs. Her very life was theirs, to be spent like a clipped copper if need be.

So-be-it.

But not her bath. This time was hers, to lie back and rest, to think, to plan, to simply be herself.

She lay back and let herself sink below the water. That was something strange about ViKay: while she floated seemingly effortlessly through her day and life, she simply could not float in water. No matter how hard her teachers had tried to teach her to swim, she simply could not keep her head above water. There was simply no use for such a quality, and ViKay resented it. She had managed to yoke her pleasures and passions to the service of the Scion and of her lord father and of the realm, but there was no way that this small thing could be made useful.

ViKay despised waste.

She brought her face to the surface and inhaled the sweet air.

Soon it would be time to end the pleasure of the bath. Kami Dan'Shir had scheduled a demonstration for the hour of the snake, and from what Lord Father had said about his last demonstration, that meant that he was prepared to expose the murderer. That it happened so quickly meant that whoever Kami Dan'Shir was prepared to accuse, it was not Arefai. Demick? Edelfaule? That tiresome Esterling, who mistook an evening of diversion for something weak and cloying? Kami Dan'Shir himself?

It didn't matter. Kami Dan'Shir would be in no rush to accuse Arefai, and therefore ViKay had no need to threaten the beautiful boy with what she would do were he not to clear her intended. That her confession would cost both their lives was irrelevant; he would know that she meant it, and that she would protect Arefai's life and position with her own.

Edelfaule was too cruel to be a proper lord of Den Oroshtai. Cruelty was unacceptable. The cold relentlessness of Lord Toshtai or of her lord father was something else; the harnessed, sophisticated brutality of a Demick or a Luchen was another. But simple cruelty was, at base, too simple.

Arefai would have to be the next lord. Lovely boy, he was faithful and earnest and passionate, as well as indefatigable beyond what she would have thought possible, but he was not clever enough to rule.

That was tolerable; that she could supply for him. That

would, in time, become her way of serving the Scion and the realm. ViKay lived only to serve.

All in time; timing was everything.

She reached out her finger and tapped tapped twice on the silver bell, then reached for a long-handled bath brush.

The bristles were delightfully coarse.

15
A Demonstration, Another Demonstration, a Remonstration, and Other Successes and Failures

PROMPTLY AT THE hour of the snake, Lord Demick received the four of us in his rooms as though he were welcoming us to Patrice itself.

Which didn't mean much. I suppose he welcomed Evan of Solway Dell with the same slight bow and open-armed gesture before removing his skin, patch by patch.

Demick had been given a broad, low suite of rooms on the third floor, overlooking the gardens separating the two wings of the keep. The centerpiece of the living room, surrounded by a low rope to warn the unwary, was a marvelous Oledi woodshard sculpture of a warrior in full raiment, his arms crossed in front of his chest as though challenging a lesser warrior to draw first.

I've always liked woodshard work, even after I learned the secret, such as it is. The original sculpture is done by the master sculptor in ice early on in the winter. During the following days, before the ice can melt, his apprentices, working night and day, glue thousands and thousands of tiny wooden slivers to each other on the surface of the ice sculpture, so that when the ice finally does melt, the shell remains, elegantly cupping the space that had been occupied by the ice. There are mundane and inelegant tricks in the process, like the necessity of inserting metal prongs to support melting pieces of ice that might break off and break through the delicate shell, but the principle is elegant: of the original work, nothing remains.

This was a particularly fine example, where the subtle colors had been expertly combined to show a raised mahogany eyebrow here, a teak swordhilt there, letting color as well as shape convey the image of a warrior about to lunge into motion.

Just outside the windows, a trio of bright green songbirds perched on a carving of a huge man's extended finger. Beaks tilted back, they burbled a liquid harmony, while within, silent servitors wrapped in Patricien purple passed among the visitors, dispensing dew-beaded glasses of icy-cold crushed raspberries and flat crackers spread with truffled confit of duck.

"I have laid on a Patricien repast," Demick said, his face as calm as the surface of a still lake, "in honor of Kami Dan'Shir's ... experiment." He gestured to a sideboard. "I have gone to some trouble, and hope it will be received with a portion of the gratitude that I have felt for the generosity and good grace my hosts have shown me here at Glen Derenai, as well as during my visits to Den Oroshtai."

Old Dun Lidjun bowed deeply, just shy of deeply enough for it to be a burlesque and insult, then straightened, the long wrapped bundle still under one arm.

"May I have someone help you with your ... package?" Demick asked, as though he hadn't a concern in the world.

"I thank you, but no," Dun Lidjun said.

Demick smiled and bowed him in, then greeted the two wizards and finally me.

"You honor us with your presence, Kami, Historical Master Dan'Shir," he said, in the same tone, I suppose, that he would have said, *We're awfully gracious to treat your bourgeois self as though you're a person.*

"I am, of course, grateful," I said, snagging a tall glass from one tray, and a cracker from another. The juice was sweet and fruity, the confit salty and heavy with garlic and sprinkled with thyme and orkan.

Demick merely smiled blankly, then turned to greet the next visitor, while I headed for the sideboard. Being clever makes me hungry.

Silver salvers held: small cubes of true Patricien ham, smoked according to a secret recipe half a thousand years old; tiny, coppery oysters that grow only in the mouth of the Demms, served on the half shell and topped with grated horseradish and lumpy begret; a small mountain of peeled hard-boiled quail eggs, each about the size of the first digit of my index finger, crowned with a peppery cream sauce; a platter of quartered honeyed apples, perhaps a trace of magic preventing them from browning in the air.

I smiled. Normally it was the condemned man who was provided the handsome meal.

Of course, there could be some sort of . . .

I turned to Narantir, who was downing a handful of the quail eggs.

"Well?" he said.

I raised an eyebrow. "Well, indeed. If you were me, what question would you be asking?"

"Any of a number," he said, "but not the stupid one you're thinking. Poison, *hagh.*" He shook his head. "If there was any poison, would I be doing this?" He bolted down another handful, then gave out a fragrant burp, then pointed at the salver of steamed turnip hearts. "Although I would caution against those," he said, passing an amber amulet over one dish. He tucked the amulet back in his sleeve. "The Law of Appropriateness finds fault with the combination of honey and turnip, no matter what Patricien custom says."

I looked away. Demick was still at the door, now greeting Esterling. The trouble with Esterling, I decided, was that he was just *too* pretty: his nose and jawline too sharp, his features too regular and even.

To my right, Dun Lidjun frowned. "He seems too self-assured, even for Demick."

I shrugged. "It's just an experiment, a demonstration, Lord. Nothing of consequence."

"Spare me your lower-class shtoi sarcasm," the old man said. "If you aren't going to indulge me with an explanation, then keep quiet."

"Yes, Lord," I said. I guess I'd been spending too much time around Dun Lidjun and was starting to take him for granted, because I heard myself saying: "Those of us in the lower classes live but to obey."

Just as the skin over my spine went all damp and clammy, he nodded gravely. "That is, of course, so."

I tried to let out my breath slowly. I guess not only the lower classes can talk in shtoi.

Lords Orazhi and Toshtai arrived in company with Edelfaule and old Lady Estrer, and a scattering of other lords. Orazhi's robes today were muted pastels in mild greens and reds, matching the dour expression on his face. Toshtai, on the other hand, was arrayed in robes of the brightest of yellows, belted across his lavish belly with a crimson sash. A noble is never without his sword, and Toshtai's dagger was stuck through the sash.

Arefai was the last to arrive, ViKay clinging to his arm as though she were frail and helpless. Lies come easily to our beloved ruling class.

I made sure my smile was simply pleasant as they approached me. "A demonstration awaits, Kami Dan'Shir?"

"More of an experiment, Lord Arefai."

He clasped my shoulder with a grip that was strong but not punishing. "I know that we can count on you," he said.

ViKay smiled at me. "I am sure of it, as well," she said, her voice perhaps half a tone too husky for safety.

Arefai didn't catch it. "You are ready?"

I nodded.

"May I?" he asked.

"Please."

Arefai cleared his throat loudly. "Kami Dan'Shir is now ready to begin his . . . tentative experiment," Arefai said. "He thought it might be of interest to the lot of us. On behalf of myself and my future wife, it is my . . . pleasure and honor to thank Lord Demick for graciously offering his rooms for this purpose."

Demick's smile was even broader than Arefai's. "It's as nothing. I've even prepared a small entertainment of my own."

Falling on your sword in shame? I wanted to ask.

Demick gestured to me, palm up. "Our attention is yours, Kami Dan'Shir."

I bowed. "I thank you, Lord Demick. Ladies, Lords," I said. "I've asked Lord Dun Lidjun to serve as a bowman this evening. As someone who has, of late, achieved some success in shooting, I think it's fair to say that he's a competent one."

Dun Lidjun had already unwrapped the bow and arrow from his package.

"I took the liberty," I went on, "of asking him to paint three bands of gold on an arrow."

Four windows looked out across the courtyard at the other wing. "Please note the open window, where Tebol ha-Mahrir stands, a lantern in his hand." Across the courtyard, Tebol stood, swinging a lantern back and forth.

I went to the window and raised a hand. Tebol slid a plain paper screen in front of the window, and was gone from sight. Still, we could see the flickering of the lantern from across the courtyard, even through the screen.

"There appears to be a flaw in the paper screen," Narantir said, on cue. Timing is everything.

"Not a flaw, good Narantir," I said, "but a mark I've made. That marking is, at the moment, in exactly the same place as the rip in the screen that covered the window last night. Lord Dun Lidjun, if you please, and quickly."

Dun Lidjun had the arrow nocked; he walked to the window and drew it back to its full extension, his expression flat and unconcerned. Mind like water, mind like the moon, the warriors call it when they raise kazuh.

"You'll see the lantern stop flickering at the moment that Tebol hangs it from its hook on the wall," I said. Light flickered and then stabilized.

"Now," I said.

Dun Lidjun loosed; the arrow flew through the night. I

could more feel than hear the thunk of the arrow connecting.

"Lord and ladies, you will be amused to note that the arrow broke the screen at the same spot as did the arrow that murdered Minch."

Tebol slid the screen aside, and took a bow.

"And you'll also note," I went on, "that the arrow sticks in the wall rather near the spot where Minch was so pinned. If Tebol had not dropped to the floor the instant he hung the lantern, he would have been killed in the same way."

I turned to Demick. "I trust you find this experiment amusing, Lord Demick."

"Oh, very," he said, clapping his hands together twice. "So much so that I've ordered up a similar one. Two demonstrations, in fact."

He turned to Lord Orazhi. "I know my lord Orazhi doesn't like to have foreign archers running about his keep unaccompanied—as who would?—so I've asked that two of your men accompany my own Verden Verdunt to the rooms above, rooms that I understand are occupied by some of Lord Toshtai's party. With your permission?"

Across the courtyard, following some signal I didn't catch, the screen was pulled back in front of Minch's window. "I've also asked a servitor to replace the screen."

Demick reached his hands outside the window and clapped them together, three times, then twice.

An arrow hissed overhead.

Across the courtyard, the screen was slid aside. "Verden Verdunt is a talented archer, as well. As you can see, yet another arrow stands next to that of the vile murderer and the estimable Dun Lidjun."

He leaned out the window and clapped his hands once more. Just once.

In the courtyard below, two warriors were helping a third up onto a branch of a gnarled oak. Limber as a young boy, the third man climbed up into the tree until he was obscured from our view by the leaves.

The wind brought the twang of the bowstring.

"To save some time, I had Eren ven Horfen cache a bow and arrow in the oak tree." Demick turned to me. "You'll find that his arrow, too, has gone both through the hole in the screen and through the spot where some coward's arrow murdered the late, lamented Lord Minch."

Demick walked over to me and put his arm around my shoulders, one companion congratulating another one on a job well done.

"Kami Dan'Shir and I want you to know that all this entertainment has been, as we have intended, a diversion. We hope that you have found it amusing, as we resume our researches into the matter of the murder of Minch." He bowed deeply to the other lords and ladies, then smiled at me. There was genuine pleasure in his grin, if only simulated warmth. "Don't we, my dear Kami Dan'Shir?"

"Yes, Lord Demick," I said, the words ashes in my mouth.

I could have beaten my head against the rough bark of the oak, but that wouldn't have made me feel any better. Although it probably wouldn't have made me feel any worse. I can't say for sure; I didn't try it. I also didn't try cutting my own throat to see if, as they say, that's really not a bad way to die.

I guess it could be, but who reports on such things?

An idiot like me wasn't going to figure that out, either.

My father used to say that timing was everything, and I had been too damn quick, and for no good reason. Well, there was one good reason: I was in a hurry to show off a solution that would clear Arefai, for all the good it had done me, which was none.

The rough bark of the old oak gave ample purchase for fingers and toes, and a dip in the low branch hung just over the tips of my outstretched fingers.

I thought about getting Narantir to help me up and decided that I didn't need to trigger another sarcastic, caustic comment, so I stepped back three paces, then took three quick steps forward, leaped, caught the branch and pulled myself up, balancing easily. I would like to say that it was the thousands of hours practice I'd put in as an acrobat that made it all possible, but I don't need to lie for practice. Almost anybody could leap high enough to do what I'd just done, and anybody a bit taller than I was wouldn't have needed to leap. Anybody with something to stand on could have done it even more easily.

Whoever had done it, if anyone, hadn't left any indication of his passing, not here. The bark was unmarked, and while there was ample evidence of old limbs trimmed off by Lord Orazhi's groundskeepers over the years, all the stumplings were old; none of the tiny branches sprouting out from the larger ones were freshly broken.

I walked along the branch toward the base of the tree, then found the right footing to climb several branches up toward an opening in the leafy canopy above, then through the opening.

Demick had found a good spot. Above and below, the spreading canopy of green leaves shielded this place from view. The base of the branch was wide enough to stand on easily, and there were two other branches off the trunk where one could rest a foot to take a differently angled stance.

I mimicked drawing a bow. Plenty of room, and only a few windows were visible from here.

I wasn't the first person to find this place. The dark bark was broken off in places, revealing the lighter bark underneath. Some ripped leaves and a half-broken green twig showed where somebody, momentarily off-balance, had grabbed in panic for support. The only trouble was that there was no way to tell if some or all of the damage had been done by the murderer or by Demick's soldiers.

Too fast. I'd been too fast, too hasty. If I had inspected things properly, I would know. Not that I could tell what good it would do me. Arefai could climb a tree as well as anybody else.

I shook my head. No, that didn't make sense. I could see Arefai killing Minch, but not by stealth. And aiming through a window screen at a spot of light? Not Arefai; he wouldn't do it. While he was by no means a friend of the lower classes—there was a spot on my cheek he had once slapped in casual demonstration of that—Arefai wasn't the sort to casually kill somebody, hoping that it was the right somebody.

Edelfaule, on the other hand . . .

Edelfaule, on the other hand, would do me no good as a murderer. Even if he did it. Unless, of course, I could use that to some other purpose. Perhaps—

"Guards, guards!" The voice from below was firm and loud, but unpanicked. Rough voices called out orders.

"You there, out of that tree. You are surrounded," the voice said, lower enough in tone that I could tell that it was Penkil Ner Condigan.

I didn't move.

"It's just me, Kami Dan'Shir," I shouted. "I have Lord Orazhi's permission to have the run of the castle and grounds."

"Well, come on down now," Penkil Ner Condigan said.

"And be slow and careful as you do," a gruff voice said, in counterpoint.

I made my way back down and carefully lowered myself to where the bottom limb joined the trunk, then came down from there.

Penkil Ner Condigan stood there shaking his head in self-disgust, a half dozen warriors scattered around him, now sheathing swords and taking arrows off the nock. He spread his hands. "My apologies, Kami Dan'Shir; I thought I'd solved your mystery." He gestured at the tree. "I understand that Lord Demick has shown that the murderer could have fired from the tree. When I heard movement, I thought that he might still be up in there, hiding."

Hiding in the oak tree ever since the murder. That was the most stupid idea I'd ever—

Well, no, it wasn't. Anything was possible, and the old oak could have concealed half a dozen assassins in its upper branches.

A chill came over me. *And it still could.* Penkil Ner Condigan's theory wasn't insane, merely unlikely. Investigating it couldn't hurt anything, and if there was somebody up the tree, that somebody wasn't Arefai, and my head was off the block.

I nodded. "You there, Lord Warrior—Penkil Ner Condigan may have an idea here. Which of your men is best at tree climbing?"

The warrior, a barrel-chested bear of a man in leather and bone armor that had been burnished until it almost glowed, laughed, and not pleasantly. "I don't know, and wouldn't ask. Tree climbing is an occupation of boys and fruitpickers. My warriors are neither. You are, so I understand it, a discoverer." He jerked his thumb at the tree. "Discover."

There are things that I've enjoyed more than climbing up, high into an old oak tree, looking for a murderer. But, since nobody was there, there's never been anything I've done that's been more pointless.

Lord Edelfaule was kind enough to join our group high in the wizard's tower.

Dun Lidjun was repeating—for the sixteenth time, I believe—his observation that the flight of an arrow was an arc, not a straight line, and that a good bowman often had to make sure that the arc traveled through one point or another before hitting its target.

"Classic hunting problem in the woods, after all. You have a straight shot at a flying gander, but you know that the arrow is going to rise after it leaves the bow, so you see with your mind not only the beginning and end of it all, but the path that it might take. Or perhaps you don't pull the arrow all the way back, and select a broader arc that will carry your arrow above a tree limb, or exchange your bow for one with a stronger pull that will send the arrow in a flatter arc. The arrow could have been shot out of there, or from above, or from the tree."

The old man shook his head. "All you had to do was ask, instead of assuming that you know everything, simply because you're a dan'shir." There was more of sadness than anger in his voice. "I've admired your audacity, boy, in the time that you faced me with a sword in your hand, in the time that you exposed the murderer of Felkoi, but audacity has its place, and its place is not to be spread all over, like jelly on a slice of bread."

Narantir chuckled. "I knew it would all end badly," he said. "You confuse authority with knowledge. Something that, of course, no members of our beloved ruling class have ever done, but that's why they are lords and ladies and you're but a bourgeois."

There was a knock on the door. Before an invitation to enter, the door swung open to reveal Edelfaule, a thin smile on his almost lipless face.

"Well, I've just failed," he said. "After spending most of the last hour trying to have Father give me your head for my wall, he finally broke down and said no." He reached out a long, slim finger and tapped me on the chest. "You embarrassed me nicely with your little demonstration in Den Oroshtai, you petty little bourgeois, but that was with money, something your kind knows far too much about.

"This was a matter of blood and honor, something you'd know nothing about, Kami Dan'Shir, eh?"

For a moment, for just a moment, I almost gave it up. Enough bowing and begging, enough mewling and groveling. I'd grab Edelfaule by the throat and squeeze, squeeze hard with hands strengthened by years of swinging from a trapeze, from years of lifting and hauling, and I'd squeeze until his blood ran between my fingers.

No, that's not what I would do. Even if Edelfaule didn't block me, Dun Lidjun stood behind me, and the old warrior could have me chopped into tiny pieces before my fingers touched his neck.

"I bid you a goodnight, useless dan'shir." With one hand, Edelfaule smoothed down the already smooth front of his robes and smiled as he turned and walked away.

Narantir tilted his head to one side. "I don't suppose you want to invite Lord Dun Lidjun to fire an arrow from Edelfaule's room, would you?"

* * *

I don't suppose that stars really snicker, although maybe there's times that they should.

Idiot, idiot, idiot, a billion stars blinked.

Toss left catch left, toss right, catch right. Juggling didn't help.

You stupid idiot, I thought, *you fell for it.*

Lord Toshtai has silently, like loose-tongued Spennymore of legend, persuaded you to trade your ox for a magic plow. And in the morning, the bones of the ox lie chewed and white on the ground, and the magic plow has become an ordinary piece of wood and iron, no more capable of moving around on its own than another piece of wood and iron.

The world doesn't care a fig for Kami Dan'Shir; it never has and it never will. And nobody in Den Oroshtai did, either.

It all began to fall into place.

I was a freden, a throw-weight.

The marriage of Arefai and ViKay threatened too close an alliance of Den Oroshtai and Glen Derenai. The combination of the large armies of Lord Orazhi, the devious cleverness of Lord Toshtai, and the field marshallship of Dun Lidjun was too much of a threat for Patrice and the Agami lords to stand still for. They probably would have redeployed their forces and marched on Den Oroshtai, but that would have left them vulnerable in the north, and they couldn't have that.

Where brute force couldn't serve, conspiracy would have to. Minch had been sent to interfere with the marriage, paid with a sword that would declare him much more than a minor lord. In return, he was to embarrass Arefai, as he had tried to do at the hunt. Members of our beloved ruling class are bloody-minded, even when it comes to their own selves. Minch was willing to risk being killed in a duel where, upon examination, it would be shown he hadn't given proper offense, which would shame Arefai.

Perhaps, just perhaps, Minch even expected to be murdered.

Now turn to Lord Toshtai, the most subtle and clever of men. He didn't know what Demick and Minch would try, but he expected something.

So, Lord Toshtai: bring along this new dan'shir, and have your idiot son Arefai prepare the dan'shir's image of great competence at anything and everything. Disposable like a peasant, but accorded enough respect and honor that, when things get hot, when the road gets tiring, when your idiot son kills a man and is in danger of being thoroughly disgraced, you throw all the responsibility and attention away with the dan'shir freden.

Nicely done, Lord Toshtai. And all you had to do was treat me with just a little lenience, just a touch of gentleness.

Nicely, nicely done.

A keep is made for keeping people out, not in.

All I'd have to do is find a length of rope, tie a loop around a battlement after a patrol had passed, then slide down the rope and be gone. The gold I'd won from the late, lamented Minch could keep me housed and fed for years, assuming I could find a way to break it down into more credible money. I couldn't rejoin my father's troop, but the north was full of intinerant acrobats; I could find work and hide among them.

Of course, my sleeping quarters here would be swept for a loose hair or bitten toenail, and Narantir could and would use that to help the horsemen of Glen Derenai track me down. I'd be lucky to escape for a day or two.

Loose hair . . . wait a minute.

I ran back up to the workroom at the top of the wizard's tower and threw the door open.

I woke up to a cold cloth slapping my face and Tebol's angular face looking down at me. "Can you hear me, Kami Dan'Shir?"

"Nicely done, Kami Dan'Shir," Narantir said, from off to one side. "Did anybody ever tell you never to bother a sleeping wizard?" The wizard's voice seemed to come from too high up; I looked over and found him stretched out in a net hammock suspended from two hooks on an overhead beam. It looked deucedly uncomfortable, but not nearly as uncomfortable as being hit, hard, by a wizard's spell.

"What happened?" I asked, although the fool words came out as a triple grunt.

Tebol felt at a pulse, then nodded and stood. "You'll be fine in a moment. But Narantir's correct; you really should make a habit of knocking before you enter."

I have, from time to time, truthfully claimed to be unheroic. That was before, lying on the cold stone floor, having been hit by a wizard's spell, I rolled to my belly and managed to rise to my hands and knees. Dapucet, the Power that holds the world together, exercises no more strength than I did as I rose first to my knees and then to my feet, the world spinning gently under them.

"That's not important now," I said with all the force available, the words coming out as a harsh whisper. "You said that there was no magic used in Minch's room," I said. "How about in Demick's?"

"Demick's?"

I nodded. "That was the part of it that bothered me. It wasn't impossible that somebody could aim at the carrier of a lantern through the window screen. But how would Demick or whoever he had do it possibly know that Minch was hanging his lantern by himself? It could have been one of the castle servitors, warming his bedding for the night or laying out sleeping clothes."

Narantir shrugged. "Which would do as well, assuming that Demick's purpose was to dishonor Arefai, no?"

"No. Not if Demick didn't know where Arefai was, too. If, say, Arefai was sitting with Lady Estrer and Lord Orazhi, the whole plan would fall through, and point an accusing finger toward Patrice and Demick. Demick had to know both where Arefai and Minch were and that Arefai was alone. For Arefai, a spy would do, perhaps— but for Minch? To be sure that it was he who was holding a lantern? How could a spy report quickly enough? Demick must have had another way."

"Of *course*." Narantir spread his hands. "A direction spell. The sort dishonorable hunters use, except made specific. Not the most difficult application of the Law of Synechdoche; whole to part, and part to whole."

Tebol nodded, quickly. "A piece of skin perhaps, or— better—hair." He turned to me. "Skin and blood change too quickly when they're separated from their owner, but hair and nails remain the same."

He pulled down a book from a shelf and brought it over to a table. He muttered a quick cantrip and touched his finger to the tip of an unlit candle; it flared too brightly, casting dark shadows all around the room. "I haven't done this sort of thing since I was an apprentice, but it should leave some effluence. Narantir?"

The fat wizard, despite himself, had gotten interested. "It should reek of it."

Tebol grunted. "I don't like sniffing around doorways, but . . . so-be-it."

I snorted. "I don't know that it exactly calls for sniffing around doorways."

"If you don't know, then shhh."

Tebol had brought out a rack of vials and set it on the workbench. Narantir took a small silver spoon and scooped out some white powder into a ceramic mortar. He added some of a red powder, and then a black one, carefully washing the spoon, then passing it through the flame instead of drying it.

Narantir took something that looked like a many-spiked ball on a stick down from a shelf and whirled it around the mortar, muttering a quick cantrip. "Basic allergenics," he said. "Come this way."

I held up a hand. "Now, wait one moment, if you please. The last time I helped out in an experiment, you turned me into a sword, and I didn't like that much. It hurt. Are you telling me this won't?"

Narantir chuckled. "No, I'm promising it will hurt you, precisely as much as if you sniffed three kinds of pepper up your nose. But it'll also make you so allergic to synechdochal directional magic that, well, you'll itch uncontrollably for hours if you come in contact with any of it."

I held up a hand. "Then why don't one of you take it?"

"Because we're wizards, you young idiot. No wizard is going to make himself allergic to magic." He held out the vial. "And it does so call for sniffing around doorways. If that sort of spell was used in Lord Demick's rooms, then all you need to do is take a hefty sniff of this, then sniff around the edge of his door, and you'll know. Believe me, with hives the size of a plover's egg all over your body, you'll know."

He tossed the vial high into the air. Somebody who had spent years as a juggler couldn't help but catch it.

There were guards, of course, on at both ends of the floor where Lord Demick's rooms were; members of our beloved ruling class always travel with their own, no matter how serious a safe conduct they travel under. It's always possible that some other lord would like to complicate the issue by inserting an assassin or two, letting the local lord take the blame for a murder . . .

Which, of course, was always a possibility for Minch. The only trouble was, it was pretty clear what the result was from Minch's death, and who would benefit.

The guards weren't eager to let anybody in, since it was the hour of the lion, and his lordship had officially retired for the evening. But I was the Historical Master Dan'Shir, and Demick had volunteered to aid me in my investigation and had made it clear to both me and them that he would rather enjoy gloating some more, so they agreed to let me into the corridor and speak to his valet, after a quick search.

Which, of course, immediately turned up the vial.

The guard's face was flat and expressionless. "I wouldn't suppose this to be poison," he said, holding it out toward me.

I forced a laugh. "If it was," I said, accepting it and pulling off the top, "would I do this?"

I tilted back the vial and inhaled sharply.

16
A Nose Full of Pepper, a Chat, a Treat, a Threat, and Other Delights and Sorrows

IT WOULD BE really nice if you could always count on wizards to lie about everything, but that would make life too easy.

Whatever else was in there, I could feel the fire of red pepper, the heat of white pepper, and the burn of black pepper not only in my nostrils, but throughout my entire head. It felt like the front of my face was going to fall off and shatter on the floor. Which would have been a good trick, considering that the floor was covered with a deep red ankle-thick Pemish carpet.

"Well, I suppose it isn't poison," the guard said. "Normally, at least in Patrice, we demonstrate that we know a substance not to be poison by putting a small sample of it in our mouths, not the whole lot of it up our nose." He laughed as he rapped on the door three times, then twice, then three times again.

Tears rolling down my cheeks, I nodded. "I thank you for the advice, Lord Warrior."

The door opened only about a headswidth, with a waft of thick, musty perfume, and a woman's face peeked out. Her skin was the color of warm cream, her lips as red as fresh blood. I didn't recognize her, although that wasn't surprising; I wasn't familiar with Lord Demick's concubines.

"What is it, dear Solan der Bereden?" she asked.

"Kami Dan'Shir to see Lord Demick, if his lordship is up and around."

She teased him with a crooked smile, and for a moment caught her pink tongue in bone-white teeth. "Oh, he's very much awake. I'll see if he wishes to see the dan'shir."

The door closed, then opened a moment later, and she ushered me in.

Lord Demick, a white silk robe tied loosely about him, rose from his cushions to greet me, gesturing at the other concubine to stay where she was, which was over by a rack of essences and a knee-height heating table. She was a lovely willowy blond woman dressed in some wisps of translucent silk belted tightly at her slim waist, her head tilted to one side, almond eyes watching me too steadily.

"You might pour Kami Dan'Shir some essence, VedaNa," he said. "Perhaps the Apricot Sunrise?" He gestured me to a seat on cushions near the window.

"Plain water would be perfect, Lord Demick," I said, trying to blink back tears. Someday, somehow, I will avenge myself on Narantir; every time he works magic when I'm around, I hurt.

I don't know how she did it; I guess either she had it ready for another purpose or perhaps there's more kazuh to the art of concubine than is commonly acknowledged, but VedaNa had a cold mug of water in my hands before I was seated. I drained it in one long swallow. It helped a lot, although my nose still burned with a distant fire.

I lowered the mug to see Demick smiling at me. "I take it you're here to discuss the progress of our investigation," he said.

No, I'm here to see if you used magic to direct the arrow that killed Minch, I didn't say. It would be worth a few hives to be able to prove that it was Demick, or at least to cast enough blame in his direction to remove enough from Arefai to get my head off the block. The only trouble was that the itching that Narantir had promised me wasn't coming on. Either this was some sort of wizard's prank, or no such spell had been used around here.

"I had an idea, Kami Dan'Shir," he said. "Perhaps one even cleverer than your notion that I had my dear friend Minch killed." His eyes never leaving mine, he held out a hand to receive a flask of warmed essence from the black-haired concubine.

I bowed. "I am, of course, interested, Lord Demick."

He gestured at the doorway. "I notice that Minch was near the speaking tube when the cowardly murderer put an arrow through his screen and into him." He scowled. "I'm afraid I must admit to being unfond of such things—we have no such in Patrice, I can assure you—but Lord Orazhi finds them useful. It occurs to me that it's possible somebody called him to the speaking tube, at which time a waiting confederate fired the arrow."

That explanation posed a few problems, the best one of which was that one of the easier places for the confederate to shoot from was the room above Demick's, which was easily available to Arefai.

"Let's experiment," I started to say, then stopped myself. No, embarrassing Demick in private wasn't likely to be a safe move. "I mean, there seems to me to be a basic problem with that, Lord." I rose and walked to where the end of the speaking tube projected from the wall, Demick by my side. This speaking tube terminated in a sculpture of a horse's head, again plugged by a carving of an apple. Personally, I would have found it more amusing had Lord Demick been forced to speak into the other end of a horse, but he probably didn't use the speaking tube himself, anyway.

"You'll note," I said, "that the tube is plugged from this end." I pulled the plug and stuck my ear to the horse's mouth.

Far off in the distance I could hear a swishing, like that of a broom on stone. "Otherwise, it could be used by the servants to spy on our—on the occupants of the rooms." Never mind that servants did—had to—do some spying on our beloved ruling class in order to anticipate their de-

223

mands; the point still stood. The speaking tubes were a way of talking down, not up.

I replaced the plug, and patted at the bronze sculpture. "With all respect, I doubt that it would be possible for anyone to have called Lord Minch to the speaking tube." I shrugged. "Besides, that would make it a conspiracy to murder Minch, and not the act of just one person."

"Hmmm . . . we can't have that."

No, we couldn't. The notion that Arefai had finally lost his temper with Minch and killed him was one thing; that two or more from Den Oroshtai had conspired to commit a murder was beyond belief. Shaming of Lord Toshtai's son would subtly shift power and influence to Demick; uncovering a shameful conspiracy between Den Oroshtai and Glen Derenai would force Toshtai and Orazhi into a direct conflict with Patrice, and far too many heads would fly.

No. If Minch was so much trouble, Lord Toshtai would have had Dun Lidjun or somebody challenge him, not commit a stealthy murder. Nobody would believe Toshtai capable of tolerating a conspiracy to murder, which would mean that nobody would, in the long run, believe that Arefai had shamed himself by committing said murder.

If I wasn't in the middle of it, I would have found it funny: two enemies with the common purpose of seeing that their enmity not get out of hand.

Perhaps Demick found the notion as amusing; his lips twisted. "Think on it, Kami Dan'Shir. I'm sure you'll find a way to vex the murderer yet."

My nose still burning from the pepper, no trace of an itch anywhere on my body, I left and headed for bed, none the wiser and more than a little confused.

She came to me that night, as I had in the back of my head wondered if she would. I opened an eye to see her slip in through the barely opened door—the door to my room squeaked if it was opened a fraction more; I wondered if she had all the squeaks in the keep memorized—and feel at the mouth of my own speaking tube before walking to my bedding and quickly dropping her robes to the floor before slipping under the thin blanket.

She lay in my arms, warm and soft on the surface, hard and strong below. I wouldn't have been surprised if she could have broken me with her legs wrapped about my hips; for a moment, it had felt as if she might.

I sighed. "I would love to know why we're doing this."

She laughed as she shifted position slightly so that I could kiss her behind the right ear. She smelled of rose and lemon. "For someone who comports himself with such . . . need, such urgency, you ask too many questions. I would have thought it obvious." She rolled closer to me, her breast rubbing gently against my chest, one hand gently stroking my back near the base of my spine.

"It isn't. And I doubt that there's only one reason."

"A way to persuade you, perhaps, to befriend Arefai. He needs you, and I hope that you'll—"

"Find a way to clear him of suspicion?" There was something perverse about discussing this with ViKay naked in my arms, but there was also something perverse in the first place about bedding the wife-to-be of the nearest thing I had to a friend in our beloved ruling class. I guess perversion doesn't bother me.

"I hope so." I sighed. "Arefai didn't do it. It's not his way. To lop off Minch's fool head in front of witnesses, sure; but to murder him in the dark? To lie in wait for him?"

No, that wasn't the way of somebody who would fish by having trout practically thrown to him. Forget matters of honor; our beloved ruling class has such a strange sense of honor that it can pull them in any direction. It was a matter of character and personality, and that just wasn't in Arefai's. He wasn't the brightest fellow in the world, but he was direct and forthright, not skulking.

"You had best hope so," she said, her voice light and breezy in my ear. "With this cloth of misgivings wrapped so tightly around him, my father will surely put off the wedding until it is cleared."

She reached down and cupped my testicles in her palm. Well, "cupped" isn't quite right. "Gripped" is better. She was not ungentle, but her grip was not unfirm, and I was not unapprehensive, nor uneager for her to let go. I was also not unmotionless, and had no intention of being unagreeable, or abandoning the unassertiveness of double negatives until she let go, something I was not unwilling for her to do at any moment.

"Lady . . ."

"And I will be the bride of Lord Arefai of Den Oroshtai, understood?" she said, a taste of iron and steel in her voice.

I wasn't disposed to argue, not with her hand there.

"It would ruin my life were we not to marry," she went on, "and I would find a ruined life easily dispensed with, as disposable as I would find the life of a dan'shir who would not or could not do his job, as easy as I would find it to pass a truth spell when I swore that the dan'shir, but a bourgeois, had me, over and over again, under the roof of my father."

She released my testicles and slipped both arms around my neck so quickly and sinuously that I was glad it was her arms and not her hands that were about my neck.

"Now, rest for a short while, while you try to figure out who killed that horrible Minch, and how you're going to clear my Arefai." She laid her head gently on my chest.

"Is there anything else you'd like me to think over, Lady?"

"Oh, of course," she said, body pressed closely to mine, her breath warm in my ear. "You must decide how you want me next, my Kami Dan'Shir."

I woke before dawn, alone, traces of honey-orange and roses along with more robust scents in my blankets. It was dark out, but it felt like the hour of the dragon, the hour when all good D'Shaians are safely asleep.

An hour when Kami Dan'Shir gets to realize what an idiot he is, was, and will be. One more day before the scheduled wedding, and the only thing I knew was that

Arefai had better not have done it and Demick hadn't done it. But how was it done? Could the how tell me who?

I dressed, got my juggling sack, and went down to the grounds, nodding to an occasional guard. Nobody stopped me or tried to engage me in conversation. I didn't quite blame them.

Above the stars snickered, while below torches flickered. The gardens, green and red and orange and blue and yellow in the daytime, were black and gray in the dark, inky leaves hanging threateningly above.

When in doubt, juggle.

It's not the beginning of wisdom; perhaps it does no good, but it can hardly do any harm. I found my concealed spot in the garden and took out three balls.

Keep it simple. A simple shower. Catch left, throw right, catch right, throw left, catch left, throw right, catch right, throw left, and all the while forget about that extra ball in the air that's looping down toward your throwing hand. All you have to do is handle one ball at a time, but you have to do it well, whether it's the solid catch or the precise throw. Never toss it away just to get rid of it.

Who can shoot through a paper screen?

Ressi the All Seeing could have done it, but the Powers don't involve themselves in the way of mortals, and even if it was one of them, I was not going to be able to present that as a workable solution. Wives who blamed an untimely pregnancy on Spennymore were traditionally flogged to death, as were shepherds who accused Evva Ugly Hands of causing a sheep shortfall. I didn't know if dan'shirs were to be punished the same way, but I also didn't know of anybody who had escaped punishment for anything by attributing it to a Power.

Who benefited?

Demick and Patrice, surely, and Demick's Agami allies, benefited from the accusation. Not anyone loyal in Den Oroshtai or Glen Derenai, except perhaps Edelfaule? No, that didn't make sense. Edelfaule was the older brother, in line to be lord. Unless, of course, Lord Toshtai passed him by to name his brother, but there was no hint of that.

Which there wouldn't be, of course. Toshtai wouldn't hint at such a thing, regardless of his intention.

Very well: assume, for the moment, that Edelfaule was the murderer. How much good would it do me to reveal that, even with proof?

Who hated Minch?

Who didn't? That wouldn't do any good.

Who would want to put me in this position? How can I get back at him?

How to find the real murderer, and blame him to let me out of this . . . Or, failing that, just to find somebody, preferably some member of our beloved ruling class, who would do. But the inconsiderate swine wouldn't cooperate. It was as though the whole purpose of this was to ruin me. Now that was ridiculous.

Come on, Kami Dan'Shir—it was unlikely beyond imagining that all this was to embarrass and discredit me. People, even members of our beloved ruling class, didn't set up elaborate schemes and plans involving possible murders just to make my life difficult. Men and women kill for reasons more personal, more intimate, than to cause me chagrin.

Sometimes kazuh feels like a well-stroked bassskin: it hums in the brain, its sound low but powerful and only in my head, not in my ears.

It hummed for me then, and it all was clear. Both the why and the how. There were two bags in the air in this problem, and I had been pretending they had been one and the same. No, of course not. Two separate problems, with separate solutions.

That was the lesson of juggling: keep one thing in mind at one time. Don't worry about the other juggling sacks rising and falling. There was merely one to be caught, or one to be thrown, and that was it. There would be time enough later for the rest.

Unless . . . I would need Dun Lidjun, and the wizard.

17

Yet a Final Demonstration, a Reward, a Wedding, and Other Rituals Both Sincere and False

THIS TIME, I knocked on the door at the top of the long winding stone staircase. Not gently.

"Wake up, if you please, Narantir," I said, then knocked again, louder.

Dun Lidjun looked old and wan in the morning, as though it took some time to apply the normal expression of agelessness and ancient wisdom to his face. His lips worked silently just for a moment. Then: "I will open it for you, if need be," he said.

It is not often that a dan'shir has a kazuh Warrior waiting his command. It is important to remember that the kazuh Warrior is not merely an object, to be moved about like a pinbone on a single-bone draughts board; the kazuh Warrior, or the bourgeois servitor, or the middle-class vegetable seller, or the dirt-footed peasant, is a person, and to respect that personhood must be the private honor and obligation of the dan'shir, even if it is not that of our beloved ruling class.

So I said, "Prepare yourself, if you please, Lord Dun Lidjun, but do nothing."

It was a treat to watch the weariness slide away from his old frame, like a drop of water skittering and vanishing on a hot skillet. The skin around his eyes stopped sagging,

and instead of forcing himself to stand upright, as though
he had stuck a pole up his back passage, he stood easily,
his feet not merely touching the ground, but standing sol-
idly as though he was the peak of a mountain, unmovable
by mortals.

I knocked again. "Wake up, Narantir; it's the hour of the
cock, and the day calls you."

The door creaked open, and Narantir stood there, rubbing at his eyes. "I take it the spell worked?"

"Yes."

"And . . .?"

"And I itched not at all, and I can demonstrate how
Minch was murdered, and who the murderer was, and
why," I said. "I just need to go over his room once more,
to prepare."

Minch's room was still dark in the distant, gray early
morning light. Figure that the sun wouldn't be high
enough to light it directly until well into the hour of the
hare, although perhaps not quite the hour of the horse.

Harsh radiance flared from Narantir's light gem as he
placed it in the lantern niche.

Bow, headless arrow, broadheaded arrow, strong will,
relentless hatred.

That was all it was.

"It's simple," I said, "once you know who the murderer
was, and what his objective was." I sighed. "Narantir, you
wouldn't happen to have a spell that will detect conspiracy, would you? It would be nice to know who else was
in on it."

It would be nice to be able to lay it on Demick's door,
but that wouldn't be necessary. I knew who could be held
responsible, and could identify him without fear of retribu-
tion.

Narantir and Tebol laughed, Tebol in his own merry
way, Narantir so hard that tears ran down his cheeks and
into his beard.

Dun Lidjun was less amused than I was, and I wasn't

amused at all. "What, may one ask, is so wretchedly amusing?"

Narantir, still laughing, pointed at the bright, shining gem. "It was a spell that Tebol and I invented, back when we were just apprentices. It makes a garnet glow in the presence of conspiracy." He stared for a moment at the wall. "A perpetual light in a D'Shaian keep, no?"

Dun Lidjun cracked a smile. "I'll go arrange the audience."

Members of our beloved ruling class don't stint themselves, or each other; there was enough room in the sitting room of Minch's suite for the lot of them. The three major lords, Toshtai, Orazhi, and Demick, were seated at the far end of the room in chairs that had been brought in for the occasion.

ViKay, having exchanged the sort of pleasantries with me suitable for yesterday's placques partner, had seated herself behind her father. If I looked closely, I could see the tension in her shoulders and neck. She was wondering if she would have to make good her threat.

Arefai stood alone, by the wall, watching me closely, perhaps too closely, or perhaps not. Perhaps he was looking for some sign of his redemption in my eyes. The idiot. Did he think that I'd call them all in to embarrass his father by naming him a murderer?

To one side of him, Lady Estrer kept her eyes on the rest of the crowd, one hand hidden in the folds of her robes, as though she could intercept an attack on Arefai with a hidden dagger there.

Edelfaule's eyes were filled with intelligence, but not a trace of liking, or even tolerance.

Toshtai, alone among the nobles of Den Oroshtai, watched me with interest, and only interest. His broad, fat face betrayed no sense of having been woken or hurried, although I knew from his habits that he had been both. His hair was freshly oiled and pulled back into a warrior's queue, and his morning robes were the usual cheery yellow.

Orazhi smiled. "I take it that you have asked that we put off our breakfast for more than some sort of . . . experiment, Kami Dan'Shir," he said.

I looked from face to face. There wasn't a pale, sweaty one among them.

"Oh, quite, Lord Orazhi," I said. "I'm here to expose the murderer, to frustrate his attempt to blame good Lord Arefai for something he would never do, something he could never do."

I hoped that would keep ViKay quiet, at least for the time being. A simple demonstration would not be enough because—

Enough, Kami Dan'Shir, my kazuh whispered to me, as though it was its own person instead of an intensification and expression of my own.

There is one ball in the air, ripe for the catching. Catch it before you think of the next.

"I'd demonstrate how it was done, except that's not good enough," I said. "There are things about this brave murder that I didn't understand."

"Brave murder?" Demick lunged for the bait. "I find myself unfond of shtoi comments about a shot in the dark."

I bowed deeply. "As well you should, Lord Demick. I spoke precisely." I picked up Minch's lax bow and string, and handed it to Dun Lidjun. "The problem was always the screen," I said, walking to the window screen and sliding it out of the way. "It's translucent, but not transparent. Enough to provide some privacy, without locking light out of the room; and, placed a hand's span from the window, it lets in cool air without the clacking of shutters."

It still had the one hole. "But why shoot through it?"

"Because," Demick said, "Minch was on the other side of it, not standing in front of it."

I shook my head. "How was the murderer to know where Minch was? The door was locked, and Minch could have as easily been standing on one side or another of the lamp as he hung it, if that's how the murderer located him.

"But, even so: imagine, you are a murderer sitting, say,

in the tree from which Verden Verdunt was kind enough to fire a bowshot last evening. How do you know when Minch will come along and hang the lamp? Do you sit there, up in a tree for hours, waiting for a momentary flicker of light and then hope that your aim will be true?" I shook my head. "No. You'd have to know more."

I went to the corner where Minch's arrows still lay scattered and took up two, one with a killing broadhead, another headless, and tapped them together.

I nodded to Dun Lidjun, who shrugged out of his robes, and stood on the carpeted floor in blousy pantaloons and sandals. He seemed somehow smaller without his robes, and the hair on his pale chest was thin and white, but beneath age-wrinkled skin, his muscles still moved under his control, and only his control.

He strung the bow in one smooth motion, and held it out in front of him, then held out a hand for an arrow.

I passed him the headless one; Dun Lidjun quickly nocked it, then drew it back, propping the blunt tip on the back of the bow. It held the bent bow, keeping it bent.

I handed the old warrior the remaining arrow, which he nocked ever so gently, its broad flat head lying on the bow, motionless, as Dun Lidjun held the backwards bow out in front of him, the arc of the bow curved away from him, the nocked arrow pointing toward his own chest. If the blunt arrow were to suddenly be gone, the broadhead would pierce the old warrior's chest.

"Raise it, if you please, Lord Dun Lidjun," I said. "We wouldn't want to have an accident."

Moving slowly, relentlessly, Dun Lidjun raised the bow, the arrow now poised to fire directly over his head.

"Thank you, Lord Dun Lidjun. Just hold it there for a moment." I turned to the crowd, moving slowly. Always watch the audience.

"You see, my Lords and Ladies, Minch wanted very much to embarrass Arefai, to interfere with the wedding of Lord Arefai and Lady ViKay. He tried first to needle him into overreacting and provoking a duel, and then to trick Arefai into making a wrongful accusation against himself."

I shook my head. "It was always the first part that bothered me. Lord Dun Lidjun, could Minch have thought to take Arefai in a swordfight?"

Dun Lidjun didn't answer immediately. "I know you would like me to say no, Kami Dan'Shir, but I cannot quite. It's enough for me to say that Minch would have had to have a much higher opinion of his own abilities than I ever did."

I nodded. "And I thank you again, Lord Dun Lidjun. One more question: with a naked sword in his hand, and Arefai's back to him, could Minch have killed Arefai as long as you were close by?"

"No." Dun Lidjun smiled. "Never."

"Quite. Minch didn't think he could take on Arefai, but as a loyal noble of Merth's Bridge, he was willing to—*now*."

All eyes were on me, but they were drawn to the wall where the arrow from the bow now quivered, half a man's height above the spot where the arrow that had killed Minch had been. Dun Lidjun reached up and drew it from the wall, then tucked it under his own arm.

"Of course, in reality, at this moment during the murder, the arrow had penetrated Lord Minch, and stuck out his back, rather than being nicely tucked under his arm, the way Lord Dun Lidjun has done." Dun Lidjun pressed a bowtip against the floor, releasing the bowstring from the other tip with his thumb, then threw the bow toward the corner where the rest of the bow and arrows lay scattered.

Only two things remained. The headless arrow lay on the floor; Dun Lidjun simply reached out a foot and swept it toward the corner.

"And the last, Lord Dun Lidjun, if you please." Dun Lidjun grabbed the feathered end of arrow in his hands and ran backwards toward the wall, thudding hard into it.

He stood for a moment like Minch had, then stepped away from the wall, as Minch had not been able to.

I forced a laugh. "Minch had failed, and had every chance of failing to interfere with the marriage of Lord Arefai and Lady ViKay. With Dun Lidjun within a swordslength of Arefai, brute force would fail. With Kami Dan'Shir to point out traps and puzzles ahead, Minch's chicanery would fail . . ."

Always end with a flourish, my father used to say. I let silence fall for a full two beats before I bowed to the assemblage, and said, ". . . as it has."

Lord Orazhi was on his feet, clapping his hands together hard. "Wonderful, Kami Dan'Shir!" he said. "I see what you mean about brave murder, eh? How did you ever think about such a remarkable . . . contrivance for firing the bow?"

Well, Lord, it's awfully similar to one of the ways I used to rig a trigger for a snare for rabbits, when I was poaching. "Way of the Dan'Shir, Lord."

"Which is a brilliant way, young Historical Master Dan'Shir. Minch was—"

"Wait." Demick held up a hand. "How about the hole in the screen?"

It's not usually safe to laugh at a member of our beloved ruling class, and it's never likely to make one look kindly on you, but I was safe here and now, and Lord Demick was never likely to look at me with any kindness, so I let myself chuckle.

"Why, that's simple, Lord Demick," I said, picking up a loose arrow from the pile in the corner and walking to the screen, "so much so that I didn't even see the need to explain that anybody can take an arrow and put a hole in a piece of paper," I said, doing just that.

"Indeed, indeed they can." Orazhi's laugh was just this side of hysterical. "I am in your debt, Kami Dan'Shir. What can Glen Derenai do to repay it?" He spread his hands. "A rise to nobility? Horses, swords, money? What can I do?"

"I've no need for anything of the sort, Lord," I said, shaking my head, then bowing it deeply. "Although there is one great service you can do for me, Lord Orazhi, impertinent though it would be for me to ask, so much so that I must ask forgiveness in advance."

Or I'll keep my mouth tightly shut.

Toshtai spoke up for the first time. "Impertinence will surely be forgiven, now of all times."

Orazhi nodded. "Of course, of course. Ask. I'm too old and wise to guarantee I'll grant a request before I've heard it, but I'd be an ungrateful wretch if I wouldn't promise you that you may speak it without penalty, and I am not an ungrateful wretch, and do so promise."

There was no ambiguity in that, but I chose my words carefully anyway. "Lord Arefai and Lady ViKay were due to be married tomorrow, in the hour of the octopus."

Orazhi frowned. "You have some . . . objection to that, Kami Dan'Shir?"

"Yes. Marry them today, this noon, in the hour of the horse. Before something else goes wrong," I said, not quite daring to look at Demick, knowing that he would take my point.

Orazhi smiled and bowed as though to an equal. "It shall be as you say, Kami Dan'Shir."

Arefai was at my elbow, although I hadn't seen him walk over. A fat tear had welled up in his right eye, and as he opened his mouth to speak, it slid down his face to become lost in his beard.

"You will stand with me," he said, "a sword through your belt, as I am married, Kami Dan'Shir, as a valued friend and companion, to whom I owe both my honor and my appearance of honor. You will have the prerogative, privilege, and honor of sampling the wedding essence, to be sure of its suitability for the ceremony, and I will trust in your judgment."

Just as I've had the pleasure of sampling the bride, I didn't say.

"I am deeply honored, Lord Arefai," sounded so much safer.

Hypocrisy is the way of our beloved ruling class, which is one of the reasons I enjoyed being in the wedding party. Look, there are advantages to hanging out with nobility—I've found that I eat better, and they're often nice enough to arrange to get one of themselves murdered for my entertainment, and they do sleep between softer, cleaner sheets and alone less often.

The only trouble with the whole thing was trying to stop myself from giggling.

Distant hints of raspberry and fire still on my tongue, I stood between Edelfaule and Toshtai as Arefai and his bride knelt before Lord Orazhi, reflecting that it's not often that a bourgeois gets to stand while nobles kneel. It was a treat to watch them kneeling in the dirt that careful servitors had spread across the cloth that now covered one end of the Great Hall; I don't often get to see plain dirt and our beloved ruling class mix. I'm told that the dirt symbolizes the soil that, in the long run, supports us all.

Me, I would have thought it more appropriate if they'd each knelt on a peasant.

Arefai was arrayed in black, red, and green. Somebody had told me what the black and green symbolized, but I've forgotten: the red was, as usual, for blood, in this case the blood of those who would endanger his new bride, which Arefai was promising to shed. Our beloved ruling class does a lot of that.

ViKay's robes were of that red-gold shading we call *surivhan* in Old Shai: it's the red-gold of a clear summer sunrise, just at the moment that the top limb of the sun breaks above the water of the Eter Enothien, shaded from an almost pure golden haze on the top to a rich dark crimson at the bottom. It symbolized beginnings, and passions, and dedication, but I liked it mainly because it was pretty to look at.

Her hair, not a strand out of place, was bound behind her in her familiar knot, and fastened there with three long bone needles. Perversely, it bothered me that the two times I'd been with ViKay, she had let down her own hair; I'd never had the chance.

"As her father, I offer my daughter to you, warranting her to be untouched and pure," Orazhi said, with what I hope was easy disingenuousness. I can't imagine that he had managed to hang onto Glen Derenai without more insight into behavior than his speech indicated. "As her lord, I bring her to you only after warranting that you have proven yourself worthy—"

By not being idiot enough to kill Minch, I interjected mentally.

"—in the search for game for the table, and I expect that you will prove yourself worthy should you be required to defend her person or honor. I put it to this company that should anyone know of a blemish or blur on your honor, I put it to him to step forward now." He raised one hand to his forehead and turned from side to side, ritualistically searching for some fool who would open his mouth at the wrong time.

This one was easy. I could remain silent in good faith instead of remaining silent in bad faith.

"And I put it to this company that should anyone challenge my warrant of my daughter's purity, let him step forward now." He repeated the searching gestures.

Line forms at the left, I didn't say.

I glanced over at Dun Lidjun, who was standing next to Lord Esterling, quite probably through no accident. Accidents don't tend to happen around Lord Toshtai, and particularly not around Dun Lidjun, whose impassive face and stone-motionless stance would have told a half-blind man that he had raised kazuh. Kazuh Warriors don't need to wave their swords in the air to become what they always are.

Esterling held silent, which didn't surprise me. I mean, no matter how badly he wanted ViKay, the matter of her marriage was settled, and nothing he could say or do now would prevent it. All an outburst would buy him would be a quick challenge and a quicker death.

At Lord Orazhi's gesture, Arefai and ViKay rose, and joined left hands—the hand nearer the heart, the seat of the soul—while maids wrapped their hands with garlands of grape leaves, symbolizing the joining of the two souls, perhaps, or perhaps just symbolizing that members of our beloved ruling class like to be wrapped in grape leaves.

238

I shifted uncomfortably in my borrowed finery, not liking the way the robes were drawn tightly around my neck, and particularly not cherishing the weight of the borrowed sword that was stuck crosswise through my borrowed sash. Swords are a badge of nobility, not of the bourgeoisie, but all of us who stood with Arefai were, in theory, here to help him carry away his bride by force should somebody interfere, as indeed they would.

"The essence, if you please, Kami, Historical Master Dan'Shir," Lord Orazhi said, beckoning.

I uncorked the sealed flask, although there was nothing particularly dramatic in that. The flask had been sealed moments before the ceremony, after the Tree's Breath inside had been tested by Narantir and Tebol to be sure that it was unpoisoned, and then again by the three of us to be sure that it was suitable for the wedding ceremony, and once again to be sure that there was no poison.

Just as well it was a large flask, I thought, as I tilted it up to my lips, letting the icy heat of the dark green essence bathe my palate. Beyond the warmth and the chill were notes of raspberry and licorice under a layer of mint, with perhaps a touch of orange and a surprisingly pleasant quiet note of burned wood.

The taste persisted as I handed the flask to Arefai. Which is the way of a fine essence. Even hours later, my tongue would find itself remembering the fire and the cold, the purity and complexity of the flavors.

Still, I might as well have substituted Weasel Piss for all the attention Arefai paid as he drank, then brought the flask up to his bride's parted lips for a quick taste. He wasted the rest of it by pouring it over their joined hands.

"It is done," Lord Orazhi intoned. "One life, one heart, one soul." One to prong away at peasant and middle-class girls as much as he wanted, so long as he didn't do it in the middle of the courtyard; one to slip into whatever rooms she pleased, as long as she didn't get caught. Although I didn't really believe that. ViKay would be careful in Den Oroshtai, which would be just as well. Fun is fun, I decided, but it would be one thing to risk being caught here, where her father's servitors would very much not want to catch her, and another entirely in Den Oroshtai, where it would take her years to find her proper place in the keep's intrigues.

The marriage having taken place according to the modern ritual, it was now time to forget what we had just done and proceed to steal the bride away. The crowd broke up quickly, servitors swiftly scurrying out of the way, noble women moving to one side, while the warriors split into two parties, those of Glen Derenai forming a half circle between the wedding party and the front gate, those of Den Oroshtai encircling Arefai and his new wife.

The tradition, so I understand it, is that visiting warriors without an allegiance to either house may choose to temporarily join either for the battle, but must join one.

I found myself standing beside Edelfaule, facing Demick, Verden Verdunt and Deren der Drumud, while off to my left, Toshtai squared his bulk off against Orazhi.

All drew their scabbarded swords with exquisite languor (except for me; I just drew mine slowly) then ostentatiously checked the knots of the ropes that bound the swords into their scabbards. Accidents can happen, and everyone remembers not only the story of how ancient Lord Vilnek the Half-Wise let one overeager retainer turn the marriage of his daughter into the slaughter of the men of Ambell, but also the story of how Kemezhi of Ambell got the scrotal skin for his drumhead.

Moving slowly, carefully, we went through the ritual of battling our way to the front gate, scabbard tapped gently against scabbard.

Click. Clickclick. Clicketyclickclick. Click. It all sounded like fidgetbugs on a hot night.

At one point, I found myself facing Lord Demick, who had been invited to join Arefai's party, and thought for a moment that he would find a way to slip his scabbard aside and slice me, but before I could work up a good fear, I saw Dun Lidjun smiling genially at the two of us, and relaxed.

Demick tapped his scabbard gently against mine, smiled

genially, and raised a finger to his brow in a friendly salute. He had tried, via Minch, to stop this, and would accept a temporary defeat with the same quiet grace with which he accepted every defeat or victory. I didn't like him, I would never like him, but he did have a certain elegance that I couldn't help but admire, although I couldn't help but hope to admire it close at hand, were Toshtai ever to conquer Patrice.

We falsely battled our way to the gate, and through it, the Glen Derenai warriors behind us already replacing their swords and heading for the waiting banquet.

Two placid horses—the listless sort of mount I usually ended up getting—waited, each held in place largely by its own lassitude, although two rather superfluous liveried attendants held each set of reins.

Arefai slid his own scabbard back into his belt. With both hands he gripped ViKay about the waist and easily lifted his bride up to the back of the waiting mare, which was caparisoned in wedding green and brown and orange.

She smiled down at him. "We seem to have fled," she said, which was slightly off form, but then turned to the rest of us. "My thanks, companions of my husband."

"I thank you all, all of stout hearts and strong arms, who have helped in our escape," Arefai said, as he climbed to the back of his own horse. He kicked the horse into a leisurely couple of steps, thereby ritually having completed his escape.

Scabbarded swords, raised to defend the fleeing couple against a horde that had already departed for the banquet, dropped slowly.

"It's done," Arefai said, then dropped back to the ground quickly enough to help ViKay down.

With the way clear, there was nothing left for the combatting forces to do but to put their weapons away and walk back into the keep and join their erstwhile ceremonial enemies in the Great Hall for the reception that would take up the rest of the day.

The cooks of Glen Derenai had been hard at work. One table held platters of seaweed on which rested hundreds of fist-sized lobsters that had been boiled, then split and carefully cleaned, leaving behind lobster meat that shone bright with a fine butter glaze and a lemony spinach compote where the unappetizing roe and tomalley had been. Another table was devoted to a demonstration of the varieties of ways a whole chicken could be prepared: I tasted a stewed older bird, surrounded by barely softened carrots and turnips, sprinkled with biting black pepper and spicy red; then another chicken that had been rubbed with honey, then carefully roasted over a slow fire until the skin turned all black and crispy, but sweet, like candy; then another that had been rolled in thyme and cardamom, then wrapped in layers of parchment before being buried deeply in coals—it was served on the parchment, which itself smelled good enough to eat; and from another platter, one of a dozen tiny birds, rolled in something magical and deep fried.

Onyx tubs filled with ices supported tiny bowls of toosweet fundleberry sherbet and little vials of icy essence; huge tureens held sorrel soups, cleverly crafted little rice boats filled with sauteed shrimp and steamed sweetfish somehow managing to float on the roiling, oily surface; and glasses glowed with a strange seven-layered drink that I'd never seen before, each layer one of the seven flavors, carefully arranged so that hot came first, letting the cold and sweet come as counterpoint and relief.

Warriors who but a short while before had pretended to war with each other now picked up plates and pretended to enjoy each other's company.

As I said, hypocrisy is the way of our ruling class, but they do eat well.

At one point, I caught Edelfaule smiling at me. I would have taken it for a genuine smile if he didn't seem to have so many teeth, and them so white, and if, after a quick look to either side to make sure nobody else was watching, his lips hadn't moved with the words *next time*.

Toshtai just watched. I went back for another plate of an

amazing lamb dish. I wasn't sure just what the cook had marinated it in, but whatever it was had removed all traces of the over-gamy taste I've never liked in lamb, while leaving every bit of meatiness, and I decided that the best way to deal with the problem was a fourth helping.

18
A Frank Discussion, a Sword, and Other Promotions and Punishments

WHEN YOU DON'T know what else to do, juggle, neh?

We were to leave in the morning, and I could pay my final courtesy calls on Penkil Ner Condigan and Tebol either this night or in the morning.

Perhaps there was somebody else I should see, and one more question I could ask, but I knew the answer to it, or enough of the answer to it. I could do it, or I could guess. Some decisions are easy enough: I had had enough of all of them for one day. Enough food, enough drink, enough company, and more than enough of our beloved ruling class. Enough of death and murder. Enough of uncomfortable noble clothing; I had changed back into a simple tunic and drawstring pantaloons.

What I needed was some time with something simple, basic.

From the small hidden rise in the gardens, the late afternoon air was filled with the sounds of birds in the trees and groundsmen cutting and trimming below, and the tur tree still had it screened off well enough for some privacy. Timing is everything; in a few more days, the flowers would fall, and the only privacy available would be below the level of the stone fence.

Which is fine for lovers, but not for jugglers.

The setting sun shone directly on the wall. At noon, the shadows would have revealed the shallow sculptures of the men holding back the soil, but it was all washed away in the direct light, leaving behind just a stone fence.

I took out my juggling bags.

Catch right and throw left, throw right and catch left. If it's not the secret of the universe, it will do, for the time being.

I started with three juggling bags, then added a fourth, and fifth, and a sixth. Catch right and throw left, throw right and catch left became catch right, throw left, throw right, catch left, and then catch right throw left throw right catch left, and finally a stream of catchthrowcatchthrowcatchthrowcatchthrowcatchthrowcatchthrow that was seamless and timeless, until I heard the footsteps on the gravel path behind me. Two people; one heavy, one able to walk so lightly on gravel that I couldn't have heard him unless he permitted it.

I let one bag fall and caught it on the instep of my right foot, then foot-tossed it over to my juggling sack, and then another, and another, before I turned slowly, conscious of the audience.

"Good afternoon, Lord Toshtai," I said, catching the remaining three bags in my hands, then tossing the whole mass of them toward the other equipment. "And to you, Lord Dun Lidjun."

The fat man's face was as expressionless as usual, no hint of a smile at the corners of his leathery lips or sunken eyes.

Dun Lidjun's eyes twinkled as he nodded to me. "And a good afternoon to you, Kami Dan'Shir," he said. He had a scabbarded sword in his hands, and another slid sideways through his sash, which puzzled me, as I'd never thought Dun Lidjun would need more than one to dice any number of enemies into assorted pieces.

"I wished to speak with you," Toshtai said, looking around for a place to sit down, then frowning in irritation when it was clear that there was nothing other than the ground itself, or perhaps the stone wall that rimmed the rise. One would be undignified, and the stone wall was too narrow for Toshtai's broad buttocks.

"I am, of course, at your service, Lord," I said. "You could have sent for me."

"Difficult," he said. "Difficult to get enough privacy, Kami Dan'Shir." A flipper of a hand barely moved: for him, a broad wave. "Just as it's sometimes difficult to extract frank speech from you, particularly when other ears listen."

I smiled as genially as I could manage. "Frank speech and long life are not often paired, Lord."

"Here and now they are," he said.

I was going to ask if he really meant it, but I stopped myself. What was he going to say? No?

Dun Lidjun bowed stiffly at the fat man. "I shall keep watch at the foot of the path, Lord," he said, then walked off.

Toshtai watched him go. "I sometimes wonder how much longer I shall have Dun Lidjun in my service," he said, then sighed. "Kazuh is pure, but the flesh dies, bit by bit."

"Or sometimes all at once, Lord."

The corners of his mouth turned up almost measureably. "Sometimes." He straightened. "I was . . . disturbed by an undertone in your demonstration. Demonstrations," he said, correcting himself. "There seemed to be something of hysteria in them, perhaps around the edges."

I nodded. "Of course, what Lord Toshtai says is true. I shall try harder in the future to give no such false impression."

He opened his mouth, then closed it. "Ah. So now I can either take your arch shtoi sarcasm as literal, or I can threaten you into a false confession of irritation over something minor." He shook his head. "You play me far too dexterously, Kami Dan'Shir."

He stood silently for a moment, which seemed to call for a comment, but I couldn't think of one that was both appropriate and safe.

"Were I to swear on the lives of my sons that you will

be held harmless for anything you say to me here and now—would that satisfy you, Kami Dan'Shir?" he asked, almost flatly, no trace of fire and anger in his voice. "Were I to swear on the good of Den Oroshtai, or on my loyalty to the Scion? Would that be enough to loosen your tongue?" His lips pursed. "Or ought I to threaten you? Need I say, 'speak frankly with me or I'll have you killed'? No." He dug into his pouch and produced a bone chit. "Present this to ... the father of my son's wife, and he will exchange it for ten oblongs of gold, ten years of what I pay you. You may have this, and a dismissal from my service, or you may speak honestly with me, here and now, as you may always speak with me in private," he said. "And this I do swear on the lives of my children, on the future of my domain, and on the soul of the Scion. Choose."

Ten years salary, or a chance to berate a member of our beloved ruling class? Perhaps if I was hungry, it would have been different, but with my belly too full, and my pouch heavy with Minch's gold, it wasn't even close.

I nodded. "Put your chit away, Lord. Let me give you something to accompany it," I said, digging into my own pouch. I handed him a small round stone.

"A stone," he said, nodding gravely. "I thank you." He waited for a moment. "I trust it has some meaning."

"It's a freden, Lord, a throw-weight, carried by travelers for when the road gets too long, for when the pack gets too heavy. Next time you have a problem that's too heavy, why not just throw it away along with this? Instead of treating me like a freden."

He held it in the center of his open palm and looked at it for a moment, and then closed chubby fingers over it.

"Next time you need to find a sacrifice, perhaps you should sacrifice this, instead of me," I said. "You saw it coming, Lord. You knew that Minch and Demick were going to do something to stop the wedding, and that's why you brought me, rather than finessing them out of appearing and interfering. Much better to show yourself as someone powerful enough to keep his enemies close to him, to escape safely, like a bullfighter waiting until the horns almost graze his naked chest before he dives and rolls to safety.

"But things went too far, and you had only one way out. Invest this new dan'shir with all the authority he would need, broadcast far and wide how great his skills and talents were, and if it was impossible for him to solve the murder, why then he could be blamed for it all, attention could be distracted. Throw him away like a freden and let him take the burden of it all into the grave, eh? Brilliant." I bowed. "I congratulate you, Lord, but I do not thank you."

"Ah." Toshtai's lips pursed for a moment. "I forget that you are still young, are new to associating with nobility, and despite your special skill, you still are a fool and a witling who is barely capable of managing to avoid drooling all over himself." A thick sausage of a finger pointed at me. "Do you think that I and my fathers have ruled Den Oroshtai since the Oroshtai Regency simply because we live in the keep at the top of the hill? Don't you understand that we don't merely demand the loyalty of the lower classes and of lesser nobles, but that we offer our own? Don't you see that we could not have survived this long were it otherwise?" He shook his head. "No, that's too much to expect of you. Let me make it simple for you: do you think I command the likes of Dun Lidjun without giving something in return?

"No. Oh, certainly, I'll spend warriors like water to protect Den Oroshtai; I've sacrificed my two eldest sons in the endless wars for the good of the realm, and never have regretted the action, just the necessity. True, I'll marry off both of my daughters to cement a tentative peace pact with lords of the Aragimlyth mountains whose forces haven't been in the south in almost two hundred years. Yes, I'll demand that peasants grow grain, and that cobblers make shoes, and that quarrymen quarry stone. And perhaps someday I'll treat you as a gambling piece, to be pushed to the center of the table over an important wager." His lips were almost white.

"But I will not do so idly, and I will not do so for the pleasure of it, and I will not do so because the power is mine, and not because it pleases or displeases a young idiot with a talent that both Den Oroshtai and the realm can use." He lowered his voice. "I'll do it, if I must, because it's necessary for the good of Den Oroshtai and the realm, and only for that." He shook his head. "But that's too much for a bourgeois to understand, eh? Very well." He raised his voice. "Dun Lidjun, to my side, if you please."

I would have expected gravel to be flying through the air as Dun Lidjun ran up the path blurringly fast, but nothing of the sort happened. One moment, Toshtai and I were alone, the next Dun Lidjun had blurred into sharp motionlessness beside the fat lord, one scabbarded sword tucked diagonally through his sash, another in his hands.

"You called, Lord," he said.

"That is Minch's sword, as I instructed?"

"Yes, Lord," he said, balancing it on his fists. "Nobody questioned when I removed it from his possessions on your behalf. Deren der Drumud ought to have taken charge of it, but the revelations about his master have him far too off-balance."

"As they should. A fine blade, so I'm told."

"Yes, lord. A particularly nice Old Lithburn, worthy of yourself."

"Full payment for risking his life to ruin my son's wedding; enough that honor would have compelled Minch to spend his life if need be, eh?"

"Easily worthy of it, Lord."

Members of our beloved ruling class have this thing about swords. Me, I don't understand it.

Toshtai nodded. "Then remove that Eisenlith from your waist, and replace it with this one, which is suitable for you."

"But, Lord, this is even nicer than your own Greater Frosuffold—"

Toshtai raised an eyebrow. "You would argue with me, old friend?"

"No, Lord." The old man did as he was told, slipping

the late Minch's sword into his belt with great care. If it was possible, he stood a little straighter.

"Now, present that sharp Eisenlith blade to Lord Kami, the Historical Master Dan'Shir."

My pantaloons were secured at the top by a drawstring; all I could do was hold the scabbard in my hands.

"Remain here; a servitor will shortly arrive with a noble's robes, including a proper sash for your fine sword." Toshtai's expression could have been a shallow smile, but perhaps not. "I had thought, perhaps, to elevate you someday in thanks for good service, rather than as a way to require you to see things as they are. I had thought, someday, to surprise you, after one of your sportive requests to be made a noble, by granting that request." He sighed. "But so-be-it. Now is the time, and timing is everything, Lord Kami Dan'Shir." He started to turn away. "One more thing."

"Yes, Lord?"

"If I ever again hear that the phrase 'our beloved ruling class' has passed your lips, I'll have Dun Lidjun slit your noble body from crotch to sternum."

The two of them walked away, leaving me with an unpacked juggling sack and the sword.

19

Two Final Courtesy Calls, an Uneaten Bowl of Soup, and Other Uncertainties

THE DOOR WAS open, and Tebol was with Narantir high in the wizard's tower. Something purple and murky was bubbling in a bubblelike vessel suspended over an alcohol lamp, sending wisps of steam into a coil of glass. I would have asked about it, but I saw something swimming in the vessel, and decided first that I didn't really want to know, and then that I really didn't want to know.

"Tebol, Narantir, you're going to have difficulty crediting what has—"

"Ah." Tebol stopped me with a nod. "Lord Kami Dan'Shir, the word has passed all over the keep of your well-earned promotion," he said, while Narantir simply raised a mug and then tilted it back.

"Oh?"

"Yes," he said. "For your brilliant work in exposing Minch's suicide. Nicely, nicely done, Lord Kami Dan'Shir."

I felt uncomfortable in a noble's robes, the sword through my sash constantly bumping into things. I also felt uncomfortable at the idea that I was in theory able to use this thing, and could be expected to do so to defend the lives of Lord Toshtai and his family. It might be interesting to see how quickly I could be run through, but it's not the sort of experiment I really want to participate in.

It wasn't the only thing I had to feel uncomfortable about, but so-be-it.

"I'm officially here for a courtesy call before we leave for Den Oroshtai in the morning," I said. "Besides, I really did want to thank you for your help and consideration. Some wizards don't think magic counts unless it hurts me."

Tebol chuckled. "I wonder who the young lord thinks he speaks of, Narantir."

I slid the sword out of my sash and thumped down into a chair.

Both Tebol and Narantir were on their feet, Narantir grunting with the effort.

"What does the young lord think that he's doing?" Narantir asked.

"It's called sitting down," I said.

"No, you certainly may not," the wizard said with a sniff. "It's not proper. It's one thing for us to sit around and drink with a bourgeois historical master; but nobles don't associate so informally with the likes of us."

But, I wanted to say, *the only good time I had on this trip was sitting around with the two of you, getting drunk and playing at being owls. I would have even settled for just the drinking and the chatting.*

I would have said it, but I didn't. Not because it was somehow not the way a noble was supposed to behave, but because the two of them wouldn't have cared.

I rose and bowed. "As you will, Narantir and Tebol." No, if they were going to be overly formal, so could I. "As you will, Nailed Weasel and Rainy Sunrise, both users of magic."

One last courtesy call. It was important to make them in the proper order; timing is, as my father used to say, everything.

It is amazingly easy for a member of our beloved ruling class, even a newly made one, to arrange for the loan of a horse and of a pair of warriors to accompany and guide him, although perhaps I should have picked a horse with less spirit. It was all I could do to keep on this one's back as he insisted on cantering most of the way, threatening to flatten my buttocks and bounce my poor scrotum chesthigh.

We found Penkil Ner Condigan's house a short but painful ride away from the keep, part of a cluster of houses between a deep stream and the dark forest. I should have remembered the way from when I had come to see JenNa, a lifetime before.

I dismissed the warriors. "The horse knows the way back; I'll be fine."

It's sometimes hard to tell who ranks who among the nobility, but surely a noble Historical Master Dan'Shir would outrank warriors on duty at the stables, particularly if he acts as though he does.

"Then we bid you a good evening, Lord," one said, wheeling his horse about.

Penkil Ner Condigan stood, filling in the doorway of his house. More of a shack, really. His long head nodded on its thin neck. "Good evening, Lord Kami Dan'Shir," he said, his deep bass voice a distant rumble. "Enter and be welcome."

"I'm just here on a courtesy call, Penkil Ner Condigan," I said. He was alone in the small, neat hut. Tools and a hiltless skinning knife were spread out over the sole table that stood in the center of the hut, under lamplight. "I hope LonDee is well?" I asked.

"She is still at work in the keep. Our worktimes do not always overlap." A kettle burbled gently in the fireplace. "Still, she has left me soup; may I offer you some, Lord?"

"Please," I said. "Just a small amount." There was no sense either in provoking Penkil Ner Condigan by refusing his hospitality or in wasting any of the soup. I had no intention of letting food or drink pass my lips in his home.

"Just as well she's not here," I said. "Your wife, that is."

"Oh?" From the desperate look in his eyes, I began to wish I hadn't dismissed the warriors.

I raised a hand. "Because she might not understand that I mean what I say, that all is well, and that I'd no more disturb things as they are than I would try to replace Large Egda at the base of a pyramid."

His face was blank. "I'm sure I don't understand."

I sat down. "Just as well you don't. Like I don't understand how easy it would be for somebody who works in the kitchens below to signal out the window when Lord Minch was calling for an evening snack.

"Like I don't understand how it would be possible for somebody in the tree in the courtyard then to fire an arrow through the screen and into Lord Minch.

"Like I don't understand how Minch's attempt to embarrass Arefai made the idea of doing so with an arrow with three golden bands delightful to somebody with a reason to hate not only Minch, but all of our beloved ruling class."

His hand didn't shake as he ladled me out a generous bowl full of soup. "Since you don't understand all this, perhaps you wouldn't understand the reason."

"Reason? To hate our beloved ruling class?" I laughed. "For a man who lost his daughter—a lovely girl, I remember—to a passing lord who thought he honored her by making her his concubine? What ever happened to JenNa, Penkil Ner Condigan?"

"He could have raised her and taken her as wife. Or he could have seen that she was properly taken care of when he tired of her. But he didn't." He looked me in the eye. "She lives with a peasant in Merth's Bridge, as his woman. My daughter works the fields, Kami Khuzud," he said. "He did it. And you knew?"

"I guessed, which was close enough." I laughed, but it sounded hollow. "The servitor in the hall with the domed tray told me that Minch had called for some food. The tension when we first met—the last thing a man with murder on his mind wants to meet is a discoverer-of-truths, eh? The killer had fired from outside, he had to have a way to locate Minch specifically—what better way than to watch for a signal from the kitchens below, then fire at the spot where you knew Minch had to be, eh? You were almost too late, Penkil Ner Condigan; he had turned away from the speaking tube, and was preparing to walk away. Another moment and you would have missed him."

He ignored the taunt. "Why didn't you expose me, then?"

I shrugged. "When I could take this sense of honor that our beloved ruling class claims to own and wrap it about Minch's neck? When I could by implication bring Demick in on it and raise my status at no cost?" Now that was worth a laugh. "Getting the blame off Arefai was guaranteed to earn me Demick's enmity; I might as well accuse him of having put Minch up to suicide, since he clearly put him up to the whole confrontation with Arefai in the first place."

Toshtai had worked that out.

But even Toshtai hadn't looked through the delusion of honor, part of the myth of themselves that the nobility wrapped themselves in. Minch? Honor? How could a man who stole another's arrows to force a false accusation have any sense of honor, much less so strong a one that he would kill himself to fulfill a promise?

But they all would rather admire the dead for his honor and resolution than think of what a worm he was when alive.

"You haven't had your soup." Penkil Ner Condigan seemed eager, whether out of hospitality or because of some poison I didn't know, and didn't much care. I wasn't going to have the soup, after all. I forced a chuckle.

"Nor will I; you may trust me not to risk that. As you can trust that I'll leave the . . . substance of this courtesy call between you and me, Penkil Ner Condigan."

"Then why?"

I didn't really have an answer for him. Perhaps it was because I wanted to repay him for the discomfort he used to ladle out when I came to call on JenNa. Perhaps it was because Penkil Ner Condigan had always looked down on me that just once I wanted him to see me as a noble, to fear me. Perhaps it was because I am a dan'shir, and there

257

is something of a revealer of truth in the discoverer-of-truth.

Or, perhaps, I just couldn't stand the thought of somebody thinking that he could fool me.

I felt his eyes on my back as I walked out the door, climbed onto the unsteady back of the horse, and rode away.

Part Three
DEN OROSHTAI

20
A Journey's End, a Greeting, a Request for Simplicity, and Nothing More

I FOUND HER at the very head of the hour of the snake, moments after sunset, that magical time when the indirect light of the fading sun turns the white stones of the east garden all red and golden, the colors fading moment by moment as the evening comes on.

She was in the east garden, perched on the edge of a white stone bench under a spreading saltblossom tree. The tree was just shy of the bloom: in two, perhaps three, days, broad red flowers the size of dinner plates would spread their pink-veined leaves, long pistils and stamens exuding a soft scent that would make this part of the garden smell like a sunspattered beach of the Inner Sea.

But now the long buds, red as TaNai's lips, hung just out of reach, promising what they would not yet give. Which is fine with me. Not yet, after all, is not a refusal, but just a postponement. There are things worth waiting for.

As usual, she was dressed in well-made cotton robes, these striped diagonally in a muted yellow and a rich black that went well with her glossy black hair. Lord Toshtai is not stingy with his retainers; she could have afforded cheap silk, but preferred good cotton.

She had been looking away from me, but when I cleared my throat, she turned.

She rose and bowed her head. "Lord Kami Dan'Shir," she said, lifting her eyes to meet mine. "Your fame precedes you."

Some things I can count on: TaNai's eyes will always be warm and brown in my memory, as they were that moment when they rested on mine. Tonight her creamy complexion was untouched by any hint of whitening, not even along her elegant gracious nose, or at the cheekbones, one caressed by a strand of hair that had escaped the knot at the back of her head. I liked her that way.

"TaNai, please. Kami Dan'Shir, or just Kami." I spread my hands. "Please."

Her smile neither promised nor conceded anything. "As you wish, of course."

I'd had a speech prepared, something modeled on Arefai's hunting speech, something about how I had gone off and proved myself, and hoped that I had earned my present station in her eyes, but in my mind the words sounded too rehearsed, too practiced, too much the product of artifice, not feeling.

"It's good to see you," I said. "I didn't realize how much I missed you."

That sounded much better than *Well, I would have missed you a lot if I hadn't been busy trying to keep my head on my shoulders.* It sounded much, much better than *And if Arefai's wife-to-be, now his wife, hadn't been busy in satisfying slightly less basic needs.* As I may have mentioned, a dan'shir is a discoverer-of-truth, and only a revealer of truth when advisable.

Besides, it was true.

She smiled, as though she had seen through me. "It's been too quiet without you. You tend to bring excitement along with you. I guess that comes from growing up with an acrobatic troupe, yes?"

I nodded. "There is that."

Silence hung in the air for a moment, and I didn't know what words would break it.

She tilted her head to one side. "Kami Dan'Shir, why are you here? What do you want?"

"What do I want?" I had to laugh. I couldn't remember anybody asking me that before.

There are harder questions to answer.

"I want *everything*, TaNai," I said. She smiled at that. "I want to sit in a hot bath and soak all ache from my road-tired bones and muscles, instead of the too-quick washing I allowed myself so that I'd be fit company this evening. And I want a fine bow and arrows, and an appropriate set of leathers, and to learn how to use them well, because I've apparently developed something of a reputation as an archer, and I may as well grow into it. I don't want to have to learn how to use this sword, but I want to resign myself to it, as Dun Lidjun himself has promised me lessons, and I have neither the heart to deny the old man that nor the courage to confront him.

"And I want to stretch out on the soft grasses at a particular spot outside the keep, over by the south wall, a flat spot of sweet-smelling grass edged by an ancient and untrustworthy retaining wall, where the night is alive with smells of mint and must and the distant ta*roo* of owls, and I want to think about many things, about just how honest Lord Toshtai has been with me, how much of a friend Arefai will be, and how great a danger Edelfaule might be.

"I want to figure out just where I belong and what being a dan'shir means—not what it means to Lord Toshtai, not what it means for D'Shai, but what it means to me. And I very much want to figure out who Kami Dan'Shir is, because that seems to keep changing.

"But right now, just at this very moment, what I most want is to hold a lovely woman in my arms, one who wants to be with me just for me, one who wants some things to be complicated enough to be interesting but this thing between us to be simple and direct right now because this is a time for simplicity, and timing . . ."

She put a finger to my lips, silencing me.

"I once told you, Kami Dan'Shir," she said, coming into my arms, "that all you had to do was ask."

"Redwall is both a credible and
ingratiating place, one to which readers
will doubtless cheerfully return."
—<u>New York Times Book Review</u>

BRIAN JACQUES

SALAMANDASTRON
———— A Novel of Redwall ————

*"The Assassin waved his claws in the air. In a trice
the rocks were bristling with armed vermin behind him.
They flooded onto the sands of the shore and stood like
a pestilence of evil weeds sprung there by magic: line
upon line of ferrets, stoats, weasels, rats and foxes.
Banners of blood red and standards decorated their
skins, hanks of beast hair and skulls swayed in the light
breeze.*
The battle for Salamandastron was under way...."
—excerpted from <u>Salamandastron</u>

__ 0-441-00031-2/$4.99